T0070979

The Curse of the Dragon God

The Curse of the Dragon God

A Gay Adventure

Geoffrey Knight

CLEIS PRESS

Copyright © 2011 by Geoffrey Knight.

All rights reserved. Except for brief passages quoted in newspaper, magazine, radio, television, or online reviews, no part of this book may be reproduced in any form or by any means, electronic or mechanical, including photocopying, recording, or information storage or retrieval system, without permission in writing from the publisher.

Published in the United States by Cleis Press Inc., 2246 Sixth St., Berkeley, CA 94710.

Printed in the United States.
Cover design: Scott Idleman/Blink
Cover photo © David Vance, 2010.
Fine art prints available at: www.davidvanceprints.com.
Text design: Frank Wiedemann
First Edition.
10 9 8 7 6 5 4 3 2 1

Trade paper ISBN: 978-1-57344-661-7
E-book ISBN: 978-1-57344-682-2

Library of Congress Cataloging-in-Publication Data

Knight, Geoffrey, 1969-
 The curse of the dragon god / by Geoffrey Knight. -- 1st ed.
    p. cm.
  ISBN 978-1-57344-661-7 (pbk. : alk. paper)
 1. Gay men--Fiction. 2. China--Fiction. I. Title.
 PR9619.4.K57C87 2011
 823'.92--dc22
                                          2010052871

For Trent,

*for all your years of love, friendship,
and encouragement.*

I

The Port City of Aden, Yemen

THE YOUNG MAN KNOWN ONLY AS THE TUNISIAN LAY ON the bed, naked and unconscious. Eden watched him from the balcony doorway overlooking the Gulf of Aden and thought to himself how beautiful the young man was; too beautiful for this line of work. Spies often die young. The choices he made, the risks he braved, guaranteed the young Tunisian would one day leave behind a good-looking corpse and a heart full of secrets. Then again, many had said the same of the handsome Dr. Eden Santiago.

Last night, Eden had met the Tunisian in an out-of-the-way restaurant and after brief, flirtatious small talk had taken him back to his hotel, where Eden opened a bottle of white wine, handed the Tunisian a glass, and then eased the young spy onto the king-sized bed. The two had been together before—once at the Hotel Descartes in Paris, once at the Chelsea in New York, and once under the stars after a secret rendezvous in a Sicilian fort that had been destroyed during the Second World War.

Strange, Eden thought to himself as he once again tasted the Tunisian's sweet, soft flesh. Strange how well he knew this body, this brown, beautiful specimen of a man. And yet, apart from the physical, he knew nothing about the Tunisian at all. Nobody did, except the Professor.

To the world, the Tunisian was a ghost.

But he made love like an angel.

After Eden poured the Tunisian a second drink, he took a condom and turned the blue-eyed spy over on the bed, caressing the young spy's perfect round cheeks before parting them and claiming that hot, tight ass.

Their lovemaking was tender and tireless. Eden made it last as long as possible, savoring every moment, knowing that any time he made love to the Tunisian could be the last.

When he came, he came with a tremendous cry, pushing himself completely inside the black-haired spy, who in turn rained jewels of cum over the bed. Eden bit gently into the Tunisian's shoulder. This time it was the Tunisian who cried out, the teeth marks in his flesh triggering another burst of cum from his perfect, rocking cock.

Eden locked his arms around the young spy and held him close, their sweating, panting bodies as one.

Afterward, they sat on the satin sheets facing each other, their legs entwined.

"You must be careful," the Tunisian warned, his blue eyes imploring Eden. "Qassim Qahtani is a dangerous man. It's not his shipping business that has made him his millions. It's his involvement in illegal weapons, and it comes at a cost."

Eden reassured him with a soft stroke of his face, "I'm only here to observe, not intervene. We need to know who's trading the diamonds and what Qahtani is offering in exchange."

"Then let me go with you."

"You've already helped enough."

"Eden, I'm coming. I owe Professor Fathom everything."

"And I owe you an apology." Eden took the half-empty wineglass out of the Tunisian's hand as the young man began to sway on the bed.

"W-what are you talking about? Oh...E-e-den?" The Tunisian's speech was beginning to slur as realization set in. "You've...drugged me...one of your potions..."

"Potions? I'm a scientist, not a witch doctor. Just take it easy now, it was a heavy dose. I had no choice—I knew you'd insist on getting involved."

The Tunisian looked at the pale wine swilling in the bottom of his glass, his face struggling with a look of surprise and betrayal as the drugs kicked in. Then a faint smile. "You know me too well."

"On the contrary. I don't even know your name."

But the Tunisian barely heard him. With a graceful swoon his body began to sink. "What—what about you?"

Eden smiled and wrapped his arms around him, laying him gently on the bed. "Shh. Sleep now. I told you, I'm only here to observe. Tomorrow when you wake you'll have a terrible headache, but at least this way you won't try to follow me and you won't get hurt."

The Tunisian's crystal-blue eyes closed as he slipped into a deep sleep. Eden kissed him lightly on each eyelid and laid the young man's head on his pillow.

Returning his attention to the harbor, Eden watched the lights of the boats and the late-night activities of the merchant shipping port. There were three ships moored at the docks: a Suezmax-class French cargo ship, an African oil tanker, and a huge, rusted Yemeni vessel. As the hours passed, he watched the last of the Yemeni ship's containers being unloaded, carted from the bowels of the ship on large heavy-duty forklifts and down a loading ramp before being stacked on the wharf.

As the sun rose over the harbor, Eden dressed and left, glancing back to make sure the Tunisian was still asleep as he locked the door safely behind him.

Sitting at a roadside café in the hot morning light, Eden dipped his head slightly and peered over the top of his sunglasses. This is where the Tunisian told him to wait as the Yemeni traders passed by on their way to broker the deal. The fast-approaching drone of a car's engine echoed somewhere out of sight down the narrow street. Sweat trickled down his forehead as a battered Fiat appeared around the corner and chugged past, blowing dust into the still air. Rowdy young Yemeni kids shouted out the open windows of the rickety car to a pretty girl across the street and were gone.

Eden pushed his sunglasses back onto the bridge of his nose and unfastened another button on his soaked shirt. He picked up his iced tea and listened to the ice spin and chime as dust from the Fiat settled on the table.

The slovenly mustachioed waiter stepped up to the table and asked him if he intended to eat.

Eden was about to answer when he heard not one but two cars approaching.

A black BMW appeared at the end of the street and sped by, followed closely by a second one. Eden stood, tossed money on the table, and hastily yanked his rented Vespa off the sidewalk and onto the street. He buzzed after the BMWs, keeping his distance while being careful not to lose sight of the cars as they wound through the dusty streets to the port.

The two BMWs steered a steady course along the dock past stacked containers and giant coiled shipping ropes, past the African tanker and the French cargo ship, heading straight for the rusted old Yemeni vessel.

Eden pulled the Vespa to a halt behind a high wall at the

entrance to the port, then walked purposefully along the length of the dock, pretending he belonged there. He made his way confidently past a group of African seamen loudly chatting and laughing as they filed down a gangplank from the tanker; past a dozen young French sailors in white caps; and straight past the office of the dozing harbor master. When he was within 50 feet of the Yemeni ship he quickly ducked behind a giant, grease-slicked chain and peered over the top.

The two BMWs had stopped at the loading ramp leading into the black bowels of the rusting ship. Several of the ship's unkempt crew stood at a safe distance on the dock, with the exception of the freighter's captain, a surly, heavy-browed man, who stepped forward to try to look through his own reflection into the second BMW's tinted windows.

As the back window began to slide down, the captain's image disappeared, replaced by a fat, hairy, bejeweled hand holding out a stuffed envelope.

"Qassim Qahtani, I presume," Eden whispered to himself.

The captain gushed with overplayed gestures as the window sealed itself shut to block out his babble. Barking orders at his crew, he waved the cars up the ramp and inside the belly of the ship.

Hastily the crew began to unhitch the ship's massive mooring lines and chains. Several charged up a narrow boarding gangplank and then winched it off the dock, securing it in a horizontal position against the ship's sheer, eight-story-high side.

Before the captain vanished into the cargo hold, he pulled out a walkie-talkie and spoke into the handset. Almost instantly Eden felt a rumbling beneath the docks, and the sea began to churn at the rear of the vessel. The ship's remaining crew scurried aboard as the loading ramp lifted off the dock like an ancient, rusted drawbridge. Eden knew his time to get aboard was now or never!

Thinking fast, he ran his hands over the grimy, slippery chain in front of him, then smeared his shirt with grease and snapped off several buttons.

He bolted across the dock, reached the edge of the wharf, and launched himself up onto the rising ramp, tumbling down the other side, into the dark, knocking into the back of the captain's legs. In a tirade of Arabic and angry spit, the captain turned and waved him inside the black void of the ship, without so much as a look.

Eden's eyes adjusted to the lack of light. He made out the other crew members piling onto a hydraulic lift at the far end of the cargo hold. With no caging and no railing on the lift, it was little more than a large, square platform with a control button mounted on a waist-high stand in one corner. A single shaft of light shone directly down onto the lift from an opening in the ship's deck, eight stories above the crewmen.

Eden felt a kick up his pants as the captain ordered him out of the cargo hold along with the rest of the men. Hastily he made his way toward the lift, quickly sizing up his cavernous surroundings.

The interior of the cargo hold was like a giant warehouse. At lower points on the walls, beams crisscrossed one another in a pulley rigging designed to move and secure containers. Chains hung from the beams like curtains bunched to the walls. Otherwise, the space was virtually empty, except for the two black BMWs, parked side by side in the center of the hold.

As Eden made his way toward the lift, looking for a place and an opportunity to hide, the driver's door of the first BMW opened. All eyes, including the captain's, watched a tall, handsome Middle Eastern man step out of the car. Eden took this opportunity and seized it, slipping unseen behind a screen of chains jangling softly by the wall.

Immaculately dressed, carefully adjusting the cuffs of

his sleeves, the man said in clear, confident English, "Our friends are waiting. We need to leave Yemeni soil—now!"

The captain gave a quick, submissive nod, uttered an apology, then hurried to join his men on the lift. As soon as he set foot on the platform, he punched the button on the stand and the hydraulics lurched into action. From below, Eden watched the captain and his crew ascend and disappear through the hatch in the ceiling.

A moment later, the sound of the ship's engines turned from a drone to a thunderous rumbling, and the Yemeni vessel was on its way.

The only question was: on its way where?

The answer presented itself sooner rather than later, in the form of Qassim Qahtani.

"How far, Yusuf?"

The immaculately dressed man's reply came in Arabic. He was holding open the backseat door of the second BMW. Inside the car, struggling to lift himself off the seat, was a large, sweaty man with four chins, a ponytail, and a small fortune in gold dangling around his fat neck. Puffs of graying chest hair sprouted from a baggy silk shirt unbuttoned to his waist.

"In English!" the fat man wheezed angrily, clambering to his feet with the help of the car door. "I told you, I want to practice my English for the visitors! Let them know that Qassim Qahtani is a man of the world and nobody's fool! Now tell me in English, how far are we going?"

"Not as far as I'd like, father," Yusuf replied. "The visitors are getting—" he looked up at the ceiling, his ears picking up a distant sound, "—impatient."

Qassim looked up too, as did Eden from his hiding place of chains. Above the churn of the ship's engines came the unmistakable *thump-thump-thump* of chopper blades cutting through the sky and getting louder, then a heavy scrape and clunk as the helicopter landed.

"Saabir!" Yusuf called. The driver of the second car quickly stepped out, a younger, shorter version of Yusuf, straightening his jacket and adjusting his pristine collar.

"Where's your gun?" Yusuf demanded.

With a cocky, gold-toothed smile, Saabir opened his jacket to reveal a semiautomatic pistol tucked into his trousers.

Yusuf shook his head, disapproving of his younger brother's weapon of choice—or more specifically its size—then returned to the first BMW, sprang open the trunk, and from the passenger seat retrieved an Uzi submachine gun, slamming a magazine into the pistol grip.

Eden felt a tingle of dread on the back of his neck, then realized it wasn't dread at all. It was whiskers. Quickly he turned and came face-to-face with a large rat, clinging to the chain and sniffing at his scent.

The rat let out a winded squeak as Eden swatted it off the chain, hitting the steel floor a few feet away, loud enough for Qassim, Yusuf, and Saabir to turn their heads.

"What was that?" Qassim demanded anxiously.

Yusuf raised his Uzi, then lowered it with a half grin when he saw it. "A rat." He watched it scurry along the wall, then snapped his head back to the ceiling as the hydraulic shaft on the ascended lift began to whine.

From the deck above, the platform descended.

Light poured in from the opening and three figures appeared on the lift: two Asian men in black suits stood on either side of a small, slender woman dressed in knee-high boots and a skintight black leather jumpsuit with a hood over her head. Each man carried a steel briefcase, laid flat in their outstretched arms, waiting to be snapped open. The sight of them made Qassim smile.

"Mya Chan," he announced as the lift sank to a halt on the floor of the cargo hold. "What a pleasure to finally meet you."

The hooded woman stepped off the lift and began to stride purposefully across the steel floor, followed by the men with briefcases. She stopped in front of Qassim, a quarter his size, yet so cold and serious that he felt distinctly threatened by the woman. It was something he wasn't used to, and an uneasy smile quivered on his lips.

"I didn't come for pleasure," she said, a Chinese accent in her voice. "This is strictly business." She nodded to the two men standing alongside Qassim, her hood billowing to reveal full, red lips; high, sharp cheekbones; and small, round sunglasses. "I thought we agreed to nobody else but you, me, and the diamond carriers."

"These are my sons, Yusuf and Saabir. I needed two drivers. I didn't want to risk carrying both devices in one car. They're very...delicate. I assure you the captain and his crew have been paid generously to keep their noses out of our business."

From behind the curtain of chains, Eden felt something heavy crawl across his shoe. He looked down and saw that the rat was back. Silently he tried brush it away, but the irritable beast reared its ugly head and squawked at him.

The sound echoed through the cavernous hold.

Mya and Qassim both turned at the shrill noise.

Saabir placed his hand on the grip of his pistol.

Yusuf unclipped the safety on the Uzi.

Eden froze.

"What was that?" Mya demanded, snapping off her sunglasses.

"Nothing but a rat," Qassim said, peering into the darkness at a thick tail trailing out from under some hanging chains.

Eden felt the rodent sniffing up his trouser leg, its wet nose rubbing against his shin.

"Enough with the formalities," Mya turned back to Qassim. "My time is short."

"As is your patience," Qassim observed. "Very well, let us do business." With a clap of his hands, Yusuf and Saabir made their way to the trunks of the BMWs, and each lifted out a small wooden crate. They placed them gently on the ground in front of Mya.

Yusuf retrieved a crowbar, then carefully pried open the lid of each crate. Mya stepped forward to peer inside.

"As requested," Qassim said, "two zidium devices. Every catastrophe lover's weapon du jour. One from a black market in Afghanistan, one from Djibouti. Both off the grid, completely untraceable. Each capable of leveling a mountain. Or destroying a city. Whatever your needs be. Which reminds me." Qassim pulled a small silver cylinder from his pocket and handed it to Mya with a shrewd, businesslike smile. "The impulse detonation device you asked for. Why you would want a toy such as this when you have two zidiums is beyond me, but a deal is a deal."

Mya reached blindly for the cylinder, for her eyes were locked on the crates sitting on the floor in front of her. Distractedly she took the detonation device, slid it between her breasts, then knelt on one knee.

There inside each crate was what looked like a silver bowling ball with a small LED panel fitted into the top of each device. Tiny rivets and screws ran around the circumference of each shining sphere.

"How do I activate them?" she asked.

"Google it," Qassim laughed. "Believe it or not, you can download a how-to guide from the Internet." He gave an innocent shrug. "Terrorism is as easy as the click of a mouse."

"I'm impressed," Mya whispered.

Qassim caught the glint in her eye. He had seen it before, many times, that lust for chaos all terrorists share. It was a look that had made him rich.

As though in a trance, Mya reached slowly—adoringly—for one of the zidium bombs. Suddenly Qassim's hand shot out and seized her wrist. In sharp response, Mya's free hand snapped a small pistol out of a holster inside her knee-high boot, its handgrip studded with diamonds. She jammed it up into Qassim's chins. In a chain reaction, the snout of Saabir's semiautomatic pressed against Mya's temple while Yusuf aimed his submachine gun squarely at the two diamond carriers, pointing it at one, then the other, then back again.

"I wouldn't touch them if I were you," Qassim breathed. "As I said, they're very delicate. Besides, they're not yours *yet*." He swallowed anxiously and his throat clicked against the barrel of the pistol. "The diamonds. The deal was for the diamonds."

Mya eyed Qassim, then Saabir, then Yusuf, then pulled the gun away from Qassim's chins and returned it to her boot.

Qassim released her wrist, Saabir retracted his semi-automatic, and Yusuf took a step back. With the situation momentarily disarmed, Mya stepped in front of the first diamond carrier, unsnapped the locks on the briefcase resting flat in his arms, opened the lid, and stepped back.

Qassim gasped.

At the same time, the pesky rat sunk its fangs into Eden's shin. He winced, gasping in pain.

Mya turned sharply and said, "That was no rat!"

With an ear-piercing squeal a writhing rat suddenly flew across the vast open space of the cargo hold like a fat furry football.

Yusuf and Saabir opened fire at the same time, shredding the air and the rat with bullets.

Instinctively, Qassim dropped to his knees, grabbing the handle of the briefcase full of diamonds in front of him. He slid it out of the diamond carrier's hands, but the lid was still open causing every last diamond to skitter and hurl across the steel floor of the cargo hold.

"Stop shooting! Stop shooting!" he screamed.

But his sons couldn't hear him over their rapid, chaotic gunfire.

Mya was already in a crouching position, ready to take flight, ordering in Chinese for her men to leave the diamonds and get the bombs.

Swiftly they snatched up the open crates.

Mya was running for the lift now. Glancing behind her, she saw the shadow of an intruder bolt from behind the curtain of chains, heading for the other briefcase.

Out of the corner of his eye, Yusuf saw him too. He spun on his heel, his finger squeezing the trigger of his gun.

Eden darted across the open space as fast as he could, sparks flying off the floor and bullets ricocheting around him.

Yusuf made a move for the briefcase as well, trying to head him off.

Eden almost reached the case, but a spray of bullets forced him left, toward the BMW. He reached the front passenger door and swung it open. On the other side of the car Saabir grabbed for the driver's door. Eden threw himself into the car, feet first. Saabir opened the driver's door and was met with the soles of Eden's shoes, both of which slammed straight into his chest, sending him reeling backward, his gun scuttling across the floor.

Yusuf caught a glimpse of his brother hitting the ground and spun his Uzi in a wide arc, blasting a rainbow of bullets through the air.

Lying sprawled across the passenger and driver's seat, Eden didn't bother to close any doors or to sit up, with the gunfire outside. He felt for the key in the ignition and turned it. The engine roared to life. Grabbing the gearshift, he jammed the car in reverse, then with his palm pressed flat against the accelerator he smoked up the floor of the cargo hold.

On the lift, Mya Chan heard the squeal of tires. "Hurry!" she screamed as her two accomplices climbed aboard the platform, each carrying a crate. "And be careful!" The second they staggered aboard, she punched the lift button.

Through the tire smoke, scattered diamonds sparkled on the floor. Mortified, Qassim crawled on his hands and knees. "My diamonds! My diamonds!" he wailed, scurrying through the smoke.

Eden's BMW swerved wide in blind reverse, swinging left and slamming into a wall of the ship's hull with a thunderous, hollow thud. Rear lights shattered. He punched the car into first gear.

Across the hold, Yusuf had already pulled Saabir to his feet and thrown him in the driver's seat of the second BMW, then rammed a fresh magazine into the Uzi's pistol grip.

Saabir kicked the car into reverse just as Eden squealed away from the wall. In the rearview mirror, Saabir grinned his gold-toothed grin as he lined Eden's Beemer up for a rear-end demolition derby smash. "Just like on cable," he cackled to his brother.

Eden saw the taillights coming, but there was no time to get out of the way. With a grinding crunch, the Qahtani brothers' car back-ended him. The momentum of the impact dragged Eden's BMW across the floor in a sliding shower of sparks. The cars skidded in a pirouette, their front and rear bumpers locked.

As the lift reached the deck above, Mya and her associates hurried out into the blinding daylight. From his place on the bridge, the captain saw the three hurry across the deck toward their black-and-silver Eurocopter EC 135. He saw the men carrying wooden crates, saw the urgency with which they moved, saw that Qassim Qahtani had not come up to the surface with them, and he knew something was wrong. He snatched up his walkie-talkie and radioed his crew on the deck below to send the lift back down—now!

Below deck, Qassim continued to scramble across the floor, searching desperately for his scattered diamonds as the two interlocked BMWs spun and screeched across the cargo hold.

Eden jerked his gears into reverse and tried to pull free. More tire smoke blew from his spinning wheels. His car dragged the Qahtani brothers several more feet across the floor, then with a jolt detached itself.

Saabir cranked through his gears and spun the steering wheel.

At the same time Eden braked, twisting his body so he was sitting upright at last, and looked through the windshield to see the Qahtani brothers facing him dead on. Yusuf was hanging out the passenger window, his Uzi pointed straight at Eden.

"Oh, shit!" Eden ducked and covered his head as the windshield above him exploded in a million shards. Bullets tattered the driver's seat headrest and smashed through the rear windshield. Eden reversed again, turning the wheel hard right. The Beemer flew in a wide circle, bullets continuing to pelt the car—and puncture the gas tank. Gasoline gushed from holes in the tank, leaving a wide arc across the floor.

While Yusuf fired, Saabir hit the accelerator and turned in pursuit, sweeping across the nose of Eden's car, unable to brake in time before plowing headlong into the ship's wall. The hood crumpled. Saabir shoved the car into reverse, zeroing in on Eden with more speed and determination than ever.

Eden peered over the glass-covered dash, saw the Qahtani brothers coming, and stepped on the brakes. Saabir was going too fast to adjust his course. Instead he braked as well, skidding to a halt directly in the path of Eden's car. Eden slammed his foot on the accelerator, wheels spinning in the pool of gas. As the tires found their grip the car headed straight for Yusuf's door.

CRASH!

Yusuf's door buckled. Eden's car pushed the Qahtani brothers all the way to the wall and pinned them there with a car-crumpling smash. The front bumper of Eden's BMW dislodged on one side, the fractured left end hitting the floor. Yusuf himself jolted across the passenger seat. The gun flew out of his hands, out the passenger window, clattered across Eden's hood, and bounced in through the shot-out windshield.

Yusuf blinked away his blurred vision, realized his gun was gone, and scrambled as fast as he could out through the bent frame of the passenger window.

Eden saw him coming and yanked the gears into reverse, but not before Yusuf threw himself on the twisted hood. As the car screamed backward, Yusuf clung to the car's hood. The half-dislodged front bumper scraped against the metal floor, sending up sparks as it followed the trail of gushing gasoline, until—*Foomp!* Sparks became flames.

Eden kept driving, trying to outrun the fire and turning the wheel to throw Yusuf off the hood. He reached for the Uzi, but as he lay his hand upon the weapon Yusuf threw a punch through the open windshield, hitting Eden directly in his face, hard enough to snap back his head and cause his hands to lose their grip on the gun and the wheel.

The car swerved precariously. Eden locked both hands on the wheel to maintain control.

And suddenly Yusuf was upon him. He had one hand on the wheel trying to tear it out of Eden's grip, and one hand flailing for the gun.

Eden returned the punch, his fist connecting with Yusuf's jaw.

Yusuf threw it straight back, smashing Eden across the cheekbone.

In the other car, Saabir glanced in his rearview mirror. He saw the quickly spreading fire, and in the middle of it he caught a glimpse of the semiautomatic pistol he'd dropped, lying on the floor amid the flames.

He reversed fast, adjusting his rearview mirror to guide him backward through the fire, keeping his eye on the gun—

—when he should have been looking out for his father.

Through the dancing flames, Qassim scrambled across the floor on hands and knees after his precious diamonds— and crawled straight into the path of Saabir's reversing car.

Saabir's BMW bounced violently as its back tires rolled over Qassim, flattening his skull.

Instantly Saabir knew something was wrong. He slammed on the brakes. Staring through the windshield, he saw the crushed, lifeless body of his father, his open palm glittering with diamonds.

"No!" Saabir howled.

He jumped out of the car and raced to his dead father.

Shock quickly turned to rage. With flames dancing in his eyes, Saabir's vengeful gaze homed in on the other car.

Eden took another blow to the jaw before slamming his foot on the brake. Yusuf slid up the hood of the car, his chest gliding over the broken glass covering the dash. He was even closer now to the Uzi and made a grab for it. Eden hammered the accelerator. The car hit 40 miles an hour in four seconds flat, blazing a fiery trail directly toward Saabir and the body of Qassim.

Yusuf got his hands on the Uzi and locked his fingers around the grip as Eden slammed on the brakes. The car slid to a breakneck halt, sending Yusuf flying off the hood and smashing into his brother.

Eden heard the lift clunk into place on the floor of the cargo hold behind him. He glanced back, slid the gears into reverse, then flew across the floor, tires aflame. He steered directly for the lift at full speed, then pulled on the emergency brake and slid onto the platform.

Far across the fiery cargo hold, Yusuf and Saabir clambered to their feet and opened fire.

Without leaving the car, Eden ducked in the driver's seat, wrestled off one of his shoes, then peered over the dash and threw the shoe as hard as he could at the large control button.

The shoe smacked its target.

The hydraulics whined into motion.

The platform began to ascend, lifting the BMW off the cargo hold floor, toward the deck. The bullets from Saabir's and Yusuf's guns ricocheted off the bottom of the platform as Eden rose higher and higher. Suddenly flames began to peel their way up the sides of the BMW. Eden kicked at the driver's door and it flung open, but he realized there was no way out. The Beemer sat squarely on the platform, and the drop was now four stories high and still rising to the deck.

As flames began to lick at the interior upholstery, Eden remembered the shirt on his back was still covered in highly flammable grease from the chain on the port. Buttons flew in the air as he ripped it open, chest first, and sent it flying out the windshield, where the flames turned it into a fireball.

His mind racing, he slid open the sunroof of the flaming BMW and saw the light of day approaching. With explosions like cannons blasting, one tire after another ruptured. Then, through the smoke, the sun filtered through the sunroof as the lift whirred to a halt, locking into place on the deck.

Eden pumped the accelerator to the floor. The gears were still in reverse, and the smoking, burning BMW squealed across the deck of the ship and slammed into the base of the bridge.

A short distance in front of him the lift began to descend, releasing a blanket of smoke from the burning cargo hold below; the Qahtani brothers would soon be on their way up.

Eden had to make his own escape before the BMW became his blazing coffin. Scrambling through the sunroof, he leaped over the flames and toppled across the deck. He looked around fast and saw the panicked looks from the captain and crew in the bridge above him. The blades of the diamond traders' helicopter swept in a wide circle, preparing for take-off, and Mya Chan was standing beside the open cabin door of the chopper, pulling her diamond-studded pistol from her boot.

She spotted Eden sprawled on the deck beneath the ship's bridge.

Her finger squeezed the trigger of the gun.

Below deck, the lift reached the burning floor of the cargo hold. Weapons in hand, Saabir and Yusuf fought their way through the flames and leapt onto the platform. They looked up at the open hatch high above, as the lift began to ascend.

On deck, Eden rolled. Sparks shot into the air inches from his turning, tumbling torso as Mya's bullets ricocheted. The black-hooded villainess pumped the trigger until the chamber was empty. Then she shouted over her shoulder at the man securing their payload. He leaned further into the cabin and handed her an M240 machine gun, an ammunition belt dangling from its feed tray, bullets ready to be chewed up and spat out in Eden's direction.

The gun looked enormous in Mya's hands, but she handled it with terrifying ease.

Eden leapt to his feet as an endless spray of bullets chased him, ripping apart the base of the bridge only inches behind him. He poured on the speed, leaping onto a nearby oil barrel, launching into the air, and crashing back onto the deck behind a large steel storage container.

With a deafening *Brrrrrrrrrr!* the machine gun's ammunition tore a path behind him, eating through the blazing BMW, up the wall of the bridge, and, to the wide-eyed horror

and the only way of slowing the ship now was to get inside the bridge. He reached the door and rattled the handle—locked. He shook it with all his strength, but it wouldn't give.

Up ahead, the port loomed closer and closer. He could see men running for their lives, fleeing the doomed port. A few gallant souls were rallying tugboats, throwing off lines and pushing the tugs out to sea.

Eden put his shoulder into the bridge door, but he felt his cracked rib snap completely. He roared in pain, wrapping his arms around his naked injured torso.

The bow of the ship cut a wake through the water, already sending waves smashing against the dock, rocking the pylons.

Eden knew it was too late to do anything but abandon ship. He raced for the railing.

As the lift rose toward the deck, Yusuf pulled himself up onto the platform, Uzi in hand, ready to take vengeance on the man who had destroyed his family. The lift stopped on the deck, Yusuf turned, and through the pouring smoke he saw Eden climb onto the railing, about to dive.

In that moment, Eden turned and spotted Yusuf.

Yusuf raised the Uzi, then saw the look in Eden's eye: Eden wasn't afraid of the man with the machine gun; he was more concerned about abandoning ship. Now!

Despite the pain that shot through his body, Eden raised his arms into a diving position and leapt from the railing.

Yusuf turned and gaped at what he saw.

Eden hit the water and plunged deep beneath the surface.

A giant wave from the charging ship surged up and over the dock. Several powerful, fearless tugs tried to ride the wave and position themselves quickly between the oncoming vessel and the port dock, and although they worked hard, engines roaring, to lessen the damage the runaway ship might cause, the port of Aden would never be the same again.

The out-of-control vessel plowed into the end of the dock, snapping the wharf's wooden planks and sending their splintered shards soaring through the air.

The Yemeni vessel tore into the French cargo ship, folding back curled sheets of steel before forcing the vessel backward, slamming it into the African oil tanker. Flames leapt from one ship to another. A sound—like a thousand car tires being knifed—filled the air as all three ships ignited. Yusuf turned to run, but he was too late.

The ball of fire that filled the air looked like an atomic blast, mushrooming into the bright blue sky and blanketing Aden in a veil of smoke that would last for days.

As the thunderous eruption sent shock waves through the ocean, the three ships began to sink. Eden held his breath for as long as he could, swimming deep and far. At one point he turned and looked back as burnt, twisted hunks of steel splashed into the water all around him. Every now and then he spotted the glimmer and sparkle of what could only be diamonds sinking through the water amid the debris. Raining down upon the seabed. Lost to the deep blue forever.

Just one, he thought.

That's all he needed to prove that these were Zhang Sen's stolen diamonds.

II

San Francisco, California

"What the hell happened to just observing, not intervening?"

Eden shrugged. "It wasn't so much a case of intervening. More like saving my own ass!"

As the two made their way through San Francisco's bustling airport terminal, Jake—dressed in a tuxedo, his shirt open-necked, and his untied black tie slung loose around his collar—took Eden's bag off him in exchange for a second, neatly pressed tuxedo in his hand. Jake was the rugged type, a New York adventurer with a penchant for deadly situations and dangerous men—a stranger to caution and care who hated pomp and ceremony. Yet Eden couldn't help but appreciate how handsome he looked right now, even with that angry furrow in his brow.

"The Professor wanted you to *see*, not *do*!"

"Is he upset?"

Jake shook his head. "Not at you. Jesus, he *never* gets

mad at *you*. If I blew up a port in Yemen, different story. But *you*, he loves. If anything ever happened to you, God help the rest of us!"

Eden couldn't suppress a smirk at Jake's accusation of favoritism. "Don't worry, I'll spare you the pain. Nothing's ever going to happen to me." Suddenly he winced and clutched his side.

"You're hurt!"

"I'm okay."

Jake lightly touched Eden's side, and the young Brazilian clenched his teeth, biting back a groan. "We're taking you to a hospital."

"No. I'm fine. Besides, don't you know that doctors make the worst patients?"

"I don't care, you're hurt."

"Later," Eden insisted. "I need to see the Professor first. I think Zhang is in trouble."

No sooner had they stepped out of the terminal and into the night air than a sleek black limousine pulled up before them. The driver was a young Chinese man, tall and muscular, wearing gloves and a chauffeur's cap. Tufts of bleached hair, white as snow, peeped out from under the cap. Eden eyed him suspiciously.

"One of Zhang's drivers," Jake informed him, noticing Eden's guarded gaze. "The party at the tower's already started."

"But we don't mind being fashionably late," said a voice from inside the limo. One of the back doors had already sprung open before the driver could offer assistance, and young Will Hunter, looking dapper in a tuxedo of his own, launched himself from the backseat of the stretch car in a maneuver that was straight off the football field. The 19-year-old college quarterback gave Eden a strong, hard squeeze, and the Brazilian tried not to let his pain show.

"Easy, kid," Jake said, stepping in and prying Will away. "Walking wounded, here."

"Jake, I'm okay," Eden insisted.

"You'll be fine once we get you to a hospital," Jake lectured him.

"After the party," Eden argued once more.

At that moment, Shane Houston, the gentlemanly Texas cowboy, stepped out of the back of the limo in his dinner jacket and cowboy hat, and embraced Eden even harder than Will did. "Are you okay?"

"I was," wheezed Eden. "Where's Luca?"

Indeed, the five of them were only four tonight; Luca was missing. "He's in Krakow," Will replied. "Still tryin' to dig up skeletons."

"It scares me to think what he might find," Eden said gravely. Then as Shane gave him another tight hug, Eden grimaced once more.

Jake hauled the cowboy off him. "Guys, you're killin' him with love. Back up. It's time the doctor saw a doctor!"

"What's all this about doctors and hospitals?" The question belonged to the Professor, who sat in the open doorway of the limousine, a look of concern on his face. "Eden, are you all right?"

"Professor, I'm fine. Probably just a broken rib or two. When we get back to the house I'll do a full checkup on myself. In the meantime, all I need is a stiff drink!"

"The bar is stocked!" Will winked, gesturing to the open back door of the limo.

"Sounds good to me," Eden said, smiling.

"Eden, are you certain you're all right?" the Professor asked again. "We're attending this party as a measure of security, not necessity."

Eden took a deep breath and said, "I'm not so sure about that, Professor." He shot another wary glance at the driver. "I'll tell you more on the way to the tower."

The screen between the driver's compartment and the back seats of the limo was closed. As the stretch car headed for the shimmering skyscrapers of downtown San Francisco, Jake helped Eden strip off his shirt, easing it off his broad brown back with care. The sleeves rolled inside out, freeing Eden's hands in time for him to receive a tumbler of scotch on ice from Will.

Eden drained the glass at once, then nodded at the rearview mirror in the driver's compartment, watching the driver's face. "Can he hear us?" The young driver didn't take his eyes off the road for a second.

Jake shook his head. "Intercom's off. So what surprises you got for us?"

Eden answered by unzipping his trousers and digging his hand deep into his underpants. He rummaged around for a moment or two, while Jake watched the sizable package shift from left to right and back again.

Shane caught the pleased glint in Jake's eye. "I don't think it's that sort of surprise."

He was right. Eden pulled his hand free, opened his palm, and everyone sat forward including the Professor, whose unseeing eyes sparkled in the reflection of the small diamond in Eden's hand.

"Is that what I think it is?" Will asked.

The Professor's sensitive fingers reached forward slowly and touched the tiny object in Eden's palm. "Zhang Sen will know for certain. Every one of Sen's diamonds contains a watermark, undetectable to the human eye. If this diamond bears that signature, then I think it's safe to assume the stolen jewels are ending up in some very dangerous hands. Which is precisely why he wants us there tonight."

"Mr. Sen wants us there to protect the diamonds?" Will asked.

"Actually, Will, it's Mr. Zhang," the Professor replied. "Sen is his first name. Traditionally, the Chinese surname comes first. And to answer your question, no, we're not there to protect the diamonds. We're there to protect *one* diamond. A diamond called the Eye of Fucanglong. It is one of the largest, most precious diamonds in the world, found fourteen centuries ago and placed in the eye of a golden dragon. It is the jewel in the crown of the Zhang Diamond empire."

"Hence the big shindig," Shane observed.

"The new Zhang Diamond Tower here in San Francisco is now complete, and the corporation is in the first phase of its expansion into the United States market. This event signifies the coming together of two great cultures, two unsinkable economies. What better occasion to unveil the Eye of Fucanglong to America? What better way to begin a multibillion-dollar international business venture than by showcasing the company's greatest treasure and putting it on display here in America for all the world to admire?"

"Or steal," Eden added.

"Why does he need us to help?" Jake asked. "Doesn't he have his own security team to keep an eye on the Eye—so to speak?"

"Sen is a very old friend of mine—we went to Oxford together. He has voiced concerns that the recent spate of thefts from his collections could be the work of someone within his own organization."

"He thinks it's an inside job?" Will asked.

"He's not taking any chances. Which is where we come in. If Sen has a concern for the Eye of Fucanglong, then we'll do everything in our power to safeguard it against those who may want to get their hands on it."

"I hate to say it, Professor, but I'm not so sure it's the diamond they want to get their hands on," Eden added. "Whoever's stealing from Zhang Sen is trading the diamonds for weapons on the international black market."

"What kind of weapons?" Jake asked.

"Bombs. I think the diamonds are being used to fund some sort of terrorist act."

"Are you sure?" the Professor asked.

"I'm positive. I saw two devices before the dealers made off with them. Professor, they were zidium bombs."

"Zidium?" the Professor breathed. "My God! Are you sure?"

"I've never seen one before, but I know what I heard and I know what those things can do."

"What the hell's a zidium bomb?" Will asked, his eyes glancing nervously from Eden to the Professor.

"I'll explain later." The Professor's tone was cool and collected, but not without a hint of urgency. "Shane, as soon as we get to the party, find us a copy of the guest list as well as a company staff listing for Zhang Diamonds. We need to know everybody who's invited, everybody who has any kind of connection with Sen, every employee who has ever worked for him. If this is an inside job, we must find out who these people are immediately. And more importantly, what they want."

"They want power. It's the curse, you see." Zhang Sen finished examining the small stolen diamond Eden had given him and put it down on the table with a heavy-hearted sigh. "And yes, this is one of mine."

Suddenly a cork popped like a gunshot and the champagne flowed, its bubbles filling up Sen's glass, although, right now, celebrating was the last thing on his mind. The waiter turned and left, closing the door to the mezzanine boardroom behind him, completely shutting out the sounds of the party that filled the 52nd floor of the glittering new Zhang Diamond Tower in the heart of San Francisco's financial district.

There were five of them in the room: the Professor, Eden, Jake, Will, and Sen, a gray-haired gentleman in his mid-sixties, small and dignified, his composure calm and his gestures understated. Yet beneath his poised facade there lingered a sense of disquiet and concern.

"It began almost fifteen hundred years ago. Legend has it, a beautiful but evil witch fell in love with a young man who lived in a village in the mountains of Shandong. He was a handsome man of purity and clarity. The witch desperately wanted his love; she wanted him to be with her for all time. But for all her spells and hexes—all her power—she could not make him love her. So one day in a fit of rage she cut out his heart and turned it into a diamond, something she could possess forever. This angered the gods, who sent Fucanglong, the dragon god of the underworld, the guardian of precious jewels and lost treasures, to kill the witch.

"Blazing a flaming trail behind him, Fucanglong burst from the mountains in a terrible explosion of fire and smoke to claim the diamond, to protect it forever. For three days the dragon god and the witch were locked in a fierce battle, one that leveled mountains and destroyed cities, until eventually the witch sliced out one of Fucanglong's eyes. But when she raised her dagger to finish him off, the dragon god seized the diamond from her and turned the young man's bejeweled heart into a glittering stone eye for himself, so that he could see his enemy with clarity and purity. Fucanglong dealt the witch one last fatal blow with his mighty tail, but before she died, she looked into the diamond eye of the dragon god and said, 'He who looks into your eye shall be cursed forever.'"

"Cursed with what?" Jake asked, his own heart turning to stone upon once again hearing that word.

"Cursed to always want...but never to have."

Sen walked over to a wall of the boardroom and pressed a button. The entire wall began to slide away, revealing a two-way mirror overlooking the party below. Concealed behind the glass, Sen and the Professor's boys watched on as hundreds of immaculately dressed men and exquisitely adorned women milled about on the floor below them, taking delicate sips of their champagne, staring with admiring eyes not at the stunning views over San Francisco through the floor-to-ceiling windows, but at the dozens upon dozens of glittering displays around them—a fortune in dazzling diamonds encased in glass.

In the center of the room, the majority of the partygoers had gathered, positioning themselves around a large, ceiling-high display case concealed by black curtains. They knew what was behind it. The rumors had already circulated and the excitement was building, and even though none of them could see it yet, it seemed that Sen's guests were already entranced by the spell of the Eye of Fucanglong.

Sen continued, "And so the curse began, fifteen hundred years ago. For centuries, blood has been spilled, men have died, feudal empires have waged war and destroyed each other, all because of the diamond. In 1936, my grandfather had made enough money with his mining company to purchase the diamond at an auction in Shanghai. He never once looked at it. He simply locked it away for fear of what it might do to him. He felt it was his duty to keep it safe from the world...and the world safe from it."

"So why bring it out now?" Jake asked matter-of-factly. "If you're worried about it, if your grandfather was so concerned about the curse, if so many people died, why tempt fate?"

Sen smiled sweetly, fondly. "My grandfather was a very superstitious man. I, on the other hand, am a businessman, one who appreciates traditional Chinese values without the hocus-pocus, and someone who appreciates true beauty. I'm not saying the curse is real or not, but I don't believe in keeping something so beautiful, so exquisite, from the rest of the world. What was it Keats wrote?"

Jake surprised everyone by answering first. "A thing of beauty is a joy forever."

The Professor smiled. "You're a curiosity, Jake Stone."

"I'll take that as a compliment."

At that moment, the door to the boardroom opened, and a handsome young Chinese man in his early twenties stuck his head in the door, sized up the room, then said, apologetically, "Oh, Uncle, I'm sorry. I didn't know you had guests."

"It's all right, Bradley. Gentlemen, this is my nephew, Bradley Zhang. He prefers a western interpretation of his name, and he's no doubt here to tell me I'm running behind schedule."

"Just doing my job, Uncle," Bradley said with a smile.

Sen smiled back appreciatively. "Bradley looks after me, and he shares the number two position in the corporation alongside a prominent Harvard Business graduate, Chad Chambers, whom you'll no doubt meet as soon as we're done here. Bradley himself went to Yale. His pipe dream of becoming an Olympic ice skater took some time to snuff out, but eventually he saw the light—or should I say, the glimmer of diamonds." Sen turned to Bradley and gave him a polite, yet authoritative, nod. "We'll be finished here in a minute...if you don't mind."

"Of course, Uncle," Bradley said, bowing courteously and closing the door behind him.

The moment he was gone, Sen turned to the others in the room. "As you can see, the future of this company is in very good hands. The only question remaining is whose hands I shall leave it in—Mr. Chambers or my nephew? Who has the fortitude to ensure that this company grows from strength to strength toward a bright shining future? That's assuming this company actually has a future. If these thefts continue..." Sen sighed before finishing his thought, then changed the subject altogether. "What is the time, by the way?"

Will, Jake, and Eden all checked their watches and began pressing buttons and turning dials. The Professor immediately sensed Sen's curiosity in the boys' fidgeting.

"Forgive them, Sen. Their watches are primarily used for global navigation. I have a tracking device inside me. It's a long story, but one that's come in handy on a number of occasions." The Professor patted his stomach. "Thanks to what's in here, my men can find me anywhere in the world."

"What an amazing world we live in," Sen marveled. "When I was a child, my mother would find me by ringing a bell." There was a hint of sadness and loss in his voice.

The Professor rested his hand lightly on his old friend's shoulder. "Everything's going to be all right, Sen. We'll find the people who are doing this, and we'll stop them before they can do any harm to you or anybody else."

There was a knock at the door then, and Shane briskly entered. He carried two manila folders in his hand. "I've got it," he said.

"Ah, Shane. May I introduce Zhang Sen." The two men shook hands as the Professor added, "Sen, I hope you don't mind. I asked Shane to gather some information on your guests."

"Your CI2, Chad Chambers, was extremely helpful," Shane said.

"We're all anxious to see this matter resolved," Sen replied, nodding.

Shane placed the two manila folders on the table and opened one of them. "This is the guest list. Five hundred and eighty VIPs, dignitaries, politicians, business tycoons—"

"You make them sound like such a boring lot," Sen joked uneasily. "These people are supposed to be my friends, my business partners. How could any of them want to steal from me?"

"Is there anyone on the list who hasn't shown?" the Professor asked.

Shane flicked through the pages. "Everyone's here and accounted for."

Sen nodded with grace and humility. "My parties are indeed popular. I like to think I have a rather outstanding reputation as a host, but in all sincerity, I think it's the lure of the diamonds. Nobody can resist being surrounded by them."

"Wait a minute," Shane interjected. "A guy named Richard Conrad hasn't shown up yet."

"I don't expect he will," Sen said. "He's currently working on a project in Dubai."

Jake rattled his brain. "I've heard of him. Richard Conrad, the British construction guy..."

Sen nodded once more. "Conrad Constructions, yes, that's him. He's only twenty-eight and already a self-made billionaire. He's very, how do you say it...hands on. He's also brash, but a smart young man and a trusted colleague nonetheless. He owns half the cranes in China and the Middle East, with more development sites on the way. We've been talking recently about future plans together. Plans I hope to unveil tonight. It's a shame he couldn't be here, but formalities bore him. He's more the adventurous type." Sen smiled. "But I've let the time run away from me again and duty calls. Gentlemen, shall we join the other guests?"

Jake led the way out of the room—almost like a bodyguard—followed by Sen, the Professor, Will, and Shane. Eden was the last to leave. He began to close the door to the boardroom behind him, then something stopped him. He turned and noticed the second folder still lying on the table, unopened. He backtracked into the boardroom, leaving the others to descend a wide swirling staircase from the mezzanine level to the party below.

Shane assisted the Professor down the stairs while Jake helped Sen.

At the foot of the stairs they were met by a dashing man in his late twenties. He was well built and fit perfectly into his expensive tuxedo. His short black hair was groomed with great care and precision, and his smooth white smile seemed to pick up the glint of every diamond in the room. "Sen, you're late. Lucky for you, being late is back in fashion, and your diamonds, well, they were never out of fashion to begin with."

Sen smiled back. "Gentlemen, please say hello to Chad Chambers, one of the brightest, most brutal businessmen I've ever had the pleasure to work with."

"I'm only brutal to be kind to the company," Chad justified with a raised finger before shaking the Professor's hand and introducing himself to Jake, Shane, and Will.

"Kind to the company? Or kind to your career?" Sen remarked jokingly.

"There's nothing wrong with a little ambition," Chad replied with a smirk.

"Absolutely not," Sen agreed. To the others he said, "Chad's a very goal-driven individual."

"Goal being the operative word," Chad happily explained. "My philosophy on achieving anything is simple. Determine your goal first, then work through the steps backward to reach that goal. Now gentlemen, if you'll excuse us. The main event is about to commence."

With a confident strut, Chad disappeared into the crowd, leading Sen toward the large veiled display in the center of the room.

Shane turned to the Professor, Jake, and Will. "If there's any trouble going down I suggest we split up."

"Where's Eden?" Jake asked.

Will looked around. "He must be back in the boardroom. I'll get him."

He crossed the floor, weaving his way past socialites and celebrities, until he reached the foot of the stairs leading back up to the mezzanine. He hurried up the first two steps before someone snagged his arm from behind. He spun around to see the concerned face of Bradley Zhang.

"I need to talk to you," he said. Without waiting for a reply he grabbed Will by the wrist and quickly whisked him through the crowd, leading him to an out-of-the way spot under the staircase.

Moving through the crowd, Sen received kisses and handshakes until he and Chad arrived at the black curtains of the hidden display. A suave smile fixed itself upon Chad's lips as he took a diamond-encrusted pen from his pocket and a champagne flute from a passing waiter and tapped pen to glass. "Ladies and gentlemen, can I please have your attention." Heads turned, as the guests quieted and gathered around them. "May I present your host, owner of the Zhang Diamond Corporation, Mr. Zhang Sen."

Applause filled the room.

Upstairs in the boardroom, Eden opened the second folder. It was a list of company employees. Slowly his finger slid down the page, his eyes scanning over each individual name, first printed in Chinese, then in English. He wasn't at all sure what he was looking for—until he saw it.

Downstairs, Jake discreetly made his way through the applauding guests, looking from face to face, searching for a suspicious sideways glance or a bead of anxious sweat on someone's brow. Shane stayed close to the Professor, watching as a small, beautiful Chinese woman in a slender red dress walked to the front of the crowd, straight up to Chad, and slipped her arm in his. Her red lips, a dazzling match to her dress, curled into a seductive smile as she whispered something in Chad's ear.

Standing before the veiled display case, Sen bowed modestly to the applause. "Thank you all for the warm reception, and thank you for coming. Some people say that the Zhang Diamond Corporation's expansion into the United States is all about money—"

"Did you see the price tag on my wife's necklace?" heckled one Southern gentleman good-naturedly.

The other partygoers shared the joke, but laughed even harder when the charming Chad piped up, "You bought your beautiful wife a necklace with a price tag? Darling, your husband's a cheapskate!"

Beneath the mezzanine stairs, Will's brow creased with unease. "You need to talk? About what?"

"I think this is deeper than just the stolen diamonds," Bradley whispered fearfully.

"What do you mean?"

"I'm not sure. All I know is, I'm on the outside. But whatever's happening *is* on the inside. I think something terrible is going to happen. Something that will change *everything*. I don't know who to trust anymore."

Upstairs in the boardroom, Eden grabbed the piece of paper from the folder and ran to the two-way window overlooking the party, frantically scanning the crowd.

"As I was saying," Sen said, "some may believe that the Zhang Diamond Corporation's expansion to American shores is all about money. I believe it's about common goals. Common dreams. And unlimited potential. I promise to surpass all other diamond-producing nations, to shun the corruption of others, and build a brand-new world industry based on smart business, fair trade, equal rights for all, and the most beautiful product in the world. And to make sure there is a guardian of that promise, I'm proud to announce tonight that my dragon—the very symbol of my family's hard work and success—has found a new home. And although my empire's protector is himself protected behind three inches of bulletproof glass, it is with great pleasure that I announce that his new home is here, in San Francisco's Zhang Diamond Tower. A new dawn has arrived!"

Audibly, a wave of excitement swept through the crowd. Sen's gracious smile spread even wider. "But before I unveil my beloved treasure, there are people I'd like to thank for making this extraordinary business venture possible, namely my two right-hand men, Chad and Bradley. As well as Chad's remarkably resourceful, and might I add stunningly beautiful, assistant—"

Staring through the boardroom window, his eyes darting desperately through the crowd, Eden saw the person he was looking for—not hidden in the crowd, but standing directly beside Sen, smiling.

Eden whispered the name at the same moment Sen said it. "—Mya Chan."

This was the cue for Mya to step forward, smile for her adoring audience, and take the gold cord that dangled from the black curtains around the display case.

"And so," Sen announced proudly, "as a gesture of my appreciation to the United States, and my faith in a long and prosperous future together, I give you the Eye of Fucanglong."

With a light, graceful tug on the cord, Mya let the black curtain drop and the audience watched it ripple to the floor. A collective gasp filled the room.

Behind thick glass casing reared a fearsome, fabulous golden dragon, its long slender body looping and spiraling around itself, its claws at the ready, its jaws open wide, and its one diamond eye casting a spell of beauty and awe across the entire room. The diamond, the size of a man's fist, radiated rays of spectral light that shone on the faces of its adoring spectators.

The giant jewel was astonishing.

It was mesmerizing.

It was perfect.

Everyone was in awe—

—except Eden.

Crashing through the boardroom doors, Eden tore down the stairs from the mezzanine level. His first thought was to get to Zhang Sen and the Professor immediately. His second thought was to find Shane, Jake, and Will and somehow detain Mya Chan. His third thought was—*gunshots!*

Crack! Crack-crack!

The crowd jolted.

Knees bent instinctively.

Short, shocked screams escaped a few frightened men and women.

Heads turned to the origin of the sound.

There was smoke near the door, yellow and choking, and a terrible commotion, then the fierce face of a colossal beast began to lash and thrash through the churning, sulfurous air.

The monster's jaws chomped theatrically.

Bright streamers rippled from its flared nostrils.

Drums began pounding, cymbals crashed, and bells chimed dramatically.

More shots rang out, only they weren't gunshots at all, but firecrackers exploding on the ground.

Relieved laughter and more sighs of awe swept the crowd, along with sporadic applause, as a shimmering, swirling 30-foot-long Chinese dragon wove a thunderous path through the crowd, arching and swooping and sweeping through the room with the help of half a dozen performers hidden beneath the dragon's silky, colorful skin.

Beneath the mezzanine stairs, Bradley Zhang looked on in trepidation. "I've got a bad feeling about this."

Will saw the unease in his eyes and grabbed his hand. "Come on, let's find the others. Fast."

Across the room, Shane seemed to share the same uncertainty as Bradley.

"What's going on?" the Professor asked him.

"A Chinese dragon show," Shane explained over the gonging bells and the hiss and spit of firecrackers.

He grabbed the Professor's arm with one hand and took hold of Sen's shoulder with the other. "If you don't mind, Mr. Zhang, I suggest we move back." Slowly he pulled away, leading the two elderly gentlemen away from the encased golden dragon with the diamond eye, all the while keeping his own eye on the theater dragon.

He did not see Mya slip away into the crowd.

Nor did he see Eden, desperately trying to push his way through.

Jake, meanwhile, was standing 20 feet away from Shane and the Professor, positioned between the glass display case and the floor-to-ceiling windows overlooking the city. His eyes instinctively zoned out the crowd and the dancing dragon and instead spotted Eden pushing and shoving his way through the packed room. Eden, too, caught sight of Jake and was trying to call out to him. But the one thing Jake couldn't block out was the sound of the party.

Eden was pointing over people's heads, shouting in vain.

Jake followed Eden's fingers across the room.

All he saw was more and more guests clapping and laughing.

Then he saw the sliver of a red dress disappear through the crowd.

Suddenly, from behind Eden, the dancing dragon reared up, opened its jaws wide, and, with an almighty thunderclap of drums, six Chinese performers—dressed in black, wearing black face masks—threw the silky beast off their backs.

The crowd's first response was to emphatically applaud the artists.

Will, however, instantly sensed danger and pulled Bradley back from the scene.

Shane tightened his grip on Sen and the Professor.

Eden saw the alarm in Jake's eyes and turned as the long, shimmering skin of the dragon costume parachuted to the floor. From that moment on, everything Eden saw seemed to happen in slow motion—as though he was counting down the last seconds of his life, carefully taking account of each and every terrifying moment.

The black-dressed performers acknowledged the applause by raising their hands in the air. Then, reaching behind their shoulders, each pulled out a Heckler & Koch MP5 submachine gun from the holster strapped to his back.

Suddenly the applause turned to screaming—

—and the sound of automatic gunfire began.

Sparks flew and plaster rained down as bullets sprayed the ceiling and punctured the walls. People ran, fell, shrieked, cried, and tripped over one another in a frenzied panic. Three of the performers began blasting open the many display cases, scooping out tiaras and necklaces and shoving them in pouches sewn into their costumes. The other three performers had their targets carefully chosen.

Shane saw the first performer turn his machine gun on Sen. As the attacker squeezed the trigger, Shane wrapped one arm around Sen and one around the Professor and threw both men to the ground, covering them with his body. Bullets whistled through the air above his head, one clipping his ear, another shredding the collar of his tuxedo jacket.

At the same time, the second performer's gun jolted powerfully in his arms as he fired a trail of bullets in Bradley's direction. But Will already had the young Chinese businessman in his arms and was sailing toward the floor, bullets splintering the steps to the mezzanine.

The third performer crouched low, placed his weapon on the ground, and pulled a small silver cylinder from his belt. He pressed a single button on the top of the device, then rolled it across the floor toward the display case containing the diamond-eyed dragon.

Jake was trying to keep as many people as he could low to the ground and push them toward the door.

He did not see the silver cylinder roll across the floor and come to rest three feet in front of the display case—and directly between his feet.

Eden, however, caught sight of the glinting device. Frantically he pushed through the crying crowd and shouted at the top of his voice:

"Bomb!"

Jake turned in time to see Eden barrel directly into him, thumping him in the chest with his shoulder, knocking Jake clear off his feet and sending him through the air. He landed with a bone-crunching crash that belted the wind out of him, opened his eyes to see Eden now over the bomb, and then—a white flash and a sonic shock wave swept out over the room, knocking everyone to the floor.

Every sheet of glass, from the huge windows overlooking the city to the bulletproof display case containing the Eye of Fucanglong, shattered into tiny shining shards that filled the air.

Jake momentarily covered his head as smashed glass shot through the air like missiles, then glanced up to see Eden, soaring across the room away from the source of the explosion, propelled by the shock wave. He was flying helplessly toward the shattered windows overlooking the city.

Jake jumped to his feet, feeling the flying glass lacerate his face.

He reached desperately for Eden as the Brazilian's stunned body sailed through the air. He stretched out his arm as far as he could, his fingers brushing Eden's sleeve, trying to grip his cuff, his hand, anything.

But he just couldn't reach him.

Unconscious, Eden Santiago flew through the air, hit the floor an inch from the shattered window, then slid over the edge, into the dark night.

Wide-eyed, horrified, Jake watched Eden vanish out the window of the 52nd floor.

"Nnooooooo!!"

His heart nearly burst in his chest as Jake scrambled for the edge.

Still shielding the Professor and a horrified Sen, Shane lifted his head and saw Jake charging for the shattered window.

"Jake?" he called out, seeing the panic on Jake's face, fearing the worst. But before Shane could lift himself up, the butt of a submachine gun connected with the back of his skull. As blackness quickly clouded his vision, he felt the Professor and Sen being forcibly dragged out from underneath him. Shane reached out in vain to grab hold of them both, but with another blow to the head he slumped to the ground unconscious.

"Professor!" Will gasped on the other side of the room, hurriedly pulling himself to his feet as he saw one of the black-suited performers pull a struggling Professor Fathom and a trembling Sen to their feet.

"The diamond!" Will heard Bradley breathe. He glanced at the golden dragon in time to see one of the performers pluck out the Eye of Fucanglong. The masked thief took the giant diamond in his fist, then turned and ordered his team of attackers to the elevator, along with their hostages: Sen and the Professor.

Will leaped to his feet and began to charge but was met with another barrage of gunfire from the submachine guns.

He covered his head and slid back to the floor.

More screams and cries filled the room.

By the time he looked up, the elevator doors were closing, with all six performers and the two old men inside.

Will glanced back at Bradley, clambering to his feet. "Are you okay?"

Bradley nodded.

"Stay here," Will ordered. He sprang across the room, leaping over the wounded and wailing, and dropped to his knees by Shane's side. The Texan's short blond hair was matted with blood. Will felt for a pulse and sighed with relief when he found one.

But his relief was short-lived.

"*Will!*"

The young college quarterback looked up and saw Jake, wild-eyed, standing at the edge of the shattered window.

"Oh, God!" Will whispered.

He bolted for the window, bounding so fast across the room that Jake had to stop him from going over the edge himself.

On the balcony of the 47th floor was the body of Eden Santiago, lying on his back, limbs tangled, a dark pool of blood spreading quickly across the tiles beneath him.

The air escaped Will's lungs in a mortified, defeated "No."

"I have to get to him," Jake blurted, a tear already streaking down his face.

"I'm coming with you," Will said, his desperate, pounding, frightened heart now breaking.

"No—the Professor. You have to go after the Professor."

Will and Jake rammed through the exit doors. Jake bounded down the stairs five at a time. Will slid down the metal banisters, crashing at the bottom of each flight, then jumping to his feet and doing the same again and again, speeding his way to the next level.

At the 47th floor, Jake slammed against the exit door, ignoring the alarm that sounded. He glanced back at Will, and for a moment Will stopped, heart thumping, eyes watering. Neither man said a word. Then Jake was gone.

Will continued his lightning descent all the way down the concrete stairwell of the Zhang Diamond Tower till he hit the ground floor, snapped open the emergency bar on the exit, and shouldered his way out the door, tumbling into an alley.

The first thing he heard was a commotion, a hundred feet down the alley.

A Chinese chef was in a rage on the ground, rolling around on his back, trying to clamber to his feet while hurling abuse through the open door of a restaurant's kitchen. Several petrified kitchen hands poured out through the door and helped their angry, shouting boss to his feet.

Swiftly Will followed the trail of chaos. He swept past the chef and the flustered kitchen hands and charged straight through the open door of the kitchen.

Under the bright lights of the kitchen, pushing against the current of terrified dishwashers and squealing waitresses all trying to escape the restaurant, Will raced as fast as he could, charging headlong through the swinging doors into the restaurant.

He was met with a blaze of bullets and the screams of patrons all huddling under round tables, trying desperately to hide. Before he dropped to the ground, Will caught sight of the six black-suited attackers weaving their way through the tables, headed for the front door of the restaurant, dragging Sen and the Professor with them. Two of the attackers yanked their hostages out through the front doors of the restaurant, while the other four remained, blasting their submachine guns in an effort to keep Will at bay.

As bullets ripped holes in the red and gold wallpaper, Will hastily belly-crawled across the floor. Through the forest of table legs, he could see the feet of his attackers near the far end of the restaurant, blocking his path to the door. Outside he could hear the screech of tires as a vehicle made its getaway.

Will had no weapon, no plan, and he was fast running out of time. He launched himself to his feet, one foot digging into the carpet, one pouncing on a chair, one hand swiftly grabbing the back of another chair and plucking it off the ground as he leapt up onto the nearest tabletop.

The guns turned on him as he landed in the center of a round lazy Susan, his momentum sending it into a spin. As he whirled, he ducked and hurled the chair as hard as he could. It flew through the air, collecting countless bullets before slamming into the head of one of his attackers. The man dropped to the floor, unconscious, his gun flying out of his hand.

Will didn't stop to watch.

He had already launched himself from one tabletop to the next. As the three remaining assailants tried to follow him with a spray of bullets, Will bent down and scooped up plates sitting on the table and threw them one after another at the men with machine guns. They flew like saucers. One plate smashed against the wall, another shattered against the front window, but the third managed to fly straight into the throat of one of Will's attackers, smashing the man's Adam's apple and sending him to the floor, choking and spluttering.

Will crouched low and covered his head as he heard the whistle of bullets inches above him. He glanced at the dishes on the table speeding by in a blur—one dish was still aflame. He picked it up and sent it hurtling through the air. Spitting fire and hissing food shot across the room and sprayed both assailants. One of the men ducked to avoid the rain of flames, but the other was too slow. Burning oil splashed across his face mask, igniting instantly. The man lurched back screaming and flailing before crashing through the front window of the restaurant.

Will pulled the table down in front of him as a shield just as the last attacker steadied his aim and pumped off several rounds. Before he could get to his feet, the last attacker appeared over him with his submachine gun in hand.

Will froze, pinned down and nowhere to go. His fingers inched their way across the carpet in search of a weapon, anything, while his eyes stared down the barrel of his attacker's gun.

With his prey sitting at close range and completely defenseless, the black-suited attacker began to laugh. When he did, Will seized a discarded chopstick off the floor in his fist and rammed it straight into the barrel of the submachine gun, jamming it in as hard as he could.

Startled, the attacker squeezed the trigger. The gun backfired, the rear of the chamber exploding in a spasm of bullets as the chopstick shot out the barrel, spearing Will in the shoulder. The attacker fell backward, his face suddenly full of shrapnel.

Will collapsed to the floor, screaming in agony, clutching at the chopstick protruding from his right shoulder. He tried to pull it out, but it had buried itself too deep to retrieve now.

As the blood began to stain his tattered tux, he stumbled out the front doors of the restaurant and saw a black van speeding away in the distance. He threw his good arm in the air and staggered into the middle of the street, trying desperately to wave down a ride of any kind. Brakes screeched and Will spun around in the headlights of a giant RV, which slid to a halt within two feet of hitting him.

He looked up through the windshield to see the startled

faces of an older couple staring down at him, clutching at their chests.

"For the love of God, Howard, what are you trying to do? Kill someone?"

"Shut up, Gladys! I can't think with you screamin' at me!"

"Forget about thinking. Just look where you're going! Oh, my God, he's bleeding!"

"Quick, lock the door. He's probably one of them homosexuals I was tellin' you about. This city's full of 'em. We never shoulda come here in the first place, but no, you wouldn't listen to me. You never listen to a word I—"

Howard was right—Gladys didn't listen to a word. Instead of locking the door, she was already opening it and in a flustered voice calling out, "Young man! Are you all right? Did my husband hit you?"

Will glanced down the street where the black van had disappeared, then looked at his watch. The tracking system had located the Professor, and he was moving fast through a gridlike map of San Francisco. Will raced around to the door of the RV and looked up at Gladys. "Ma'am, I need a ride."

"To the hospital?" She looked at his bloodstained clothes. "Is that a chopstick in your shoulder?"

"Goddammit, he's been fightin' with the Chinese!" Howard muttered disapprovingly. "This city's full of 'em. We never shoulda—"

"Oh, shut up, Howard!" she shouted, then smiled politely at Will. "My husband's lost—again. If you need a ride I'm afraid we won't be of much help to you at all. We're not from around here."

"That's okay," Will said, climbing aboard. "I'll drive."

"Oh, Lord Jesus!" Howard cried, springing out of the driver's seat with his hands in the air. "Is this a carjacking? Just please don't touch me inappropriately. I pray to God above to spare me from this homosexual."

Will rolled his eyes, dropped himself into the driver's seat, and turned to Gladys. "Has your husband always been this way?"

Gladys sighed and nodded her head yes.

Howard gave Gladys an incensed glare.

Will smiled and said, "Ma'am, you might wanna take a seat and buckle up. It's gonna be a bumpy ride."

As Gladys strapped herself into the passenger seat and Howard sat down at the kitchenette table in back, Will crunched the gears, flattened the accelerator, and spun the tires of the RV. The 30-foot vehicle took off with a squeal and rocketed down the street.

Gladys clung to her seat as though she was about to be ejected into space. Howard's hands slid back and forth along the edge of the table, trying desperately to hold on. Horns blasted and drivers screamed abuse as the RV hurtled through the night.

"Ma'am, do you know how to read a map?"

"Better than my husband."

"Poppycock!" Howard shouted from the rear as Will spun the wheel and turned a hard left.

The young man winced at the pain in his shoulder, straightened the wheel, and jerked through the gears once more, then held his left hand out to Gladys. "Take my watch. It's a tracking device. We need to follow that flashing red dot."

More shocked than ever, Gladys unstrapped Will's watch. "What are you, some kind of secret agent?"

"Not quite. I'm a history major. And I play football."

"Oh, my," Gladys gushed with a flutter of her eyelids.

"Where's the red dot now?" Will asked urgently.

"Oh, of course! The dot!" She tried to focus on the watch in her hands. "Oh, dear, I think it's behind us!"

"You've got the damn thing upside down!" Howard shouted from the back.

Will turned the wheel a sharp right, and the sour old man rolled off the cushioned bench seat and onto the floor. "Excuse me, sir, there's no need to talk to your wife like that!"

"I see it!" Gladys shouted excitedly, pointing to the flashing red dot on the grid. "It's moving parallel now. Turn at the next corner, left, then—"

Suddenly Gladys shrieked.

The next corner was a hell of a lot closer than Gladys bargained for, but Will did as instructed. He slammed on the brakes, hauled the wheel sharp left, and everyone held on tight as the rear of the RV sailed wide. The vehicle took the corner, straightened up, and kept going at top speed.

"Hold on," Will warned again, as the van hit the rise of a hill and for a moment became airborne—lifting Will and Gladys out of their seats while Howard rose off the floor—before slamming back down in an explosion of sparks. The chassis groaned, as did Howard at the unmistakable rattle of RV shrapnel trailing away on the road behind them.

"There!" Gladys pointed ahead, surprised at the level of excitement in her own voice. She felt as though she'd stepped straight into a movie, one with a handsome hero for a leading man—and Gladys at his side! "That's it up ahead! Can you see?"

Will spotted the taillights of the black van weaving in and out of the night traffic ahead. "I see 'em." His fist seized the gearshift as he pumped the clutch and gave the accelerator hell. The engine strained and the RV flew up the hill.

Will changed gears again and swung out onto the other side of the road to avoid a slow-moving station wagon, only to find himself directly in the path of a flower delivery truck sailing down the hill. The truck veered left, right, not sure what to do.

Howard moaned fearfully in back. Gladys held her breath and gripped her seat even tighter.

As the truck sped toward them, Will watched the driver clamp his eyes shut. Then, at the very last second, the delivery truck turned out of Will's path—

—only to reveal the Powell-Hyde cable car, which had been tailing the truck, racing down the street, about to collide head on with the RV.

Will tried desperately to accelerate clear of the station wagon, blasting his horn.

Panic gripped the cable car driver. At first he started ringing his bell like a fire alarm, but quickly abandoned it to crank on the brake lever with both hands. A terrible, ear-piercing grinding sound filled the street, the cable car squealing as it tried to grind to a halt, passengers screaming.

The station wagon peeled over to the side. Will spun the wheel hard, but by now he was too close, traveling too fast, to avoid some sort of impact with the oncoming cable car.

A split second later there was a loud *CRACK* as the corner of the cable car connected with the RV, snapping off the left mirror. The cable car scraped along the entire length of the motor home in a lightning storm of sparks.

Panels from both vehicles buckled, ripping loose and spitting out onto the road. The cable car finally screeched to a halt as the motor home kept speeding in the opposite direction.

"Is everyone okay?" Will shouted.

Howard was too stunned to answer. Gladys nodded and began to laugh. "Okay? I've never felt so alive in all my life!"

Will smiled, then glanced ahead to see the black van reach the crest of the hill, brake, and make a sudden turn, as though the driver was acting on a hunch. "Where's he going?" Gladys asked.

"I don't know, but wherever it is, that's where we're going."

As the RV hit the top of the hill, Will turned the wheel

sharply to follow, then gasped, "Oh, shit!" suddenly regretting the move, trying to spin the wheel out of the turn. But it was too late. He'd missed the signs. Now the almost unmaneuverable 30-foot motor home had just careened nose first down steep, zigzagging Lombard Street.

The RV didn't stand a chance of negotiating these hairpin bends.

In a single glance, Will realized that if he attempted a single corner he'd either wedge the RV or be unable to turn at all and crash headlong into one of the houses on the first bend. So instead he did the only thing he could—he turned the wheel straight down the middle of the slope, taking the RV off-road completely and plowing a beeline through the winding curves, churning up the gardens and leaving a trail of destruction.

The black van smoked its brakes at every switchback as it raced down the crooked street. But the RV was gaining fast, thanks to Will's desperate move. Gladys held on to her safety belt for dear life, while Howard was thrown relentlessly up and down in back.

As the van reached the bottom of the street, the beaten-up RV crunched through the last concrete retaining wall, flew into the air, and hurtled into the back of the van, sending it into a spin. In a shroud of burning rubber, the vehicle performed three full revolutions, and for a moment Will thought they had caught them. But the driver of the van regained control and hightailed it down the street.

"Son of a bitch!" Will wiped the sweat from his brow and revved the engine of the RV. It didn't quite sound the same this time—the motor rattled and clunked.

"You've broken it!" Howard hollered from the floor.

"Not yet, I haven't." Will put his foot to the floor once more, and the motor home buzzed and sputtered as fast as it could down the street, dragging twisted chunks of metal behind it.

With Gladys navigating, the RV raced as fast as it could through the streets of San Francisco, heading west, then sweeping north toward the Golden Gate Bridge. On the tracking grid of Will's watch the distance between the RV and the van grew wider and wider until they could no longer see the van through the windshield.

Then—

"They've stopped!" Gladys yelled.

"Where?"

"The bridge!" she gasped. "I think they've stopped right in the middle of the bridge!"

The motor home skirted the Presidio as signs to the bridge passed overhead.

And up ahead they saw that Gladys was indeed right. Dead in the center of the Golden Gate Bridge, to a chorus of blaring horns, the black van had pulled over to one side.

As cars swerved dangerously to avoid hitting it, the van's side door slid open and the two remaining black-clad diamond thieves jumped out, barking orders in Chinese through their masks, dragging Sen and the Professor out of the vehicle. With guns jammed into the back of their skulls, the two elderly men were forced to the side of the bridge and held at the railing. Through the fierce winds the men barked orders at Sen and the Professor.

"My God," Sen cried in fear to the Professor. "They want us to climb. I think they're going to throw us off the bridge!"

At the south end of the bridge, the whirring, beaten RV veered from one lane to another, overtaking as many cars as it could, racing toward the middle of the bridge, where Will could see the abandoned van.

As the diamond thieves dragged Sen and the Professor to the top of the bridge railing, one of the black-clad kidnappers pulled a small remote device from his pocket, turned back to the van, and pressed a button.

Through the cracked windshield of the RV, Will and Gladys watched as the van suddenly exploded in a ball of flames, bursting outward from the van's windows and sending the roof of the vehicle flying high into the air. A bright orange plume of flame rolled upward, and every driver on the bridge slammed on his brakes, the cars spinning and smashing into one another.

Will stood on the brakes of the RV as hard as he could, skidding out of control, watching the pileup getting closer and closer until eventually the RV became part of it. The second the motor home slammed into the car in front, Will unsnapped his safety belt and grabbed Gladys.

"Are you all right?"

She nodded, stunned and breathless, but lucid enough to hand Will's watch back. "Here, I think you'll be needing this."

"Thanks." Will gave Gladys a peck on the cheek that made her eyelids flutter once more, then leapt from the RV to the sound of an angry roar from Howard.

"Shut up, Howard!" he heard Gladys say.

As the ball of fire swept into the black sky, people began to stumble out of their cars, panicked and confused. Will jumped onto the crippled hood of a sedan and looked quickly toward the blast zone. Across the pile of smashed vehicles, he saw four figures standing high on the edge of the bridge railing, facing outward, as if to jump.

"Oh, God!" Will whispered, then sprang as fast as he could into action, avoiding the wave of fearful motorists hurrying away from the burning van by leapfrogging from one car roof to the next, sliding across hoods, bounding and bouncing until he managed to jump clear onto the bridge walkway and bolt toward the figures on the railing.

He didn't take his eyes off them. He saw one of the black-clad figures strap Sen to the front of him, while the other did the same with the Professor. He saw both diamond thieves unzipping parts of their outfits.

Will poured on one last burst of speed.

He was almost there. He had a chance. But then—

"Professor!!"

As Will hit the railing, the two black-clad figures jumped off the Golden Gate Bridge, taking Sen and the Professor with them.

Will gasped in horror, pulled himself up on the railing, and stared down toward the water. The van fire lit up the night, enough for Will to see the black-clad figures free-falling, plunging toward certain death until—

Foomp! Foomp!

Parachutes opened, turning their fall into a swift glide as they spiraled toward the waters below, where a large cruiser awaited them, its well-lit back deck forming a landing pad.

Amazed, relieved, helpless, Will looked on as the kidnappers touched down on the boat, the sound of the cruiser's motor revving into high gear and moving swiftly out to sea.

Back at the Zhang Diamond Tower, Jake had burst through the balcony doors and stopped, his heart pounding in his throat. For a moment he tried to convince himself this was all a bad dream.

But the blood spreading out from under Eden's body was real.

Jake fell to his knees beside the still body, the trousers of his tuxedo soaking in blood.

"Eden?" he whispered, praying for a response.

But none came.

With a slow, trembling hand, Jake placed his fingers against the side of Eden's neck, feeling for a pulse, all the while thinking, *It was supposed to be me. Why wasn't it me?* A tear spilled from his eye, and for a moment Jake realized he had just lost the one thing he thought we would never find.

Then, ever so faintly, he felt it.

pum-pum...

pum-pum...

III

THE BILLOWING BIG TOP TENT TOOK UP ALMOST THE entire area of Krakow's Market Square, between the Cloth Hall and the Palac Pod Baranami, where Krakow's famous cabaret had been running since 1956. The Cirque des Trompettes—a multinational circus troupe formed in the late 1960s—was renowned for gathering the most talented performers from all corners of the earth and had been touring the globe for decades. But there was no city in the world that loved the Cirque des Trompettes as much as the city of Krakow.

Surrounding the big top, forming a tiny mazelike city within a city, were the dozens of caravans and trailers that housed the circus crew and countless performers.

Thousands of Krakow's citizens flooded through the intricate network of trailers to behold the big top. There were children sitting on the shoulders of men, with balloons in one hand and red-and-white-striped candy in the other.

There were dozens of brightly lit sideshow stalls blaring carnival music, their stall keepers shouting at the crowd in Polish and German, inviting showgoers to test their skills and win prizes. Men and women on stilts stepped through the crowd like giant insects. Mimes, jugglers, trumpeters, drummers, and clowns of all kinds were everywhere.

There were so many clowns that Luca didn't know where to begin looking.

"Don't you want to see the show?"

Luca turned and saw a handsome, young blond man standing behind him. He had a flaming torch in each hand. He wore nothing but a pair of red tights with an orange flame motif leaping up each leg. His torso was tanned and well muscled, the body of a circus performer, someone who had spent his life pitching tents and training hard.

"That's what most people come to see." His accent was northern European. "The show, I mean. Out here, we are just the first act, a prelude to the main event to spark your sense of adventure."

As if to prove his point, he tilted his head back, lifted one of the flaming torches to his lips, then blew a giant ball of fire high into the air. He gave Luca a large white smile.

"I am Tomas, the fire-eater from Iceland. Here to ignite your imagination."

By the time Tomas was done, nothing had been left to the imagination.

The eye contact between Luca and Tomas had led swiftly to a much more intimate exchange in the tiny trailer Tomas called home. The second Tomas shut the door, their lips met.

"I'm looking for someone," Luca said, pushing the words from his lips as they smothered Tomas's.

"You found me instead," Tomas breathed.

"I'm somehow glad I did. But I have to ask."

"Ask what?"

"Does it burn? Does the fire burn your throat?"

Tomas pulled away and grinned. Luca could tell right away he was the kind of guy who lived every day as it came. Tomas laughed a little. "Not if you do it right. But it doesn't hurt to follow it with something soft and soothing."

The young Icelander stood back and Luca's eyes fell upon the bulge in his tights, the orange flames on the legs pointing up toward his throbbing, growing crotch.

Luca pulled off his jacket, unbuttoned his shirt, and let Tomas peel it away from his broad, muscled shoulders.

Tomas let the shirt drop to the floor, then placed both hands on Luca's chest, palms flat against the mounds of his firm, sparsely haired pectorals. He looked directly into Luca.

"My mother was a gypsy," Tomas said, holding his hands in place on Luca's chest. "A magical woman. A wise woman. She taught me that touch is everything. What you feel, inside and out, even just the nearness of it, is everything. I feel the heat of the flame, and I have to trust my instincts. When to breathe in—"

Luca unwittingly inhaled deeply.

"—and when to breathe out."

Luca exhaled.

Tomas closed his eyes, as though drawing energy from the simple rise and fall of Luca's chest. When he opened them again, his brow was creased in sympathy. "You don't know who you are, do you."

It wasn't a question, and if it had been, Luca didn't have the answer. Instead he leaned forward to stop the Icelander from delving deeper, and planted a long, hard kiss on Tomas's lips.

For several minutes their tongues probed the inside of each other's mouth. Luca's hands locked with Tomas's and their fingers explored each other's touch. The skin of

Tomas's palms was tough, from pulling ropes and lifting tent poles; likewise, Luca's hands were rough and ready from too much action and adventure. And yet, both men handled each other with such tenderness, such delicacy, that even their palms and fingers felt soft and inviting.

Luca—who had come in search of answers to his past—was suddenly dizzy with an unexpected sense of longing. And belonging.

He pulled out of the kiss, realizing he hadn't told Tomas his name, suddenly feeling the need to introduce himself properly. He opened his mouth to speak, but Tomas simply smiled and placed a finger on Luca's lips. "Shhhh."

Then, slowly, Tomas lowered himself to his knees.

The young Icelander's hands were undeniably sure of themselves as they unbuckled Luca's belt, unzipped his jeans, and pulled them to the floor.

There was no way possible anything but a fully erect cock was going to spring from Luca's jeans. Sure enough, what Tomas unleashed was thick, huge, and hard, the foreskin already pulled back down the shaft, revealing the head of his cock full and brimming.

Tomas slipped his moist lips around it without hesitation.

His juicy mouth wet the head of Luca's cock, then his entire penis as Tomas opened his dexterous throat all the way and swallowed him whole.

The young Italian felt the almost crushing pressure on his bulbous head as it was forced down the narrow passage of the Icelander's throat. It was at once excruciating and exquisite. Luca turned his face upward, his head rolling back on his neck. He opened his mouth and a gush of ecstasy escaped him.

His hands reached forward and found Tomas's short blond hair. He gripped the head of the Icelander and tried to ease him back, but Tomas resisted. The muscles in Tomas's throat constricted, and Luca felt an even greater pressure on the head of his cock.

The sound that escaped Luca now was a loud, tortured grunt.

He let go of Tomas's head, surrendering himself to the young fire-eater.

After years of training, Tomas had complete control over the muscles in his throat. He released the hold on Luca's cock a little, allowing the slightest relief, before doubling the pressure. Squeeze and release. Squeeze and release. Not letting go. At the same time, Tomas's tongue began running up and down the thick purple vein on the underside of Luca's captured cock, tickling and teasing it.

The young Icelander's hands slid gently up Luca's stomach, fingers trickling up his torso inch by inch until they found Luca's nipples and began to twist and roll them, gently at first, then harder.

Luca flinched and groaned again, but he was unable to move a muscle, frozen in a state of agony and ecstasy. This was like nothing he'd ever experienced before; it was a blow job, but instead of friction and motion, it was all about muscle manipulation. All about—

"Ooohhh! God!"

Squeeze and release.

Squeeze.

Squeeze harder.

Release and squeeze even harder.

Luca's head fell forward on his neck, his eyes watering, his brow creased in pain, and his mouth gasping for air—for relief—as he breathed, "I'm going to come. I'm going to—"

Suddenly Tomas's throat released the head of Luca's cock.

He pulled back slightly.

Luca moaned with relief but it was too late—he could feel the gush inside his balls.

His cock slid back into the cavern of Tomas's warm, wet mouth, and there he felt the surge of his semen erupt, filling Tomas's mouth with cum.

He shot once.

Twice.

But Tomas didn't swallow.

Instead, his muscles shut off the passage to his throat.

Gently he let Luca's still hard and seeping cock slip from his mouth, then he quickly rose and planted his lips on Luca's lips once more.

This time, as their mouths sealed tightly together, Luca not only felt Tomas's tongue enter his mouth, he also tasted the flavorsome swirl of his own cum.

They drank it together, lapping it up, swallowing it down.

When every last drop was gone, Tomas pulled away with a smile and looked down. Luca was still stiff.

"Where did you learn to do that?" the Italian whispered.

Tomas smiled, his lips glistening. "Before I was a fire-eater, I swallowed swords."

"No kidding!" Luca continued kissing Tomas madly. His hands seized Tomas's shoulders then groped his arms, his chest, his stomach. They reached the top of Tomas's tights and at long last yanked them down, unleashing the Icelander's stiff, swinging cock.

Tomas's humble bunk was only a few feet away.

With his jeans still wrapped around his ankles, Luca hastily began stepping Tomas backward toward the bed, shuffling frantically, till the back of Tomas's knees hit the bed and both men tumbled onto it, Luca on top.

As his lips and tongue lapped up every inch of Tomas's neck, shoulders, and chest, Tomas reached across the bed to a small bedside table. He retrieved a condom and a bottle of lubricant from the drawer. He bit open the condom packet.

"Here," he said, pulling Luca's face off his stomach and showing him the condom.

Luca grinned, took it, then slipped it on over his own engorged cock. His shaft was still wet with Tomas's saliva and his own cum, and the condom went on easily.

The moment it was on, Tomas grabbed Luca by the shoulders and in one graceful move he threw the young Italian onto his back on the bed, while Tomas flipped himself up and over the top, straddling Luca's hips, hovering above his anxious cock.

Tomas took the lube and squeezed a long glistening wad into the palm of his hand. To the delight of the young Italian, he slowly greased Luca's sheathed cock, taking his sweet time, enjoying every moment, every inch of Luca's bountiful length and girth. Kneeling over Luca, he swiveled his hips teasingly, hovering an inch or so out of reach of Luca's cock.

Unable to resist the temptation, Luca thrust his hips upward, the head of his cock nudging against Tomas's anus, and Tomas gladly relented. He spread his cheeks and lowered himself down onto Luca.

The young Italian grimaced, his cock—although hard—still tender after the first orgasm. He let out a strained and pleasured sigh as Tomas placed his palm on Luca's chest for support, then gently...

...sank...

...down...

...onto his cock.

Tomas drew in his breath and held it as the hard, meaty shaft filled him and his ass cheeks came to rest on Luca's pelvis. There he stayed for a moment, his breath held, his chest bursting, his rectum on fire with the heat radiating from Luca's cock. Then, slowly, with as much control as he could manage, he released the air from his lungs, at the same time lifting himself up, pausing an inch from the end of Luca's shaft before sliding back down for more.

Faster this time.

Then faster again.

Tomas took his hand off Luca's chest and leaned back a little, using the muscles in his hips, thighs, and ass to support himself as he slid up and down. He arched his back, pushing his hips forward to get a better angle on Luca's cock. He placed his hand behind him now, gripping Luca's thickly muscled thigh. With his right hand he began to stroke his own gleaming cock.

"Harder," Luca breathed.

Tomas did what he was told, ramming himself down onto Luca's cock harder, faster. His ass cheeks slapped against Luca's pelvis louder and louder. At the same time, he jerked himself off more vigorously, more ferociously.

With one hand, Luca reached forward and grabbed Tomas's balls. They were a moving target, rising and falling with ever-increasing speed up and down, but he homed in swiftly and seized them and squeezed hard.

The sensation sent shock waves of pain and pleasure through Tomas's body. His pectoral muscles flinched, the mounds of his large strong chest spasming for a moment or two. He grunted in pain. But his rhythm did not falter.

His head rolled forward, his chin pressing into his chest. He tilted his cock upward, still thrashing it as hard as he could—so he could watch his balls swell as Luca squeezed them, harder and harder, until Tomas thought they would surely burst.

"Don't..." Tomas gasped breathlessly. "Don't...stop. Don't stop. I'm about to...!"

Before he could finish his words, a huge spurt of cum jetted from his cock. It shot into the air and graffitied its way up Luca's chest and throat in glistening white spirals, hot against Luca's warm skin.

Luca thrust his hips upward as hard as he could, forcing

his own cock as far into Tomas as he could manage, about to come again. He cried out as he exploded, the head of the condom catching his reservoir of hot cum.

The scorching pulse inside Tomas triggered a second, then a third jet of cum, decorating Luca's torso all the way from his stomach to his chin.

Tomas moaned.

Luca gasped for breath.

As the thrill of their orgasms slowly rippled away, Tomas shook the last drops of cum from his thick, meaty cock, then gently pulled himself off Luca and collapsed next to him on the bed.

There they lay side by side for a long, lingering moment until their panting eased and their glistening cocks settled and lay wet and spent against their stomachs.

Tomas said, "You were looking for someone. And it wasn't me."

Luca propped himself up on one elbow and said, "No, but I'm glad I found you." He kissed Tomas on the lips, and when he was done he lay back down again, staring at the ceiling of Tomas's modest little trailer. "I'm looking for a particular person. Someone from long ago—he used to be a clown named Valentino."

This time it was Tomas who propped himself up on one elbow. He had a curious look on his face. "The name, it's familiar. But I can't say there's anyone working here now called that. But there is someone who might know."

"Who?"

"A woman. She has worked with the circus for many years." Tomas lowered himself back onto the bed. "I don't know much about her, she doesn't talk much. She sells roses and keeps to herself. Her name is Elena."

"You think she knows him? You think she knows who Valentino is, where I might find him?"

Tomas shook his head and yawned, exhausted. His

encounter with Luca had made his eyelids heavy. "I don't know. But she's seen a lot of faces come and go. She's certainly the first...person...I'd...go...to." Tomas's voice trailed away, as his eyelids closed and his head slid down one side of the pillow.

Luca looked at him, smiled sweetly, then kissed him once more on the lips. Tomas didn't stir.

Carefully, Luca climbed over him and out of the tiny bed. Quietly he pulled up his jeans and slipped his shirt back on. Before he left he glanced back once more at Tomas sound asleep. Silently Luca opened the door and stepped outside the trailer.

It was dark.

He quietly closed the door behind him. From a short distance away he heard the cheers of the audience packed inside the big top—

—and from somewhere much closer, he heard the panicked, clip-clop of shoes against cobblestone, of someone scurrying away in a mad dash.

Luca saw a shadow disappear through the maze of trailers.

He raced after it, turned a corner, and heard the footsteps stop.

He saw a figure a short distance ahead, looking back at him. A small, lean shadow in a cloak.

He called out to it. "Wait! Who are you!"

But the figure only turned and scurried away.

Luca put on the speed, trying frantically to follow the figure as it disappeared behind trailers, weaving in and out between circus carts and stacks of wooden crates and boxes.

"Hey! Wait a minute! I want to talk to you!" But the figure didn't stop.

Luca lost track of it for a moment behind a mountain of burlap sacks, then he rounded a trailer and the bright sight of the big top filled his senses.

He spotted the figure again, at the foot of the big top, lifting the bottom of the tent high enough to vanish inside. Luca charged forward and grabbed the canvas where the figure had disappeared, hoisted it up and ducked underneath.

Inside, the noise was deafening and visibility was almost nonexistent. Luca realized he was under a huge grandstand. Above him he could hear the sounds of the crowd, feet stomping excitedly on floorboards in time with drummers somewhere in the middle of the arena. The drumbeat was getting faster and faster, and with it the thunderous stomping.

Suddenly it stopped. The crowd fell silent, and Luca heard a man's voice over a megaphone. It was the circus ringmaster.

"Ladies and gentlemen, may I present, all the way from the fair city of Dublin, the Flying Fitzpatricks! Performing with no safety harnesses—and no safety net!"

The crowd cheered.

By this time, Luca's eyes had adjusted to the dark enough to see the shadowy figure scurrying along the perimeter of the tent underneath the grandstand. It reached a steel ladder that ran all the way up the side of the big top and began climbing. Luca sprinted straight for the ladder.

The figure was already halfway up, ascending toward a massive lighting rig in the ceiling of the tent. Luca started climbing, his hands and feet tearing up the rungs. He clambered up so fast the whole ladder shook with his weight.

Three-quarters of the way, he glanced up and saw that the figure in the cloak had reached the top and was now making its way rapidly along a narrow gangplank that led to the center of the big top, above the staging lights.

Luca ascended past the highest point of the grandstand now, and looked over the heads of the audience. All the lights and action of the big top came into full view. The massive crowd was captivated by the midair performance of four men flying through the big top, leaping from one trapeze to another, catching each other by the wrists and ankles, forming a pendulous human chain before flying free and performing their next acrobatic stunt.

Luca didn't have time to spectate. The cloaked figure on the gangplank was already nearing the middle of the lighting rig, heading toward the opposite end of the tent where another ladder led down the other side.

Luca had to catch the figure before it could make it to the opposite end of the gangplank.

Giant lights shuddered and vibrated on the rigging as the young Italian reached the top of the ladder and pounded his way along the narrow gangplank.

A huge cheer rose from the crowd as the Flying Fitzpatricks flew into another death-defying leap.

High above them, Luca was gaining on his target, but as the figure reached the middle of the rig, it bent low, unlatched two hooks, and with some effort slid a 10-foot section of the gangplank away from Luca, leaving a massive gap between them.

"No!" Luca shouted, his voice competing with the cheers below.

Just then, the figure looked up, directly at him.

Luca caught his breath, skidding to a halt at the edge of the gangplank where the section had been removed.

Only 10 feet of empty space and an 80-foot drop lay between Luca and the figure. He could see her now. It was a woman in her early fifties—the same woman Luca had seen selling roses before the performance.

"Elena?" he whispered.

She looked at him almost pleadingly. "Please do not follow me! Please, turn back! For your own safety. Luca, I beg you."

Luca stood staring at her for a second, trying to put

together an impossible puzzle in his head. Who *was* this woman? How did she know his name? Why was she running from him? Did she know Valentino? Was he in danger? And from whom?

She was the one who could answer his questions.

Determinedly Luca backed up, then sprinted as fast as he could along the gangplank before launching himself into the air, leaping across the 10-foot gap.

He made the jump—

—almost.

At the other end he fell short, slammed into the gangplank, and slipped.

The woman dived to her knees and tried to grab his hand, but missed.

Luca's fingers clawed at the grating in the gangplank but couldn't hook on. He dropped down below the walkway, fingers still clutching at the air until they found something.

A chain. A short, oily chain dangled below the edge of the gangplank, hanging over the drop into the middle of the giant arena. Luca's fists clutched the chain and held on tight.

Far below him the acrobats swung back and forth, unaware that Luca was dangling perilously above their heads. Above him, the cloaked woman leaned as far over the edge of the gangplank as she could, trying in vain to reach him.

"Climb!" she shouted, her voice panicked. "Try to reach my hand!"

But the chain was oily, and as the woman spoke, Luca's fingers slid further and further down the slippery links.

"I can't..." He struggled to hold on.

"Try!" The woman begged. "You have to try!"

But Luca's fingers slipped again, only inches from the end of the chain now.

The woman leaned over as far as she could.

Then something slipped out from her cloak, something from around her neck.

A delicate necklace. A small silver cross on the end of it. The same silver cross as the one Luca had worn around his neck his entire life, until the day it was lost forever in the molten rivers of Vulcano.

Luca gasped. His fingers slipped from the chain completely. He fell into the air.

The woman's eyes opened wide in sheer horror. She looked down, saw the acrobats, and shouted as loud as she could over the applause of the audience, "*Shamus!!!*"

Standing on a ledge, one of the Flying Fitzpatricks somehow heard his name above the crowd. Instantly, almost instinctively, he looked up and saw a man falling from the rig, about to plunge right through the middle of the acrobats to his death.

"Liam! Devlin! Aidan!" Shamus Fitzpatrick shouted desperately to his brothers. At the same time he launched himself off his ledge and swung toward Luca.

As Luca plummeted into full view of the entire stadium, a spotlight swung on him. Spectators gasped and the circus crew on the ground immediately started to unravel an emergency net. "Faster, faster!" someone shouted.

With a *whoosh*, Shamus soared into the middle of the ring, swinging upside down by his knees now, reaching out as far as he could with both hands.

As Luca plunged he saw Shamus coming toward him out of the corner of his eye. He tried to grab for the acrobat's hands. He clipped his fingers, but missed by an inch.

Then suddenly Luca had the wind knocked out of him by Liam, swinging in from the opposite direction and crashing straight into him. Liam almost fell from his swing but held on tight with one hand, his other hand grabbing the back of Luca's shirt.

The shirt ripped and slid straight off Luca's back.

The young Italian continued to fall, but was suddenly flipped upside down as Devlin, the youngest Fitzpatrick, flew in from the side, grabbing Luca by the shoe.

They swung over to the far side of the tent and back again, but as Devlin tried to inch his grip higher to grab Luca's ankle, the shoe slipped off completely and Luca flew in an arc, heading straight for the audience.

Just then, Aidan, held by Liam, held by Shamus, came flying across in the human pendulum formation, grabbing Luca's wrist and snapping him back before he could crash into the crowd. They looped back toward the center of the arena, then, as surely as Aidan had grabbed Luca's wrist, he suddenly let him go.

Luca fell straight into the emergency net, now stretched tight over the ground. He bounced once, twice, then sank into the net on his back, startled and breathless.

As the crowd let out a thunderous roar and the circus crew lowered the net to the ground, Luca looked up and saw, far above, Elena still leaning over the gangplank. Her teary eyes filled with relief as she quickly stood.

Something red and green fell from her cloak as she vanished from sight. It fluttered through the air toward Luca.

As it neared, he saw it was a rose. A single red rose. He took it in his hand.

As the circus crew charged across the net toward him, Luca quickly searched for any signs of Elena, in the rigging, on the ladder, in the crowd. But she was gone.

At that moment the circus crew seized him by the arms, hoisted him to his feet, and brusquely hurried him away so the show could go on. High on their ledges, the Flying Fitzpatricks bowed to a standing ovation from the crowd.

Outside the big top, Luca landed facedown on the cobblestones. The circus crew grunted angrily at him, dusted their hands clean, and returned to the activity inside the tent.

Over the cheers and applause of the crowd inside, Luca heard the faint ring of his cell phone. He sat up, pulled the phone from his jeans pocket, checked the caller ID, and answered it quickly. "Shane?"

"Luca, we need you back here right now! Somethin' bad has happened. Somethin' real bad. You gotta get to San Francisco as fast as you can."

IV

The Island of San Sebastián, Caribbean Sea

A NEW YORK STREET KID LIKE SAM HAD NEVER SEEN THE sun shine so bright, never seen sand so white or a sky so blue or an ocean so vast, stretching all the way to the far horizon. It was, indeed, the perfect day.

The only thing spoiling it was the huge islander with the three-day stubble and the bitter coffee breath. The man was hauling him backward by his backpack, kicking, past the paying customers on the small, island-hopping boat, who leaned across each other to get out of his path.

"No ticket—no ride!" the big man bellowed.

"Get your goddamn hands off me!" Sam argued, his arms flapping like the wings of a captured bird. "I told you, I can pay you at the other end. I have a friend on San Sebastián. He'll pay for my ticket!"

The burly man scowled. The kid was talking about the new owner of the little plantation island. "If he's as mean as the last bastard who lived there, I'll be lucky if he pays me with coconuts!"

With a forceful shove and a boot up the ass, Sam was jettisoned off the boat, landing flat on his face on the wooden plank wharf.

He didn't take it personally. Since catching ride after ride down the East Coast to Florida, then stowing aboard a trawler and spending a night undetected in its oil-stinking hull till it arrived on Grand Cayman, he knew his luck was bound to run out sooner or later.

As he picked himself up off the wharf, he heard the motorboat drone away. Then he heard laughter coming from somewhere above him. It was a relaxed, amused laugh.

Sam rolled over and shielded his eyes from the sun to see a young Caribbean man standing over him, wearing nothing but a pair of crisp white shorts, a necklace of seashells, and a huge grin of white teeth. His body was black and toned, skin glistening in the bright sunlight. Sam could see every muscle in his taut stomach ripple as he laughed.

"You have a splinter in your chin," the young man observed. With an easy air, he put down the rod and sack he was carrying, squatted beside Sam, and plucked a long sliver of wood from Sam's chin.

"Thanks," Sam muttered, not sure what to make of the stranger's friendly nature.

"So you need a ride to San Sebastián? Come, I'll take you."

"But I don't have any money."

The young man shrugged indifferently. "Don't matter to me. I'm going there anyway." He reached into the sack on the ground and pulled out an envelope. "The new residents have their first letter."

Sam saw the sender's address printed at the top of the envelope: *From the office of Charles Hunter, U.S. Embassy, Cairo.*

He smiled. "You're the postman?"

The young islander grinned. "It's the perfect job. The

amberjacks near San Sebastián are much bigger than the ones in these waters. Come. I'll teach you a thing or two about how to catch a fish."

The young man gave him his hand and with a mighty yank snapped Sam to his feet and led him to a tiny wooden boat bobbing up and down in the water, its ancient outboard motor dipping in and out of the sea.

Two hours later, Sam was standing on a different wharf—leading toward Professor Fathom's house on the island of San Sebastián—waving goodbye with one hand to his newfound friend the postman as he putted away in his tiny wooden boat. In his other hand Sam held three large, freshly caught amberjacks.

"Don't forget the mail!" the young postman called across the aqua-blue waters before chugging out of earshot.

"I won't!" Sam shouted back. The letter was in his pocket. He supposed it was a good enough excuse to show up unannounced on someone's doorstep. That and the fact that he had caught enough dinner for everyone, including Jake, who was probably still pissed at him for running away.

Sam would bet his last dollar—if he had one—that Jake was already here, waiting for him, knowing that this was where the kid would end up, in the safe haven of Professor Fathom's care. After all, Sam and the old man had bonded in France. There was a moment, after Sam's tantrum-throwing and the Professor's book-throwing, when the two of them actually understood each other, if only for a brief moment. Sam had decided he liked the Professor very much. Not to mention his housekeeper, Elsa, who was a damn good cook—and right now Sam was hungry!

Taking a deep breath for courage, dreading the thought of facing Jake—although he couldn't deny he'd missed him—Sam began striding down the jetty toward the beach.

He only got as far as the white sand before two figures came rushing out of the two-story colonial house. Through the palms, Sam instantly recognized the stout, lovable shape of Elsa as she barreled across the bright-green lawn. Beside her was an even larger woman of island origin Sam did not recognize. At first, he thought the two women were rushing to meet him.

But then he noticed the suitcases, one in Elsa's hand, one in the other woman's hand.

Then he noticed the look on Elsa's face. Distraught. Frantic. Full of fear.

Sam realized she hadn't even seen him—until now.

"Sammy? Sammy, is that you?" she shouted in her thick German accent. She was breathless, her voice filled with panic, the suitcase banging against her leg as she lumbered desperately toward him. "*Mein Gott!* What are you doing here!" With a dramatic toss of her arm she dropped the suitcase and ran to embrace him.

Sam dropped his fish. "Elsa? What's wrong?"

"Something terrible! Eden! The Professor! Something terrible has happened, I—" At that point she began mumbling and crying and Sam couldn't make any sense out of her.

The second woman, having picked up the suitcase that Elsa discarded, joined them and tried to translate Elsa's emotional ramblings. "There's been an accident. In San Francisco."

"Jake!" Sam said, the panic spreading quickly. "Is Jake okay?"

"I'm not sure. The phone call was brief. Elsa's on her way to California now."

"I'm going with her," Sam said determinedly. He grabbed the two suitcases from the island woman, who seemed a little relieved by his decision to take control.

"There's a boat already on its way," the second woman

said, pointing out to sea. Sam turned and saw a small charter craft speeding across the water toward the wharf. "It will take you to Grand Cayman. There's a plane leaving in two hours for the mainland."

The woman took Elsa's shaking hand while Sam took the suitcases, and all three of them hurried along the wharf to meet the charter boat. "Take care of her," the woman said, helping Elsa into the boat.

"I will," Sam said, nodding.

"My name is Big Zettie, by the way."

"I'm Sam."

"I'm sorry we didn't meet under better circumstances," Zettie said, warmly embracing Sam as though she'd known him all her life. "Don't worry, everything will be all right. One day soon all of you will be back here, sitting around the dinner table. I'll cook you all the biggest fish coconut curry you've ever seen."

"Blargenwurst," Elsa muttered from the back of the boat, sniffling into a handkerchief. "My boys like sausage!"

"Blargenwurst it is, then," Big Zettie said with a smile.

Sam turned to Zettie. "I'll take care of her." He jumped into the boat and the driver cast off the lines.

Zettie stood on the wharf and watched the charter all the way to the horizon. She crossed herself, then quickly made her way through the palms to the island's tiny whitewashed chapel, dedicated to the island's saint, Sebastián. There she knelt and prayed as hard as she could for the safe return of the Professor and his boys.

V

San Francisco General Hospital, California

WILL FLINCHED AS THE NURSE GRIPPED THE CHOPSTICK with a clamp and slowly eased it out of his right shoulder. It came free with a sickening squelch, followed by a small but steady stream of blood that poured down the young man's bare chest and stomach.

The nurse was quick with gauze, then glanced over her shoulder at Bradley Zhang, who had accompanied the Professor's men to the hospital and was now watching squeamishly. "Are you a friend?"

"Yes," Bradley replied, not really thinking about the question at all. He was too transfixed by the wound to take in much else.

"Then grab yourself a pair of those latex gloves over there and press down here, nice and firm."

Bradley did as he was ordered while the nurse dropped the chopstick and clamp into a metal tray.

"I'll be back with some sutures. Till then, sit tight. Don't go anywhere."

Frustrated, Will glanced at the tracking grid on his watch as the nurse left the room. He was sitting on the end of a bed in the emergency ward. He could see Bradley's eyes staring intently at the wound, concentrating hard, so careful not to release any of the pressure that he was now in fact hurting Will.

"I think you can probably ease off a little."

"Sorry, I guess I'm just—distracted. I knew something was going to happen. I should have said something. I should have told someone."

"You told me."

"I mean my uncle."

Will lifted his arm and, with some pain, pointed to his watch. "It'll be okay, we'll find them, I promise. We have a tracking device on the Professor. Actually, it's *inside* the Professor. They took him north a short distance, then it looks like they've gone airborne, moving west across the Pacific."

"Heading straight for China," Bradley said.

"You told me earlier you didn't know who to trust." Will leveled his gaze at Bradley, his blue eyes staring deep into the young businessman's dark brown eyes. "I'm telling you, you can trust us."

Just then, Bradley's cell phone rang. He answered it and heard Chad Chambers's voice on the other end of the line.

"Bradley! Are you okay?"

"I'm okay."

"Oh, thank God! Where are you?"

"I'm at the hospital." He almost mentioned who he was with, but thought better of it.

"Listen, Bradley, we have to tell the board. We have to instill some confidence in them now, before shares start dropping and the industry panics. We have to let them know the corporation is unsinkable. I'll call a meeting, straight away. I'm leaving for Hong Kong now."

"I can be on a plane in an hour."

"There's no need, Bradley. You should stay here, assist the police with their investigation as much as you can. Sen needs your help. He's your only family. Mya and I can take care of the company."

"No, Chad. I'll be in Hong Kong by morning." With that, he hung up the phone.

Will looked at him. "Need a friend to tag along for the ride?"

Luca's eyes darted from face to face as he raced through the hospital corridor leading to the intensive care unit, searching for a face he knew, until—

"Shane!" Luca rushed to greet him with a hug, his worried eyes taking in the bandage wrapped tightly around Shane's head. "What happened?"

"The diamond's gone. So is the Professor."

"What!?"

"It gets worse." He put a hand on Luca's shoulder, bracing him for the news that was to come. "It's Eden."

He turned and pointed. Jake was standing alone at the end of the corridor, looking through a window into the intensive care unit, one hand pressed flat against the glass.

Luca raced toward the window, Shane close behind.

Inside the ward was Eden. A doctor was thumbing the unconscious Brazilian's eyelids open and shining a small flashlight into his unseeing, unknowing pupils. Two nurses checked instruments and gauges, and secured the many tubes running in and out of Eden's mouth and nose with strips of tape. An elevated bag fed clear fluid into his veins, while a second bag replenished his blood supply. The only indication there was any life left in him at all was the beep of a heart monitor and the thin green line that raced across the screen, jumping with each faint beat.

Jake blinked as a tear streaked down his cheek. He rested

his forehead against the glass. "It was supposed to be me," he whispered, his breath fogging up the glass. "The curse was meant for me."

Gently, a hand pressed down on his shoulder and squeezed. Only then did Jake notice Luca standing beside him.

"He pushed me out of the way," Jake's voice croaked, trying to explain. "He was trying to tell me something, and then—"

He couldn't finish his sentence. He turned quickly back to look at Eden, not wanting to take his eyes off him for more than a minute.

The doctor inside the intensive care room looked up, saw the three worried men standing at the window, and exited the room. Once out in the corridor, he took off his mask and gloves and introduced himself to Jake, Shane, and Luca.

"My name is Doctor Angelo Dante."

"You're Italian?" Luca asked, picking up on the name and the accent.

"Yes, I'm a specialist from Rome, currently doing some research and field work here in San Francisco. There's a shortage of doctors on tonight. I happened to be working late when you're friend was brought in."

"*Mi chiamo Luca*," Luca said with a handshake. "These are my friends Jake and Shane. And that's Eden," he added quietly.

Jake swallowed hard before asking, "Is he—is he gonna live?"

Doctor Dante took a moment, then sighed. He was a handsome man, in his late thirties, olive skin, distinctly Roman nose, jet-black hair peppered with streaks of distinguished gray. Despite his natural good looks, he had that heavy-hearted sigh of a surgeon who had broken bad news too many times.

"It's not good. We've put him in an induced coma. Your

friend has lost a lot of blood, and there's internal hemor-rhaging, some of which we've managed to slow with the surgery, although we may need to open him up again. There's no guarantee we can save him. I'm sorry, but you should prepare yourself for the worst." Doctor Dante returned to the intensive care unit.

Suddenly the corridor was filled with a distraught yet familiar voice.

"Oh, *Gott in Himmel!*"

Luca, Shane, and Jake turned to see Elsa blubbering and barreling down the corridor toward them. Beside her was Sam, a suitcase in each hand.

Luca and Shane hurried to embrace the weeping Elsa while Jake rushed toward Sam.

For a moment, Sam braced himself for Jake's wrath, but what he received instead was a bear hug of an embrace. He felt Jake kiss him ceaselessly, on the forehead, on the face, on his scruffy black hair.

"You're not pissed at me?" the kid asked, squinting back the kisses.

"Yeah, I'm pissed. And you shouldn't be here. But hell, I'm so happy to see you. I needed to see you."

As Jake released Sam, Elsa sobbed, "Where is he? Where's Eden?"

In silent response, Luca, Shane, and Jake all glanced at once toward the intensive care unit. Elsa fixed her tear-filled gaze on the window, then slowly walked toward it as though in a trance.

The moment she peered through the window and saw Eden's motionless body lying on the bed, her face became still and silent. The sniffing stopped. The tears seemed to freeze in the wells of her eyes. For now that she could see Eden, Elsa Strauss's defense mechanisms finally kicked in and she began to do what she did best: organize things.

"Sammy, the suitcase. There's a box of strudels. Get

them out, everyone eat, you must be starving! And clean clothes, there are clean clothes for all you boys. Pajamas for Eden too. Look at him, he must be frozen in there. Where's the doctor? I want to see his doctor. We need to put his pajamas on him." She was on her knees now, rummaging desperately through the suitcase.

Sam took her by the hand. "Elsa, it's okay. There's no hurry. He'll be okay."

At that moment, Will and Bradley came rushing down the corridor. Will's shoulder was bandaged now, and he was already easing his arm out of a sling. "How's he doing?" Will asked anxiously.

Shane lied in front of Elsa. "He's fine. He's gonna be just fine. But right now we need to figure out how to get Sen and the Professor back."

"No prizes for guessing China's where they're headed." Will said, trading the sling for a T-shirt from Elsa's suitcase. "Bradley's got a meeting with the board in Hong Kong tomorrow. I'm gonna ride shotgun to see if there's anything suspicious going down at Zhang HQ."

Shane checked his own watch and turned to Luca. "You feel like chasing the little red dot?"

"The company's headquarters are in Hong Kong," Bradley offered, "but the mines themselves are in Shandong, south of Beijing."

"If you two cover Hong Kong, we'll head for Beijing," Luca said.

Jake turned to Bradley. "Any other leads you can think of? Anyone else with a major interest in the business? Partners, suppliers, anyone with a stake in the company's dealings?"

Bradley shook his head. "The only other person I can think of is Richard. Richard Conrad."

"Conrad Constructions," Jake nodded. "Sen said he was in Dubai, right?"

"I'm coming with you," Sam piped up, jumping to his feet.

"You're staying right here. Elsa needs you. And *he* needs you." Jake glanced once more at the window to the intensive care unit. He put a hand on the kid's shoulder and said, "Sammy, you got the most important job of all. Make sure nothing happens to Eden."

Elsa took Sam's hand then, patted it firmly, and assured Jake and the others, "We'll keep him strong. Don't worry. Just find the Professor. Bring him home safely."

One by one the boys hugged Elsa and Sam and raced for the elevator.

Before he left, Jake stopped at the window one last time. "Don't you die on me," he said softly. "We'll be back. I'll bring everyone back, I promise. Just don't you die."

Then, without looking back, he raced from the hospital.

VI

Beijing, China

BEIJING BETTY'S WAS A RAMSHACKLE, FOUR-STORY deathtrap. It was also the raucous, polluted heart of the city's slum district, thrashing and thumping to the beat of neo-Asian electro-pop strip music, illegal booze, experimental drugs, and lawless gay lust. There were no rules at Betty's apart from every man for himself when the police came, which was often. Yet Betty had enough friends and incriminating photos to keep the place open and her many customers happy—from the highest-ranking officials to the lowest dregs of modern China. Everyone here had an addiction—opium, crack, sex, or simply a need to watch, and this was the place to set your demons free.

Demons like the small, skeletal Chinese man with the tattered black patch over his left eye, the man known only as Doctor Cyclops. He was not a visitor to Betty's. He was a resident who lived on the third floor above the nightclub, calling this place of debauchery home. His entire world. He only left the building to buy noodles, cigarettes, and alcohol from the cluttered little corner store down the street. Sometimes he'd venture into the private back room known as the Den to score some opium from Betty, but that depended on who she was entertaining at the time. Sometimes the cigarettes and the gin just had to do.

Occasionally Doctor Cyclops parted with a little cash to feel up some young man's crotch. More often than not, though, he simply enjoyed watching the show, intently observing the men for sale, studying the contours of their bodies, their flesh, fantasizing about what their muscles looked like *under* the skin. He wished the striptease would keep going, even after the clothes were gone. He wished they could peel away the flesh on their bodies. Yes, the thought of it intoxicated him. Desperately he wanted to see what they looked like on the inside. He wanted to open their chests and see their hearts pounding. If he could see their hearts beat, then surely it meant they loved him.

This was his nightly ritual.

Tonight, however, the pattern would be broken. Doctor Cyclops had been contracted for a job.

"This way," he called over the dance music that thundered through the walls.

"I can't hear you," shouted the white-haired Chinese man behind him.

"This way. Through the garbage room."

They were in the back of Betty's, pushing their way through bags of overflowing garbage. The tall, young, white-haired man pushed two smaller, frailer men in front of him, both wearing black hoods over their heads.

Behind him, a small, slender woman in a red evening gown followed, stepping precariously across the slippery floor in her expensive heels. Mya Chan glared past the white-haired henchman and her two captives and shot

Doctor Cyclops an unimpressed sneer. "This had better be worth it!"

"No questions asked, no face remembered, no health care card required." Doctor Cyclops started snickering and spluttering at his own joke, then almost tripped on the first step of the backstage staircase.

Mya noticed. "Are you drunk?"

Doctor Cyclops rubbed at his eye patch, grinning a little uneasily, showing his jagged yellow teeth. "You're two days early. This job is very short notice."

Mya took a small item from her pocket and handed it to him. "Here's your down payment. You'll get the cash when everything's over."

Doctor Cyclops took the wrapped object. Unfolding the paper, he beamed at the sight of a large glass bead with a diamond embedded in the face of it. Like the pupil of an eye. "Oh, it's beautiful," he breathed, then quickly shoved the bead into his pocket. "Don't worry, I won't let him die on the table. Not unless you ask me to."

"Perhaps I should just crush both their spines now and be done with it," the white-haired man suggested, grim-faced.

"No, Xi!" ordered Mya sharply, hurrying up the steep stairs behind the others. "This detour has already put the whole operation at risk. I'm supposed to be in Hong Kong in the morning, not here in this fucking rat's nest! We have a strict plan. We must return to the schedule we agreed upon as soon as possible."

Indeed up until a few hours ago, everything had gone exactly to plan. Zhang Sen and the Professor had been successfully kidnapped, and the Eye of Fucanglong was in her possession, as were the two zidium devices. Of course there had been one or two close calls along the way, including the destruction of Qahtani's ship in Yemen and the young college kid's overly enthusiastic efforts to prevent a smooth exit from San Francisco. Even Mya could not deny there were cracks appearing in the plan. Yes, she had managed to flee in the Zhang Corporation's private jet at an abandoned airfield north of San Francisco; she had successfully taken a sample of Sen's and the Professor's blood before Doctor Cyclops could contaminate it. But after that point, things seemed to hit another unexpected snag. Thus the need to call ahead and rearrange Doctor Cyclops's schedule.

"You hate it when things don't quite go as planned, don't you, Mya," Sen said now, his voice muffled beneath the black hood covering his face. "You always did."

"Silence!" Mya barked as they reached the door to the doctor's room.

Breathlessly, Doctor Cyclops jingled through his keys, unlocked the door, and pushed it open.

Once inside, Mya stood in front of the two captives, then snapped the hoods off their heads.

The Professor stared blindly ahead of him, asking, "Sen, are you all right?"

"I'm okay," Sen replied. "We're going to be all right." But the expression on his face indicated the exact opposite as he took in their surroundings.

The room had no windows, four grimy walls, a rickety old chair and table, a sink in one corner with a cracked mirror cabinet above it, a murky brown toilet, and a stained, tattered mattress.

"Put him here on the table, face up. Use this to tie him down," instructed Doctor Cyclops, handing Xi a rope and clearing the tipped-over gin bottles and spilled ashtrays off the table.

Xi seized the Professor from behind and roughly laid the blind old man on the table. Sen tried feebly to stop him, but Mya locked his forearm in a strong, painful grip.

"Mya, for God's sake! Why are you doing this? I'll give you whatever you want. Just don't hurt him! Max has nothing to do with this! Please, let him—"

Mya shut the old man up with a backhanded slap across his face so powerful it knocked him to his knees. "Silence!"

The Professor heard the blow and struggled to lift his head and shoulders off the table, as Xi strapped him to the table with the rope. "Sen? Sen, can you hear me?"

"Shut up! Both of you!" Mya ordered, then turned to Doctor Cyclops. "Do you have everything you need?"

Rummaging through the mirror cabinet, Doctor Cyclops nodded excitedly. "Yes, I think so," he said, rushing to the middle of the room and dumping a metal tray on the table beside the Professor. "For tonight's operation I have this." He pointed to the contents of the tray: a blunt scalpel, a rubber tourniquet, a rusty syringe, a clamp, a cigarette lighter, a crumpled piece of foil, a small package wrapped in old newspaper, and a bandage that looked as though it had been used before. Doctor Cyclops smiled broadly, then headed over to his mattress on the floor in the corner. "And for the operation in the mine—"

His yellowed fingers dug inside the tattered mattress, through one of the many tears in its lining, and pulled out a large set of shears, like a giant pair of scissors. He opened and closed them several times in rapid succession, cleaving the air. He laughed maniacally at the thrill of what was to come.

Still on his knees, Sen looked from the crazed doctor to the impatiently pacing Mya. "What are you going to do to us?"

"I said shut up!" she shouted, storming up to the old man in her sleek red dress and striking him so hard he crashed to the floor, unconscious. "You!" she pointed at Doctor Cyclops. "Put that down and get on with it! You've got twenty minutes, otherwise you'll lose more than this contract!"

The deranged doctor's glee quickly disappeared as he

scurried over to the table, nodding emphatically. "Yes, of course, twenty minutes, twenty minutes!"

On the table, the Professor tried to fight against the ropes, but Xi had fastened them firmly, the knots cutting into the old man's wrists and ankles. He could smell the gin-stinking breath of the doctor hovering over him now. He could hear his trembling, nervous fingers fumbling through the items on the metal tray.

The Professor's sightless eyes turned toward the end of the table. That was where the sound of Mya's heels had stopped, where she had last struck Sen, who was no longer making a sound. "What's this all for?" he asked sternly in Mya's direction, not a hint of fear in his voice. "You've got your diamond. What else do you want?"

For a moment, the Professor expected her to tell him to be quiet. Instead, Mya Chan decided to indulge her captive.

Slowly she walked to the side of the table and leaned over him. "You're asking the wrong questions. It's not a matter of what else I want. It's a matter of what *don't* I want. The answer is quite simple. There's *nothing* I don't want, and there's *nothing* I won't have. The diamond is but a small part of the sum of my desires. Cash, control, chaos—these are the things at my fingertips now. These are the jewels I will possess. The Eye of the Dragon is a key. You can't imagine what's hiding behind the door it opens. You can't imagine what lies ahead. The world will never be the same again."

"The Eye of the Dragon isn't a key, it's a curse."

Mya laughed. "Come now, Professor, I thought you were a man of reason."

"I am. And it's a reasonable assumption that although you may not believe in the curse, your actions will fulfill it."

"The words of a moral man. Unfortunately for you, moral men always wind up dead." Mya leaned in close and smiled. "I'm just chasing my dream, just as your men are no doubt chasing the dragon, or at least what was stolen from it. Which is precisely what you're about to do now."

"What do you mean?" the Professor asked.

Suddenly Xi seized the old man's arm and held it up straight while Doctor Cyclops strapped on the tourniquet. The doctor took the small newspaper bundle and unwrapped it. Inside was a sticky brown substance like resin.

Mya watched the veins on the old man's arm bulge. "Do you know what dragon-chasing is, Professor? It's a term used by drug addicts, referring to the injecting of raw opium directly into the bloodstream. Trust me, it's for your own good. You don't want to be awake when Doctor Cyclops here cuts into your abdomen to retrieve that tracking device lodged in your intestines."

"How do you know about that?"

"It's not important how we know. What's important is that we get it out of you."

Doctor Cyclops was already using his scalpel to scrape as much of the sticky brown substance as possible onto the piece of foil. Once the foil was full, he molded it into the shape of a small bowl, then flicked the cigarette lighter and began to wave the flame beneath the foil. Soon the brown substance gave off a tendril of smoke that twisted into the air.

"Beautiful," he observed with his one mesmerized eye. "They call it dragon-chasing because of the smoke. It's like a dragon rising up in the air. See its claws curl in search of prey. See its body writhe and snake, escaping the pool of opium."

As Xi continued to hold the Professor's arm out, the doctor took the rusty syringe and filled it with the liquid opium. Then, slapping the Professor's forearm, he placed the tip of the needle against the old man's skin and slid it into his flesh.

The Professor gasped.

The doctor emptied the syringe, then pulled the needle free.

"The opium works fast." The doctor grinned. "Sweet dreams, Professor."

Almost instantly, the Professor's eyelids began to flutter as his blind eyes rolled back into his head. But before the demons of his opium-induced slumber came lurching out of the shadows of his mind, he whispered groggily to Mya, "You're not doing this alone, *are you*." It was not a question.

Mya pursed her lips in a sly smile and shook her head. "There's an old Chinese proverb. Treat your flaws like holes and fill them in with someone else's strengths. After all, what's a business empire without a consortium to back it?"

Slowly the Professor's eyes closed completely. His arms and legs fell limp and his entire body sank against the filthy table surface.

Doctor Cyclops put the syringe back into the metal tray, unbuttoned the Professor's shirt, then picked up the rusty scalpel still smeared with sticky raw opium. Without iodine, antiseptic, or gloves, he made a random incision in the Professor's belly and began probing inside with his rotting, nail-chipped fingers.

It was the first incision of many.

VII

Hong Kong, China

RAYS OF EARLY-MORNING LIGHT BOUNCED OFF THE ZHANG Diamond Tower as it stood tall and proud next to the soaring Two International Finance Center and the other high-rise buildings of Hong Kong Island's financial district. It was barely 7:00 A.M., yet the streets were already bustling with briefcase-carrying businessmen and financiers all hurrying to work.

Even at this early hour, the air was thick with the smell of the salty harbor and the sweet scents of sticky rice congee pouring out of street stalls.

Through the smells and the crowd of workers raced Will and Bradley. They had leapt from a water taxi and were now charging as fast as they could from the wharf, across the financial district's waterfront toward the Zhang Corporation's Hong Kong Headquarters.

They hit the revolving doors of the tower and spun into the lobby of the building.

The elderly Chinese security guard at the desk immediately stood at the commotion, not recognizing Bradley for a moment.

"It's okay, George, it's just me," Bradley told him.

"Oh, Mr. Zhang, I'm sorry," a flustered, concerned George apologized as Bradley and Will bolted past him for the elevator. "Mr. Zhang!" he called after them. "Mr. Chambers has canceled all office work for today. None of the employees will be coming in except for the members of the board. Some kind of emergency. Is everything okay, Mr. Zhang?"

"It will be," Bradley replied, hitting the elevator button. He smiled at Will confidently, recalling the young college student's comforting words on the way here. Will beamed back as the elevator doors opened before them and the pair hurried inside the lift.

On the flight from San Francisco, Will had noticed how agitated and tense Bradley seemed. As Bradley's hand clutched the end of the armrest, Will placed his hand firmly on top of Bradley's. Bradley smiled and let Will's fingers interlock with his. "You're very sweet, do you know that?" Bradley said, his voice still a little anxious. "I only just met you, yet you make me feel...I don't know...safe, I suppose."

"It'll be okay," Will said, speaking softly so as not to wake the other passengers. "You'll see. Everything will be okay."

Bradley sighed and whispered back, "I'm scared for him. And I'm scared that perhaps I never told him enough how much I love him."

"He already knows."

Bradley shook his head. "I'm not so sure. My uncle can be a hard man. After my parents died, he raised me. I love him, and I need his respect, it's part of our culture. He knows who I am, deep down, but we never discuss it. I've never tried to hide who I am, but sometimes he does. Being gay in the world of Hong Kong business can be difficult. China's a very traditional place. Homosexuality isn't illegal there but it's hard to be—different."

"Being gay isn't about being different. It's about being you. You're not some kind of freak and you're not alone."

"Sometimes that's how it feels. My uncle likes to think he's open-minded, but sometimes I think he questions my ability. I can see it in his eyes, as if he wants to disown me. That's how it was with my figure skating. I could have been a champion, you know. But he told me all I'd end up being was a laughingstock. He told me he could offer me a job at the company, an honorable job, but only if I started at the bottom. Which I did. I worked hard, all the way to the top. I tried to become something he could be proud of, but even now I feel like an outsider. Even now I feel—dispensable."

"Is it what you want? A future at the company?"

"The dream of being a skater is long gone. I've worked long and hard to get to where I am now, so yes, it is what I want. I like what I do. I'm good at what I do. I just need others to see that. It's hard. Sometimes I think it would be easier to just give up."

Will shook his head. "Never give up. Someone told me that once, and I've never forgotten it."

"Someone special?"

Will nodded. "Someone I think of as my father. Although he's not really my father. He's my friend. I had an accident once. Ended up driving my motorbike off a cliff into the sea, nearly got myself killed. But Felix was there for me. I remember lying in the hospital bed. I think he thought I was unconscious, maybe I was, but I heard his voice. He told me: Never change, never apologize for who you are, and when things can't get any harder, do whatever it takes to pull through. But never give up."

He looked Bradley in the eye then and said in a quiet

100

voice, "I'm only young, but I'm lucky to have a bunch of older, wiser people around me. And those assholes who can't see that you're good at what you do? Screw 'em!"

Bradley smiled and looked into Will's eyes, and then, before he could stop himself, he leaned in and planted his warm, soft lips on Will's.

For a moment he thought the young American might refuse his bold advance. He thought Will might pull away, embarrassed or even worse, offended.

But Will only closed his eyes, lost in the moment, and savored the sweet, moist taste of Bradley's lips. He clenched his fingers, interlocking them with Bradley's even tighter than before, and gently pushed his tongue into Bradley's mouth.

The handsome young Chinese businessman took him in, cherishing this tender moment amid all the anxiety.

Will's free hand reached across and began to unbutton Bradley's shirt, unfastening two, three, four buttons before sliding his hand down the front of Bradley's shirt, feeling the tensed mounds of his stomach muscles beneath the fabric, gliding further down over his bulging crotch.

Bradley quickly broke away from the kiss.

"I'm sorry," Will whispered.

Bradley put his finger on Will's lips to silence his apology. "Don't be." With that, he stood from his seat, made his way quietly past the sleeping passengers, and then, with a single glance back at Will, opened the bathroom door.

When Will reached the lavatory, he saw the door was unlocked. He pushed it open and suddenly Bradley's arm appeared and yanked him inside.

Bradley closed the door, slid the lock across, then seized Will by the neck of his shirt and hauled him into a powerful and passionate kiss. He pressed his hips hard against Will's, making his intentions more than known.

Will grinned through the kiss, feeling the long, stiff

shaft of Bradley's keen cock pushing against his leg. It was trapped inside Bradley's trousers, ensnared inside his underwear. It had done its best to extend sideways, forming a horizontal bulge, the length of it reaching all the way to Bradley's hip, but Will couldn't bear to see it tortured and trapped like that.

In one swift move he unbuckled Bradley's belt, then unclipped and unzipped his trousers, pushing them down several inches, revealing his white designer underwear and engorged bulge beneath. Will grabbed the swollen shaft through the white cotton, squeezing it hard in his fist, forcing a pained groan from Bradley and a drop of precum that seeped through the material and turned the cotton slightly transparent. Will pulled out of the kiss and looked down. He could make out the eye of Bradley's cock through the moistened fabric. He squeezed again and pushed out another drop.

Will had become instantly hard the second he'd laid his hand on Bradley's, back in their seats. Now, with the sight of Bradley's throbbing underpants in his fist, Will's own hungry cock strained in pain.

His hands trembling with impatience more than nervousness, Bradley unsnapped the buttons on Will's jeans, his jittery fingers brushing the delicate delight of Will's blond pubic hair before the thick stem of his cock appeared. There was no hope of getting all the buttons undone before the young college student's dick sprang into the air. Inside the tiny compartment, Bradley jerked Will's jeans down around his knees, freeing his full round balls and exposing his tanned, athletic thighs.

Before the jeans went any further, Will reached down, groping through his pockets in hope. He smiled, and pulled out a condom packet. "Thank you, Elsa," he said, looking up at the ceiling as though the Professor's housekeeper was some kind of guardian angel.

He threw the condom on the bathroom basin, then awkwardly heeled off his boots and clambered out of his jeans, taking high steps to pull his legs free in the small space.

Standing in only his T-shirt now, with his thick young legs spread wide and his cock standing high, Will attacked Bradley's shirt, quickly unsnagging the remainder of the buttons before pulling the shirt wide open, revealing Bradley's thick smooth chest and ripped abs. Bradley flicked the shirt from his arms while Will forced the young businessman's trousers down. With only the straining underpants left, Will dropped into a squat, his face level with Bradley's bulge.

Bobbing on his powerful haunches, Will took the waistband of Bradley's underpants in his fingers and slowly pulled the elastic down. Bradley's sparse black pubic hair sprouted and blossomed first, then Will caught a glimpse of his brown-skinned cock, stretching all the way to the left, a thick trunk positioned just beneath the waistband. The shaft pulsated. Then, as Will slid the underpants all the way down Bradley's legs, that sweet, stiff cock bounced free.

The slippery wet slit of its eye opened and gleamed as another desperate drop of precum escaped it, then without another second's hesitation, Will took the swollen head of Bradley's dick in his salivating mouth.

As Bradley clutched his breath and held it, Will teased the head of Bradley's cock with his tongue, savoring its beautiful flavors, his teeth nibbling at the soft sensitive skin.

"God, I'm going to—" Bradley panted, his voice quavering.

Will quickly released his head, kissing it as he looked up at Bradley and winked. "Not yet, you don't. We've only just started."

Will stood, his hands sliding up Bradley's firm thighs and slipping between his legs, his fingers molding and kneading

Bradley's high, tight balls before gripping the base of his shaft and milking its length.

Bradley gasped, trying desperately to control his ready-to-erupt loins, his face pleading and full of pain. Will released Bradley's cock once more and kissed the tormented expression away.

His own cock, stiff and bouncing, thumped against Bradley's burning shaft. Their dicks played together as Will lifted his T-shirt over his head, revealing his hard, youthful torso—the rippling stomach, the defined, hairless chest, the small solid gems of his nipples—but as he reached high, his hands thumped against the low ceiling of the tiny compartment and his arms became locked and tangled in his twisted T-shirt. There was no room to move. Bradley tried to help him off with it, their smooth chests and stomachs now touching, their rock-hard dicks rubbing and bumping against one another, but all he managed to do was tangle the T-shirt even more around Will's forearms, effectively tying the young American's hands together above his head.

"Looks like you're in a bind," Bradley laughed.

Will kissed him hard on the lips and winked. "That works for me."

Bradley welcomed the notion. Taking the quarterback's solid, contoured hips in both hands, he managed to turn him around, their flesh grinding, muscles rubbing, until Will was facing the mirror, with his toned, perfectly rounded ass to Bradley, his arms bound above his head.

Will gave in to the captive pose and rested his balls on the rim of the basin. His hairless sack spilled several inches over the edge and into the sink. His throbbing dick was so stiff and long it reached all the way across the basin, the head of his cock tapping the faucet. He leaned his sculpted torso forward, pushing his ass out and pressing his chest and one cheek against the mirror. He opened his mouth slightly, misting up the glass. He closed his eyes. Then he heard the sweet sound of the condom wrapper opening.

A moment later, the splayed fingers of Bradley's hands traced their way around Will's hips, slid down the deep, defined ridges of his carved obliques, feathered Will's light pubic hair, and arrived at the base of his shaft. His fingers slowly crossed the bridge to the faucet where Bradley let the water flow before squeezing soap from the dispenser into both palms.

When Bradley's fingers made their way back down Will's shaft, they left a tingling, frothy trail. Foam dripped and squelched as his right hand remained behind, squeezing and massaging Will's cock to the soft, melodic moans of a young man being pleasured, while his left hand returned to Will's perfectly formed ass. There his wet fingers slid between Will's ass cheeks, turning his crack into a slippery, inviting crevice.

Bradley sponged his own condom-covered cock then, working up a lather that almost made him come. Before he could explode, he took his stiff, soaped shaft in his fist and guided it gently between Will's ass cheeks.

He felt the velvety ring of Will's well-trained ass already opening up, the lips of his anus sucking hungrily on the head of Bradley's cock. It was the warmest of welcomes, and Bradley didn't hesitate for a second. With a confident, forceful thrust he pushed himself deep inside Will.

The air clicked in Will's throat and a ripple shot through the muscles in his back. His biceps locked, his hands bunched into fists and instinctively tried to pull themselves out of their bind. The T-shirt ripped a little, but Will held his pose, sliding his ass closer to Bradley's hips, forcing Bradley's cock even deeper inside him until it could go no further.

Bradley let out a long, tremulous sigh, one that felt like it had been pent up inside him forever. At the same time he tightened his grip on Will's cock and began jerking him off in long, firm, soapy strokes. When Bradley pressed his lean, muscular body hard against Will's back and bit gently into the taut muscle running from Will's shoulder to his neck, the young American knew this wasn't going to take long at all.

Bradley's wet, panting mouth ventured up Will's throat and reached his ear. His drenched, foam-filled fist began pounding Will's cock harder and faster.

He pulled his own dick out of Will, then plunged it inside him again and again, working up a strong, swift rhythm, the suction from his thrusts forcing tiny bubbles out of Will's sweet, soaked, soapy ass.

"Fuck me," Will uttered, his soft tongue licking and flicking at his dry, parted lips. "Fuck me, fuck me harder!"

Bradley did as he was told, pumping his cock into Will with all the force and grunt he could muster. Will too had fallen into rhythm now, slamming his ass back against Bradley's straining hips as Bradley hammered forward. The beautiful, young Chinese businessman was groaning softly now in time to the beat, his pitch rising quickly, his brow twisted in desperate yearning.

Will too let out a gasp with each blow, feeling his balls slide up the rim of the basin now, turning into solid spheres ready to burst. He could already smell the cum, even before a single drop was spilled.

Then, suddenly, he could hold himself back no longer.

The first shot of cum slapped against the mirror, stayed there for a moment, waiting for the second blast to join it before sliding down the glass. But Bradley did not stop or even slow his pounding fist. With relentless determination, he forced a third, fourth, fifth jet of cum from Will's aching, bulging cock. With each jolt of semen, Will let out a groan louder than the last. His fists unfurled and his bound hands pressed themselves against the mirror, palms flat, fingers spread. He forced himself back hard on the cock he was still riding. Then it was Bradley's turn to fire his load.

His feet—strong and dexterous from his years of skating—hoisted him up onto the tips of his toes, and with him went Will, whose feet actually left the ground altogether. Bradley pushed his shoulders flat against the wall behind him, thrust his hips as high as they would go, and with a spasm that Will felt all the way up his ass and through his tight, tensed stomach, the Chinese businessman shot off a blaze of cum into the head of his condom.

Another quiver rocked his body as a second load was released.

Then a third.

A fourth.

And then—after holding his breath for an endless moment, his body frozen in a state of sheer pleasure and relief—Bradley slowly lowered them both back down to the floor.

Will smiled and let out a long, heaving sigh. He could hear the fireworks of Bradley's heart pressed against his back, the euphoric *thump-thump-thump* of his own thunderous heart, their hot, heavy, happy panting, and then—

Ding!

The seat-belt sign.

The boardroom of the Zhang Diamond Tower in Hong Kong was situated on the 40th floor of the building. There was a long mahogany table in the center of the room. On one wall was a showcase of Zhang Sen's favorite diamonds, while the opposite wall was all glass, a vast floor-to-ceiling window overlooking Hong Kong's bustling Victoria Harbor. Beyond that were the high-rises of Kowloon and the old Kai Tak airport.

None of the men in the room, however, were looking at the view. They had seen it many times before. All of them had their eyes fixed squarely on Chad Chambers at the head of the table.

"Gentlemen, a decision has to be made," Chad was

saying, sitting forward in his seat, demanding everyone's attention with a hand that cut the air like an axe with each stern, serious word. "Investigations are taking place as we speak, but while the authorities take care of finding Sen alive and well, we need to take care of this company. We need to put someone in charge, right here and now."

"It seems to me you're the logical choice," offered one of the men at the table with a matter-of-fact shrug.

Chad nodded respectfully. "As vice president of the company, I'll do my humble best to get us through this."

"What about Bradley?" another board member asked. "The two of you share the same title. Where is—"

"Bradley did the right thing and chose to stay in San Francisco," Chad answered. "He told me he needs to be hands-on with the investigation right now, which will no doubt take up all his energies. He's more help to the authorities than he is to us."

The members of the board looked at each other and nodded, some of them sorrowfully, concerned for Bradley and his uncle. None of them could deny that Chad was the obvious man for the job.

"Gentlemen," Chad continued, ready to close the deal for leadership once and for all. "This company's future now hangs in the balance. The mines in Shandong are producing diamonds at a record rate, more than twelve thousand carats each month, with more and more deposits being tapped every week, not to mention the plans for our expansion into the U.S. We are about to reach a pinnacle in this company's history. We don't have a lot of time for discussion."

"How about another ten minutes? Just to let me have my say!"

Suddenly, the entire room turned to see Bradley Zhang in his disheveled tuxedo standing inside the glass doors of the boardroom, behind him a young American in a slightly ripped T-shirt and jeans.

Chad simply smiled. "Bradley, it's so unnecessary of you to—"

"You knew I was coming to this, Chad. The last time we spoke—"

"The last time we spoke, you were clearly shaken. You were worried about your uncle. My God, there were guns! An explosion! Nobody blames you for giving me control of—"

"I gave you control of nothing."

Bradley glared at him angrily while Chad took on a caring, sympathetic facade. "We all understand you've been through a lot. It's your job now to help find your uncle, not to be burdened with *this*." With a sweep of his hand he gestured to the board members, the room, the entire office.

"*This* is what my uncle would want me to take care of."

"Are you sure about that?" Slowly Chad's caring expression transformed into the shrewd look of a calculated businessman. "Bradley, do you truly understand what's at stake here? Sen's been kidnapped and the chances of him returning in one piece are remote to say the least, given his financial standing. It's a crisis point for this company. We have to take certain steps to get through this. It's time to sort out the men from the—" he paused, eyeing Bradley up and down, no longer with a look of concern, but a look of doubt, something he wanted the others to see. "It's time to sort out the men from *your* kind."

Bradley cocked his head, at first puzzled, then appalled. "What the hell are you trying to say, Chad?"

"Admit it, Bradley. You may be blood, but what you lack is courage. Leadership. The kind of fortitude that will ensure that this company grows from strength to strength toward a bright shining future. You lack the fortitude of a real man."

Will suddenly stepped forward, ready to take Chad for every swing and punch he was worth, but Bradley put his arm out and stopped him. His hand settled on Will's chest with a certain familiarity and stayed there, feeling the angry hammer of his heart. Everyone present stared at Bradley's hand positioned on the young American's chest, and a sense of unease rippled through the room. The board members whispered into each other's ears and looked at Bradley with misgiving and mistrust.

Bradley didn't care. Instead he cast a quiet, controlled remark over his shoulder to his blond friend. "It's okay, Will. Wait for me in reception. I can handle this."

Fighting the instinct to stay and defend his friend, Will respected Bradley's decision to stand his own ground and slowly backed out of the room.

Will didn't quite get as far as reception. As he made his way through the silent, empty corridors of the Zhang Corporation's Hong Kong offices, Chad's words rang through his ears: *The kind of fortitude that will ensure that this company grows from strength to strength toward a bright, shining future.*

They were words he'd heard before. Almost verbatim.

Will suddenly took a detour through the building. Instead of heading back to reception to wait for Bradley, he followed a nagging suspicion that led to an office door with Chad Chambers's name on it. He opened it and disappeared inside.

Chad's office was enormous, elegant, minimalist. All his furniture was white and silver and perfectly streamlined. The place was almost too sleek and cool. It was practically icy.

Swiftly Will made his way through the vast space, past the low-lying furniture to Chad's desk. He didn't know what he was looking for, but something told him Chad Chambers was a man with secrets, one of which might well be the whereabouts of the stolen diamonds, and of Sen and the Professor.

Chad's pencil-thin laptop computer sat closed on one side of the desk. Will sat himself in Chad's high-back chair, swiveled to face the computer, and opened it. The screen came to life with a welcome message.

Good morning, Chad.

Please enter your security password now.

Below the message was a text box containing four individual spaces. The computer was waiting for four digits or letters to be typed.

Will tried the obvious.

C-H-A-D

A new message appeared.

Incorrect password. Please try again.

Will realized his chances to get this right were no doubt limited. Chad was not the sort of guy to use his year of birth or a cute nickname, and he definitely didn't strike him as the kind of guy who'd ever owned a pet.

He was, however, a numbers man.

Will glanced at the phone on the desk. As with any Touch-Tone phone on the planet, each letter had a corresponding number, 2 to 9. Will typed Chad's name on the computer keyboard using the corresponding number sequence.

2–4-2–3

A message flashed up on the screen.

Incorrect password. Please try once more. Failure to enter correct password will result in a security alert.

"I know you're a numbers man, Chad," Will muttered to himself. "And you're arrogant enough to use your own name. What clue am I missing? What is it about you that—"

Will stopped, suddenly recalling Chad's philosophy for achieving anything. Determine your goal first, then work through the steps backward to reach that goal. "Go through things in reverse first."

Quickly, confidently, Will typed the numbers into the computer in reverse order.

3–2–4–2

The screen went blank for a heart-stopping moment and Will clutched his breath. Then a new message appeared.

Password accepted. Thank you, Chad.

Will smiled to himself. "Yeah, thanks Chad."

Now that he was inside Chad's system, he was granted access to the network. Instantly he began searching the archive for certain file names.

He was sure that if Chad was up to something, he certainly wasn't stupid enough to bury it within the archive. But he may have left a thread *through* the archives, a trail of breadcrumbs, and maybe, just maybe, Will might be able to trace the file names back to Chad's personal folders.

He typed in *Zhang Sen.*

Just about every file in the archive began spilling down the screen. Will canceled the search instantly. He knew it was just a matter of time before the meeting in the board-room ended and Chad returned to his computer.

Will had to think outside the box, and fast.

He typed in *United States.* That's where all of this had begun. Half a dozen files came up immediately:

SF_HQ_Contracts and Legal

SF_HQ_Town Council/Project Plan

SF_Launch

SF_Strategy_5 Year Marketing and Sales

SF_Submissions and Quarterly Projections

Will could only assume the *SF* referred to San Francisco and that these files contained documents pertaining to the setup of the U.S. office. But a single file name stood out: *MT Project.*

"M-T," Will pondered. Not a reference to the word *mountain*—the *T* wouldn't be in upper case. No, *MT* was a state.

Quickly he left the archive and returned to Chad's personal files. He went straight into the search function and began to type *Monta—*

Suddenly he stopped, deleted the letters, and typed *Tcejorp Anatnom*

He pressed ENTER.

A single file appeared. Will opened it quickly, only to find the *entire* document had been written in reverse. Every word. Every letter.

"Jesus Christ," Will whispered to himself, hurriedly rummaging through Chad's drawers. He knew Chad was a neat freak, the kind of guy who would surely possess—

"A grooming kit." Will smiled, pulling a slender silver box out of the drawer and opening it up. He took out the mirror, spun the laptop around, and held the mirror in front of the screen.

The letters were reversed in the mirror's reflection, but the words no longer were. They were in the right order now, giving him enough of a clue to piece together the document's headings:

The Montana Project: Confidential

To begin implementation prior to The Beijing Project

Head of Insurance Portfolio: Chad Chambers

Head of Planning & Execution: Mya Chan

Head of Excavation, Engineering & Construction: Richard Conrad

Will stopped reading and turned the computer back to face him. He frantically clicked PRINT. A beep sounded behind him. Swiveling in the chair, he saw the printer light flashing *Out of Paper.* He shot a glance at the glass doors, feeling the seconds slip away. There was no sign of anyone outside in the corridor yet, no indication the meeting had finished.

Desperately he began opening drawers once more, sifting through cupboards, looking for paper to refill the printer. He shuffled through stationery supplies as fast as he could, knowing full well he couldn't afford to be held up another moment. Time was running out.

* * *

Time was running out. The holdup in Beijing had cost Mya Chan valuable hours, but Mya was a beautiful woman, and beautiful women had a way of forming friendships with the wrong people in the right circles. Or, in her opinion, the right people in the wrong circles.

Regardless of perspective, those people in those circles meant that, in an air traffic delay, while all the usual domestic and international passenger planes queued up and circled the skies over Hong Kong, Xi managed to land the Zhang Corporation jet at a completely different location—Hong Kong's infamous Kai Tak Airport. The old airport proved to be the perfect place for discreet landings and departures. Like getting the Zhang Diamond Corporation jet in and out of Hong Kong as quickly and quietly as possible.

And while Mya Chan was now considerably late for the boardroom meeting at the Zhang Diamond Tower, from Kai Tak she could take the Zhang high-speed motor cruiser directly across the harbor and still be at the company's Hong Kong Headquarters in time to help solve the problems that really mattered.

"The problem is obvious," Chad declared to Bradley in front of the entire board. "Everybody knows your—how shall I put it—*leanings*." With that he pointed to the glass doors through which Will had exited earlier. "And leanings like yours give you a tendency to be flippant, feeble-minded, unpredictable—"

"When have I ever been any of those things?" Bradley challenged confidently.

"—and as I was about to add, defensive. I'm simply stating the facts."

"You're simply stating your prejudices!"

Chad suddenly turned, his patience gone, his agenda pressing. He hammered the boardroom table with his fist.

"Let's face it, Bradley—and I speak for every last member of the board when I say this, including your uncle—you know as well as I do that you're not capable of running this company."

"Give me one good reason why not!"

Chad delivered his response as though it was common knowledge or simple logic. "Because everybody knows the gays don't have the balls to run empires."

"*The gays?*" Bradley repeated, incredulous. "Right now, Chad, you sound like the Nazis! Is that how you plan on running this company?"

More murmurs swept the room and the tables suddenly turned as the looks of misgiving and mistrust swung toward Chad.

"Don't be ridiculous!" was all the Harvard graduate could muster.

Bradley shook his head. "You're not a businessman. You're just a bully. Empires are built on respect, not rhetoric. You're all talk, Chad."

As though a glove had just been slapped across his face, Chad's expression changed once more, from disdain to an undisguised glee. "*Am I?*"

"Gentlemen, please," interjected one of the board members, standing at his chair. "We're all under a great deal of pressure. Now is not the time to argue. Nor is it the time to act rashly."

"I agree," added another. "It's becoming quite obvious that the two of you have your differences, but the decision to put someone else in charge is supposed to be Sen's."

"He's not here!" Chad shouted.

"I don't believe we should be making this decision for him," a third board member said, standing firm. "We should wait."

"Wait for what?" Chad questioned angrily.

"For my uncle," Bradley answered resolutely.

Chad fumed quietly and wiped his sweating brow.

Will wiped his sweating brow. He had found the blank paper, crammed it into the printer behind Chad's desk, and listened as the machine began pumping out the pages of the *Montana Project* document. Quickly he turned back to Chad's computer. "The Beijing Project? What are you up to, Chad?"

He typed in the words *Beijing Project*—backward.

One file appeared, one that had to be retrieved from the computer's trash and unlocked. Again the entire document had been encrypted in Chad's secret code. Again Will hit the print button, then slipped the mirror into his back pocket. He could work on it later, scour through every inch of it once it was printed off and in his hot hands. As the printer pumped and buzzed out the pages, he quickly glanced through it onscreen. Several words stood out.

Neda—

Aden, he quickly deduced.

Edart dnomaid—

Diamond trade.

Ecived DZ—

ZD device.

"ZD device?" Will quickly exited the document, logged on to Chad's Internet connection, and began typing in letters. It sounded like some sort of scientific acronym or chemical symbol. He extended the search and found *zidium*, a word he'd heard in the limousine in San Francisco, a term that the Professor never had a chance to explain. "What the fuck is a zidium device, anyway?"

"It's a bomb," came the reply. "One capable of leveling mountains. And cities."

The words came loud and clear. At the same moment the snout of a pistol pushed its way through Will's messy blond hair and pressed itself into the back of his skull. He froze. He didn't have to turn around. He already knew from the voice and the brief glimpse into the files who was on the other end of the gun.

"Mya Chan. How nice to finally meet you face-to-face—or rather, gun to head."

"Don't get cute!"

Suddenly the snout of Mya's diamond-studded pistol left Will's head for a second, and the butt of it came down hard and heavy. Will's forehead crashed against the keyboard as Mya knocked the young man unconscious with a somewhat satisfied smirk on her face.

Chairs whispered across the white carpet, rolling back from the table as the board members rose to leave.

"Gentlemen, please, sit down," Chad insisted. "We need a resolution on this."

"No, Chad," Bradley responded firmly. "We have a majority vote on this matter. We wait for the outcome of the investigation into Sen's disappearance, whatever the news may be."

"And so we just let the company slide into the ground without a leader?" Chad was trying to stop the board members from leaving one at a time, but they simply side-stepped him.

"No, we run the company jointly," Bradley said. "You decide *nothing* without my consent. You *do* nothing without me."

As the last of the board members headed for the elevators, leaving Chad and Bradley alone in the vast boardroom, Chad turned on Bradley, his face red with resentment. "I'll do as I damn well please."

"Is that a threat?"

Chad stormed up to Bradley, physically trying to intimidate him, physically trying to force him to back away. "No, it's a warning. Just like I warned you not to come here. Stop getting in my way or I'll—"

Bradley stood his ground. "Or you'll do what?"

Their chests met, Chad's snarling teeth only inches from Bradley's face. "Or I'll bury you alive." He smiled and made a starburst gesture with his hand. "Kaboom!"

Suddenly a cold, callous voice came from the boardroom doors. "There's no time for that."

Both Bradley and Chad turned to see Mya standing there, a sly red-glossed smile on her lips. Beside her stood Xi with an unconscious Will dangling under one arm. Mya crossed her arms. "I'm afraid this situation needs to be dealt with now."

VIII

Dubai, United Arab Emirates

ON ONE SIDE OF THE SHORELINE STRETCHED THE glimmering aqua gulf, on the other a vast expanse of desert as far as the eye could see, and in the middle, shooting up out of the white sands, was a narrow oasis of buildings made from shimmering glass and precious metals, tall and splendid and dazzling under the bright Arabian sun. It was a city like no other on Earth. A designer paradise. A rich man's fabricated fantasy, where credit cards and business cards were currency and everything that glittered was indeed gold. Where every Rolls Royce purred like a cat down Jumeirah Beach Road—

—while one particularly sleek yellow Lotus roared down the avenue like a lion.

Richard Conrad pushed the lavish locks of blond hair away from his sunglasses and turned up the radio. He suddenly decided he adored the song that was playing, although he had no idea who the artist was, and for a moment he entertained the thought of buying the record company that had the foresight and business savvy to sign up such an artist. Then came the song's bridge, his adoration waned, and just like that his interest was gone. The young Englishman's thoughts suddenly switched to something else: the new Mumbai contract that had landed on his desk at 9 A.M.; then switched again to the yacht he'd recently purchased in Monaco and what he was going to name her despite the old seafarer's warning that doing so was bad luck; and speaking of names, what the fuck was the name of that hot Eurasian model he'd left in his bed this morning? Alex? Aaron? Andy? Who cared! Richard shrugged it all off, including the song. All that mattered was today was a good day, and the next few days promised a lifetime of good days to come.

At the age of 28, Conrad had made the list of the Top 20 Richest Men in the World Under the Age of 30 three years running. His swiftly acquired, self-made fortune in the construction industry was mostly spent on investments, expansion, expensive toys, and endless adrenaline-fueled antics. Races to the polar ice caps, spaceflights in zero gravity, nautical expeditions in search of long-lost ships, privately funded (and very secret) scientific experiments involving particle collisions—these were the fun, shiny trinkets on which Richard Conrad spent his pocket money. Because without the fun, shiny stuff, money was nothing.

"Anthony, that was his name," Richard said to himself, clicking his fingers. "Fuck, I hope he didn't steal anything on the way out."

He adjusted the rearview mirror to check his hair, stroked his blond waves, then twisted the mirror back in place. That's when the glare of the sun bounced off the hood of a silver 4WD BMW trailing two cars behind. It caught Richard's eye, and so did the driver of the car. Even from this distance, he got enough of a glimpse to discern that the man behind the wheel was reasonably striking.

He changed lanes so that the two cars between them were no longer blocking his line of sight. He adjusted his rearview mirror again, and his assessment of the driver shifted from reasonably striking to undeniably handsome.

He could now make out the silhouette of a square-chiseled jaw. Short dark hair. Eyes concealed behind a pair of sport sunglasses, the kind you wear on a snowy slope or, as the case was, in the desert.

Richard eased his foot off the gas a little with the intention of falling back and letting the BMW cruise alongside him. He planned on getting a much better look at the handsome driver, and perhaps even do a little tailgating, first in the streets, then in the sack.

But as the Lotus slowed, Richard watched in the rearview as the BMW slowed as well. Strange, he thought. He kept his eye on it, ready to turn in case the BMW turned, checking the clock to make sure he still had enough time to get to the dunes.

The BMW signaled, but instead of turning off, it simply slid into the same lane as Richard, again keeping two cars between them. Suddenly Richard Conrad realized he wasn't the cat in this game of chase.

Suddenly he found the situation a hell of a lot sexier!

He smirked at the now obscured view of the BMW in his rearview mirror, then without warning, stamped his foot on the accelerator, slid effortlessly through the gears, and turned a hard right.

Smoke rippled from his back wheels.

The Lotus cut across the traffic and vanished in a black cloud up a side street.

Richard stole a single glance back before leaving Jumeirah Beach Road in a state of angry chaos. He smiled again to see the silver BMW speed up, skillfully gliding past the horn-blasting cars to take up the chase.

Richard turned the Lotus again, this time into a narrow

alley congested with delivery trucks loading and unloading. The Lotus moved in a swift, gentle zigzag, slipping easily through the gaps as shop owners and van drivers jumped out of the way. All the while, Richard glanced from the alley ahead to the view behind.

The BMW weaved its way quickly down the alley, veering left, twisting right, missing crates and clothes racks by mere inches.

"I like you," Richard said to the reflection of the pursuing BMW. "Let's see what you're like behind the wheel of something a little more fun."

He peeled out of the alley and back toward Jumeirah Beach Road before continuing on toward the marina then heading south out of town. The silver BMW kept pace as the hotels and towers faded away behind them like a desert mirage, leaving nothing but a seemingly endless drive ahead. That is, until Richard wrenched the wheel and took his Lotus off-road. A yellow cloud bloomed in the air as the sports car spat sand from its broad tires and tore across the desert.

A moment later, the BMW did exactly the same, following the cloud's trail. Here the desert ground was firm, the sand relatively compacted to give the cars enough grip to continue their pursuit. But the dunes on the near horizon were tall and unclimbable, at least for the Lotus.

The sizzling air at the foot of the dunes began to ripple in waves, revealing new shapes and colors. At first the shapes looked like molten wrecks in the shimmering heat that rose from the desert floor. Then slowly they materialized into cars. Dozens of cars. It looked as though a small parking lot had been plucked from the city and transplanted here in the middle of nowhere, with one exception—not all the cars were roadworthy city vehicles.

Off to one side were five dune buggies. They were large at the back due to their oversized rear tires, looking like strange creatures positioned on their haunches on the golden sand, ready to pounce. Their skeletal shells were dented and scraped. Their eyes were cracked headlights. They watched the Lotus approach, as did several dozen men standing in a group between the parked cars and the dune buggies.

While the Lotus drove straight up to the group of men, the BMW peeled away to the far side of the parked cars.

Richard stepped out of his sports car and looked back to where the silver BMW had disappeared. He couldn't find it among the cluster of other cars.

"Ah! Mr. Conrad! Always a pleasure to see you. Although for a minute there we thought the race was going to start without you."

"I was—distracted." Richard stopped craning his neck, trying to see over the parked cars, and now made his way toward a large man in a long white tobe—the robelike tunic of the Persian Gulf states—seated at an old fold-out card table. He was facing the gathering of similarly dressed men who now parted like a biblical sea for Richard to approach. Money quickly exchanged hands as a wave of excitement swept the crowd.

At the card table, the fat man's kaffiyeh—the traditional Arab headpiece—billowed in a short-lived yet welcome desert breeze. "Let's hope you regain your concentration quickly," he said, beaming to Richard, his hands grabbing at money now coming from all sides. "Otherwise you may lose yourself another small fortune."

"Oh, Jahmar, you know how much I enjoy giving you a reason to smile."

The smile on the man at the table suddenly brightened, literally, as the sun hit him. A long-missing front tooth, now replaced by a diamond that Richard had recently lost in a bet, shone like a lighthouse.

"Mr. Conrad, what would the Dubai Dune Derby be without you?"

"Still dangerous. Still underground. Still highly illegal," Richard answered in his plum British accent. "But probably not half as much fun."

"Well, it's always *fun* taking your cash," Jahmar said with a grin. "Or are you still digging into that secret diamond stash of yours?"

Richard shot a glance into the excited gathering of men and saw a face at the back of the crowd—sunglasses, short, dark hair, square-chiseled jaw—then answered Jahmar by throwing a small black pouch on the card table. Jahmar cooed, his fingers dancing delicately as they untied the pouch string and poured a night sky of tiny glittering stones across the table. "My, my, that supply of yours seems endless," he said, reaching under the table to hand Richard a helmet.

"No, not exactly. But enough for two to play." Richard took the helmet and pulled a second small black pouch from his pocket. He handed it to Jahmar and watched the Arab's jeweled smile grow even brighter. "I want to enter a new driver in the race."

"Who?" Jahmar asked, caring less about the answer than about the twinkling diamonds he emptied into his sweaty palm.

Richard turned to face the crowd and pointed assertively. "Him."

All heads turned, one by one, following Richard's pointing finger, which seemed to cut a path straight through the group directly to a single man—the last man in the crowd.

Jake Stone.

With all eyes on him, the handsome American cleared his throat awkwardly. "You've got me confused with someone else," he said, pushing his sunglasses further up the bridge of his nose then quickly turning to head away.

It was all an act. From the brief amount of research Jake had done between San Francisco and Dubai, he had learned that Richard Conrad was a man who enjoyed chasing bait. Jake had deliberately made the catch easy—but he was careful not to make it too easy.

Conrad hastened after him, pushing through the crowd before grabbing hold of Jake's arm and spinning him around with considerable force.

"Race me," he challenged. "You've been tailing me for the better part of an hour through Dubai. Let's see if you can keep up on the dunes."

"I told you, you're mistaking me for someone else."

Jake pulled away.

This time Richard overtook him and blocked his path. He offered his hand. "I'm Rich."

"I could tell."

"Richard Conrad. And you are?"

"I'm Jake Stone."

"And *I'm* very rarely mistaken, Mr. Stone. There's something you want from me. What is it? Work? Fun? Money?"

"No," Jake said, giving up the facade and cutting to the chase.

"Then you want answers of some sort. Information. Very well, I'll tell you anything you want. But first"—Richard thrust the helmet in Jake's stomach so hard it knocked a grunt out of him—"you'll have to catch me."

For a moment Jake hesitated, looking down from Richard's goading gaze to the helmet, and back again.

"What's the matter?" Richard mocked. "Ready to give up the game so soon?"

On the contrary, Jake had the feeling the game had only just begun. He threw down his first gauntlet. "Did you know Zhang Sen has been kidnapped?"

Richard raised one eyebrow. "So you do want answers. The first being, yes, of course I knew. He's a dear friend and business colleague. But if you want to know anything else, that depends entirely on how good you are behind the wheel of one of those." His head tilted toward the five dented dune buggies glinting in the sun.

Jake took a deep breath and grabbed the helmet. "All right, then. How fast can they go? They look pretty beat-up."

"For good reason. The Dubai Dune Derby isn't so much about speed. It's more about...durability." Richard then said to Jahmar without taking his charming eyes off Jake, "Jahmar, we're ready to race!"

With an excited bellow, the oversized Jahmar rose to his feet and announced, "Gentlemen, start your engines!"

Like a wave sweeping along behind them, the crowd followed five men to the waiting buggies. Richard walked alongside Jake, guiding him to a scratched-up once-red vehicle. "The course stretches a quarter of a mile that way. You'll see a red marker—if you get that far. Then down to the water, along the shore, and over this dune to return here." As he spoke he pointed to the massive mountain of sand separating them from the sea. "I advise you to climb the last dune as fast as you can, otherwise you'll lose friction, what little there is. Trust me, when these things topple down a hill that big, they don't just roll. They bounce. So make sure you're strapped in properly, otherwise—"

Jake was already climbing into the battered buggy. "Otherwise what?"

Richard gestured to the roll bar above Jake's head. "See that patch of reddish-brown? That's not paint. That was Shakil Antoun's final mistake."

"I take it he doesn't mind me driving his car."

"No, not at all. You automatically forfeit your place when you're dead."

"Are there any other rules I should know about?"

"No. In fact there are no rules whatsoever except to finish first. Entry fee is anything over $50,000 and the winner takes all, so you can imagine rivalry gets a little heated at times. But since you're brave enough to join in the fun, it's only fair I give you a few tips." He looked over at the other three drivers now fastening helmet straps and seat belts. "That guy in the yellow-striped buggy over there, his name's Scalper. Watch him, know where he is at all times, otherwise he'll jump a dune on your blind side and take the top clean off your bug."

"Hence the name," Jake figured.

"Over there," Richard continued, "getting in the blue buggy, that's Khalil Khoury—Killer Khoury to his friends."

"Because he likes to kill?"

"Not as much as he likes to maim. He says it leaves a more lasting impression than death. But Maimer Khoury just doesn't have the same ring to it." His gaze moved to the third driver. "And over there, getting in what's left of that purple buggy, that's Elvis."

"Elvis?" Jake looked quizzically at the bald, badly scarred Arab who didn't look remotely like Elvis at all.

"One day on the track," Richard explained, "his car was completely demolished, and Elvis there, well, for eight and a half minutes he was actually dead. Then suddenly, in front of everyone's eyes, he came back to life. If you ask me, I think Death is still chasing him. The question is, how long can he outrun it?"

"What about you?" Jake strapped on the seat belt that formed an X across his chest.

"Are you asking how long I can outrun Death? Like everything else I do, that's a race I intend to win."

"No, I don't mean Death. I mean, what's your nickname?"

Richard smiled, took a helmet from Jahmar, and slid it over his blond head. "Me? I don't need one. My real name carries all the clout I need." He made his way over to a hammered black dune buggy with a smashed headlight. "Watch for Jahmar, he'll give the green light. And remember, no rules!"

"No rules," Jake whispered to himself nervously, putting on his helmet and finding the key already in the ignition. "Jesus Christ, Jake. What the hell are you doin'?"

Jake turned the key and the battered red buggy roared to life. Suddenly the other four buggies did the same. As Jahmar made his way to the front, the crowd fell back, cheering and chattering and exchanging money down to the last second.

Jahmar lifted both arms high in the air. "Gentlemen. On your marks. Get set..."

Engines revved. Clutches burned.

Jake desperately sized up his dead man's buggy. He found the gears, pedals, gripped the wheel.

"Go!" Jahmar bellowed.

Like a volcanic eruption, the spinning wheels of the five buggies sent so much sand into the air that it momentarily turned the bright white sun into a burnt-out ball in the sky. The engines roared, gears squealed. Then, one by one, the vehicles took off. First Scalper, then Killer, then Richard, then Elvis, and bringing up the rear, red tail still whipping and sliding, was Jake Stone, his fists wrestling desperately with the wheel.

Flying sand stung his face and quickly clouded up his sunglass lenses. Praying he wouldn't crash into an unseen vehicle, he simply tightened his grip on the wheel, straightened his trajectory, and laid his foot all the way to the floor.

All five buggies rocketed across the blazing desert, speeding over the first undulating dune and setting sail into the air from its sandy peak. They landed one at a time with a crunch and bounce before continuing their charge toward the distant red marker.

Consumed by the dust cloud from the other buggies, Jake

began to veer, cautiously, a little to the left, then over to the right, trying to clear the cloud and gain greater visibility. His buggy sloped up a dune, and suddenly he was out of the cloud bank, racing along a sandy ridge parallel to, though still lagging behind, the others.

Up ahead he could see Scalper and Killer vying for the lead, with Richard close behind and Elvis closing in fast. The engines screamed, the wheels devoured the desert. Ahead of them, a stake with a red flag protruded from the ground. Scalper tried to make a clean break, but Killer suddenly veered his buggy toward his competitor and the nose of it clipped the left side of Scalper's tail bar.

The impact was enough to jolt the rear of the yellow-striped buggy off track, and before he knew it Scalper lost control of his vehicle. He heaved on the wheel, too hard, trying to overcompensate, and the buggy flew into an uncontrollable spin, creating a tornado of sand as it pirouetted off course and out of the lead.

The remaining buggies slipped into single file in their new rankings, first Killer, then Richard, then Elvis. Flying along the ridge, Jake punched his gears, made a swift, smooth descent down the dune, and took fourth place as Scalper's yellow-striped buggy finally twirled to a halt.

As Jake roared by, Scalper watched him with the menacing gaze of a shark that had just spotted the silver streak of the last fish in a spooked school. He grabbed the wheel in one hand and his gearshift in the other.

Up ahead, Killer's blue buggy sprayed a wave of sand in the air as it rounded the red marker, turning so fast that it almost flew into a tumble. He maintained control of his car and the lead, heading straight for the turquoise ocean.

Behind him, Richard took the corner with even greater speed and precision, followed by Elvis, whose buggy wobbled precariously for a moment and then stabilized quickly.

In fourth place, Jake took the turn, splitting the difference between caution and speed. As the red marker disappeared behind him he glanced back to see whether Scalper had rejoined the race. But there was no sign of him.

Without taking his hands off the wheel or his foot off the accelerator, Jake instinctively glanced over each shoulder, taking in his blind spots. On the right he saw nothing but the vast desert. On his left there was a low dune.

Jake slammed both feet on the brakes.

The tail of the buggy reared up, the front wheels dug in hard, and the vehicle slid to a long, shuddering stop just as Scalper's buggy launched itself clean off the dune on the left. The yellow-striped buggy cut low and fast in front of Jake, slicing the air where Jake's buggy would have been had he not braked.

But instead of scalping the top of Jake's vehicle, Scalper's buggy soared straight into a nosedive. Metal crumpled and glass smashed as the buggy's nose plowed into the ground, the momentum of the jump flipping the vehicle over completely until it crashed flat on its back like an upturned turtle, engine whining and wheels spinning uselessly in the air.

Jake put his buggy into gear and quickly pulled up alongside the smashed car. "Are you all right?" he called, twisting his neck to see Scalper upside down inside the buggy, angrily trying to unbuckle his seat belt while screaming abuse at Jake. Jake let out a karmic chuckle and said to himself, "Yeah, you're okay."

Scalper finally managed to unlatch his belt and fell flat on his face inside his wreck. Jake simply revved his engine and roared back into the race.

The three lead buggies were charging through the sand, jumping the low dunes one after the other, heading straight for the beach, with the fourth buggy catching up fast.

Jake was now starting to master his untamed beast, getting a handle on the heavy steering and the burnt-out clutch and the unpredictable traction in the sand. He cranked through the gears again, and soon he was spearing through Elvis's sand cloud and coming up behind him fast.

The ground beneath his wheels became firmer, the driving became smoother and easier, and Jake realized they had just driven onto wet, compact sand. Instead of churning, they were flying faster than ever, the sand clouds now watery jets.

Killer turned left again, just before he hit the waves, and made a beeline straight down the length of the beach.

Richard did the same, staying hot on Killer's heels.

Elvis went to turn his wheel. Suddenly a neck-jarring jolt from behind rocked him. His hands slipped from the wheel. There was another sharp impact from the rear. Elvis tried to grab the wheel, but it was too late. He was speeding straight ahead—no, he was being pushed straight ahead—directly into the water.

Jake's bumper slammed into Elvis's tail bar once more, enough to send the purple buggy plunging into the sea with so much speed that a fountain of water exploded into the air.

Rather than sink, the vehicle's thick, air-filled tires kept it afloat, sending it out into the Persian Gulf. If Elvis could swim, he would live to race again, but Jake wasn't about to hang around and find out. He reversed out of the knee-deep water that the shove had carried him into, then spun the steering wheel left, in hot pursuit of Killer Khoury. And more importantly, Richard Conrad.

The spray from the wheels of the two leading buggies shot up in their wake. Jake kept the accelerator flat to try to gain on them, following their tire lines in the wet, glassy sand, quickly gaining on the tall masts of water spraying up into the air behind their buggies.

He saw on the left the mountainous sand dune looming large, getting closer and closer, steeply gobbling up the sky—the last challenge before the finish line. On the other side of it, he knew that Jahmar and his crowd of bidders would be eagerly watching the peak of that dune, laying bets to the last second on who would come soaring over the crest of the dune first.

Jake didn't give a shit about winning. All he cared about was getting closer to Richard.

He was closing the gap fast, but Killer Khoury closed it for him even faster. As Richard tried to steal the lead, Killer snapped the wheel and knocked Richard into a spin that sent him hydroplaning across the slick, wet sand. By the time Richard managed to regain control of his buggy, Killer had already veered away from the sea and was climbing his way up the steep final dune.

Jake was also now slicing an arc in the shining shore as he turned from the beach toward the giant sand hill.

Richard jerked his gears and sprang into motion, accelerating fast and cutting a line straight for Jake.

As the foot of the enormous dune approached, Jake began pulling back on the gears, the engine revving loud and high, when suddenly—

SMASH!

Richard's buggy sideswiped Jake's so fast and so hard that the two vehicles locked together, side by side, heading at full speed toward the sand dune. Metal screeched and groaned as Jake tried to pull away from Richard, but the side bars of the buggies had hooked one another and refused to give.

The vehicles hit the base of the dune and started to climb as fast as they could. Richard and Jake battled with their gears, trying to keep their buggies moving as fast as possible, all eight wheels spinning madly up the dangerous incline.

"You're gonna kill us both!" Jake yelled, feeling the strain of the weight of both cars vibrating up the gearshift.

Richard only laughed. "What's the matter? You strike me as the kinda guy who enjoys getting up close and personal!"

"I am! But I also enjoy being alive!" Jake rammed through the gears, his engine struggling.

Richard did the same, smiling through his clenched jaw, enjoying the thrill and danger a little too much.

Up ahead, nearing the top of the slope, Killer Khoury's engine was howling, his wheels perilously churning through sand. But Killer didn't care. All he could see was the prize awaiting him at the finish line.

The one thing he didn't see was the bolt that had come loose when he slammed into Richard, the same bolt that now bounced and jumped until eventually—

Poing!

It leapt free, springing out of its joint and rattling down into the engine and lodging itself in the fan, splintering the blades instantly. There was a spark, then a dreadful gasp from the buggy as the fan spluttered and stalled and the engine's temperature skyrocketed in the heat of the Dubai day.

Within a moment, Killer stopped cackling. Within the next moment, his buggy coughed up a lungful of smoke and radiator fluid, then seized completely. The vehicle's momentum pushed it upward for a few hopeful seconds, carrying it within a few feet of the dune's peak, before gravity took hold and dragged it back down the mighty slope.

At first the buggy simply slid backward, as though it was reversing back down the dune, then the vehicle veered sideways. Killer unbuckled his belt and tried to jump free, but before he could escape the left front and back wheels sank deep into the sand and the entire buggy flipped sideways, sending the vehicle into a high-speed somersault—

—heading straight for Jake and Richard.

"Pull away!" Jake shouted, eyes fixed on the oncoming blur of blue and silver, Killer's screams getting louder and louder like the siren of a fast-approaching ambulance.

"I can't!" Richard shouted back, snapping desperately at the wheel. "We're locked."

Jake jerked his own wheel, but the twisting front tires of the two buggies only slowed their ascent, putting them in danger of sliding backward too. He cocked one leg out of the cabin and began kicking at Richard's buggy as hard as he could.

Killer's howls grew louder.

The spinning buggy began to hop and bounce like a boulder rolling down a mountain, changing shape with each bounce.

A headlight whistled through the air.

A wheel flew off.

Jake kicked at Richard's buggy harder still. "Faster!"

"Are you crazy! That thing's coming straight for us!"

"Faster or the same thing'll happen to us!" Jake kicked again. The side bar gave a little.

Killer's buggy hurtled toward them.

Jake's boot connected with the side bar again. He heard the sound of metal grinding against metal, the sound of the side bars unlocking. Then he heard Killer's scream mere feet away.

Jake turned his wheel hard left.

Richard turned his hard right.

The two buggies separated just in time to let Killer's pulverized bowling ball roll straight between them, so close it turned Jake's side mirror into a desert relic.

As Killer's runaway buggy vanished behind them, Jake and Richard tore up the remainder of the dune, heading directly for the blinding sun, noses pointed to the sky, feet flat to the floor.

Richard took the lead.

Jake fought back.

Richard nudged ahead.

The two buggies burst over the crest of the dune in an explosion of sand and speed.

Richard hit the downward slope first, followed closely

by Jake, barely in control, touching down, then skimming off the sand, springing into the air once, twice, before the wheels took hold of the sliding sand and devoured the descent. Despite the steep angle of the dune, braking down the hill did not appear to be an option for Richard. The roaring engine and the suck of gravity sent the buggy plummeting toward the foot of the hill as the needle on the speedometer quivered north of 110 miles an hour.

Richard shot a wink over his shoulder, as if the race was already won. But Jake was much closer than he thought, and there were still 300 meters to go before the finish line.

Suddenly the incline leveled off, sharper than Richard or Jake anticipated.

The buggies gave a loud crunch and shudder as their noses scraped the sand, digging out great divots before the vehicles fired off on the straight, flat homestretch. Up ahead, Jahmar stood surrounded by the cheering, jeering crowd, his arm raised, signaling the invisible finish line.

Jake shifted gears one last time and nosed ahead, but only for a moment.

Richard clenched his teeth, biting against the violent tremor and growl of his buggy, pushing it faster and harder than he had ever pushed before. He took the lead by mere inches.

As the finish line raced toward them, the crowd began to part, men hurrying left and right, clearing a path for the two oncoming buggies.

Jake's needle spiked at 122 miles per hour.

He gave it just that little bit more and nudged it up to 123, enough to slide into the lead as the finish line approached. Only 80 meters away now.

70.

60.

Richard swore over the roar of his engine, trying in vain to regain the lead.

Only 30, 20, 10 meters.

Then suddenly—

—Jake hauled as hard as he could on the emergency brake.

The red buggy twisted into a whiplash spin.

A cloud of sand erupted in the air.

Richard blinked, stunned and confused—and suddenly he crossed the line first.

Jahmar's arm fell, announcing the winner, as Jake's buggy spiraled to a halt three feet short of the finish line.

The spectators whooped and howled and shouted abuse at each other before descending upon Richard, whose buggy finally braked another 50 meters down the track. But Richard ignored the pats on the back and the handshakes. Instead he leapt out of his seat, threw his helmet in the sand, and stormed back to the finish line.

Just as Jake pulled himself free of his red buggy and peeled off his helmet, a furious Richard Conrad pounced on him, slamming Jake in the jaw with a right hook so powerful it knocked Jake off his feet.

"Why the fuck did you throw the race!?"

Jake spat out blood. "Because I don't want your damn prizes! All I want is information!"

Richard let go of Jake's shirt and pushed him back to the ground. The look of anger turned to one of gleeful control once more as he pulled himself to his feet, not taking his eyes off Jake. "All right, then. Jahmar, I want to change the prize."

Bewildered, Jahmar came running over. "Change the prize?"

"Yes. Keep your *loot*. Instead," he pointed to Jake, "I want him."

Jake squinted at the silhouette of Richard against the sun. "You're buying me?"

"I'm not buying you. I won you. No rules, remember.

You lose? You lose everything!" Richard pulled a tiny cell phone from his pocket. "Now, why don't you and I finish this somewhere more private."

As Jake wiped the blood off the corner of his mouth with the back of his hand, Richard flicked open the phone. "Stevens, bring the chopper."

Richard scrunched the Egyptian cotton sheets in his fists, twisting them in savage swirls as he bit down hard on the soft, cloudlike pillow. He was facedown on the bed, already naked, his round hard ass exposed, lifting itself into the air, searching blindly for something to fill it. That something came in the form of Jake's index and middle fingers, shining with lube.

Richard let out a muffled moan into the pillow and shut his eyes tight. The room was spinning. Or more accurately, the four-poster canopy bed was spinning.

Slowly the lavishly adorned walls and glistening water view from the master bedroom of the Burj Al Arab's Royal Suite rotated, but Jake was more interested in the handsome young construction tycoon splayed on the crisp sheets beneath him than the panoramic Persian Gulf vistas. After all, he had some construction work and digging of his own to do.

With another pained groan from the pillow, Jake's ring finger joined the other two fingers already excavating a passage into Richard's ass.

"Fuck!" Richard growled, his teeth releasing the pillow. "I want it fucking harder. Deeper, fucking deeper!"

Jake did as he was told, scooping his fingers deeper into Rich's begging ass, using more force, the lube making succulent sucking sounds. It made Jake's mouth water; it made him want to taste that exquisite ass for himself. He removed his fingers and buried his face between Richard's bulbous, beautiful cheeks.

Twenty minutes earlier they had arrived at Dubai's landmark hotel—standing like the white, wind-filled sail of a traditional Arab dhow skimming across the gulf—via Richard's personal chopper, which he insisted on flying himself and landing on the hotel's helicopter pad before being escorted down to his usual suite on the 25th floor. The young Englishman quickly dismissed Stevens, his personal butler, before swiftly leading Jake up the marble and gold staircase to the master bedroom, leaving one shoe by the library entrance and one on the leopard-print tufted carpet. His shirt set sail across the floor and settled on the Carrera marble. His jeans he flung over a mahogany chair. His tanned naked body splayed across the bed, stomach down, ass up.

Jake had been slower to undress on the lightning trip to the bedroom. He managed to get the buttons on his shirt undone—at least, the ones that Richard hadn't already ripped off. But while the handsome Englishman gave Jake plenty to look at as he rapidly revealed his tight, beautiful body, there was something else that caught Jake's discreetly straying eye as they entered the master bedroom: a first-class Emirates ticket sitting on a side table by the bedroom door.

Later, Jake had thought to himself at the time. First there were a few other things about Richard Conrad that needed exploration. Like his ass.

Richard pulled lubricant and a condom out of the top drawer of the bedside table. He left the condom on the sheets and smeared lube all over Jake's fingers, then picked up the phone receiver and stammered into it, "Dom...Dom...Peri ...gnon. Two glasses. Ch...ch...chilled," while his ass was being ravaged by Jake's roughly probing fingers. After the fingering came the tasting.

Jake was still almost completely dressed apart from his open shirt. He knelt on the bed over Richard's naked face-down body, his lips nuzzled between Richard's ass cheeks, his tongue rimming the young Englishman's hot, wet anus, occasionally plunging inside, lapping up the sugary gel of the lubricant mixed with a salty serving of man sweat—a cocktail of pure pleasure.

It was too tantalizing for Richard to bear. He wanted Jake's tongue to lap him up completely. He wanted him to lick his aching balls, he wanted that mouth to suck his cock, he wanted those perfect white teeth of Jake's to bite his nipples. He wanted Jake's dick to finish the job his tongue had started on his ass.

"More," Richard grunted. Suddenly he twisted around, the fullness of his erection swinging through the air and slapping against his flat stomach as he settled on his back, hands grabbing impatiently at Jake's clothes.

Jake yanked off his own shirt while Richard made fast work of his jeans, unclasping the buttons hastily, watching the bulge on the inside throbbing and pulsating, ready to tear its own way out of those jeans if somebody didn't set it free soon. Jake couldn't help but moan with relief as the buttons popped open, the vein-rippled trunk of his cock seeing the light of day first before the last button sprang open and Jake's giant, oversized dick lunged out.

Richard's eyes flared with delight.

His own cock began to beg, flicking against his stomach and leaping up toward Jake's dick, desperately wanting to play.

Jake seized both cocks in one large fist and began to squeeze and rub the hard shafts together, the two stiff dicks enjoying each other's heat, exploring each other's hardness, feeling each other's hunger.

Richard gasped, the exchange so tormenting he almost couldn't breathe. A bead of cum slipped from the eye of his cock and he hit Jake's hand away, releasing both cocks before it was too late.

Jake raised his eyebrows. "What's the matter? Ready to give up the game so soon?"

As was his usual defense, Richard responded by seizing control, grabbing Jake by the shoulders and flipping him on his back then taking the upper position, his thick thighs pinning Jake to the bed. He grabbed the condom, tore open the wrapper, and unfurled the sheath down the long, meaty length of Jake's cock.

He raised himself into a squatting position over Jake's pole, then nuzzled the head of Jake's cock into his crack and eagerly sank himself down onto the shaft, biting his lip at the pain. His ass was tight, like his tensed chest muscles, like his clenched stomach. His own beefy cock slapped enthusiastically against Jake's stomach now, and a few dewdrops of precum sprinkled warm and shiny beads across Jake's abs.

The moment Richard melted all the way down Jake's shaft, filling himself up completely with the thick, pulsating meat, he swiftly slid himself back up again, establishing an ebb and flow, plunging himself down, then pulling up once more. His appetite for Jake's dick was voracious, his tolerance for the pain higher than any man Jake had ever fucked.

Jake let Richard ride him as hard and fast as he wanted. He rolled his head back on the pillow, eyes shut, mouth open wide to let out a groan of pleasure. Along with a whispered word: "Eden." It escaped him so effortlessly, so naturally, Jake wasn't even aware of it.

Richard, on the other hand, noticed, but he didn't let it break his stride. In fact, the mistaken whisper turned him on even more. He picked up the pace, sliding up and down Jake's cock ever harder, heavier.

Eyes still closed, hands now taking hold of Richard's hips, Jake began to reciprocate, thrusting his pelvis up off the bed as Richard's ass slammed down upon him. The air from Richard's lungs came accompanied with noise now— a shallow moan with each breath. His stiff, bobbing cock seemed to be floating free, out on its own, unattended.

Occasionally it snapped upward and smacked him on the stomach. Or it bounced so hard with the rhythm of sex that it slapped against Jake's clenched abdomen, making a clapping sound. Jake opened his eyes and reined the cock in by seizing the shaft in one hand. He began stroking it, his fingers and palm still wet with lube. As the pace of penetration grew more and more intense, Jake's fist squeezed Richard's cock harder, pounding it faster and faster.

Richard's groans grew louder. They started to form words.

"Fu...fuck! Ahhh...I...I'm...com..."

Jake pushed deeper and faster into the young tycoon.

Richard slammed harder down on Jake's pole.

Jake grunted, teeth clenched. With his other hand he suddenly squeezed Richard's balls, painfully.

Richard cried out, words twisted up in his pain. "I'm com...I'm com..." But before he could spit them out, the head of his cock bloomed large and purple.

Jake's eyes squeezed shut, his mouth fell open, and his body arched, ready to welcome the hot spray that was about to shower upon him. Within seconds, Richard fired a blast of cum that soared clear over Jake's stomach and splashed spectacularly up his chest.

As soon as the sizzling jism hit his skin, Jake's balls opened their own floodgates.

He felt the rush of cum shooting up his shaft and arched his back even higher, pushing himself as far into Richard as he possibly could. Richard, still groaning and rocking with ecstasy, pressed his ass cheeks down hard against Jake's pelvis to the point of maximum penetration. He felt Jake's head high inside him.

Then he felt the temperature skyrocket as the head of Jake's condom bulged with an immense load of boiling hot cum. Jake's body quivered once, twice, and again, and again, each time shooting another pulse of cum up his shaft.

In response, Richard's cock shot a second load of cum onto Jake's heaving chest.

Jake massaged Richard's cock roughly, squeezing the last of the juice from him with a few more spasms and groans. Gradually he lowered his hips back down onto the bed as the last of his own cum drained from his exhausted body into the condom inside Richard's clenched, spent ass.

For a few moments, both men remained rock hard, gasping for air. Leaning forward, still sitting on Jake's cock, Richard delicately licked every last drop of his cum from Jake's large, panting chest, then continued to lick his sweating stomach and sides, tasting every inch of his enviable torso. With several small white jewels still beading on his lips, Richard sat up and smiled. "Now that you've whetted my appetite, shall we eat?"

At that moment the doorbell to the suite rang.

Richard's eyes lit up. "Ah, but first, a little drink." He pulled himself off Jake and the bed and, stark naked, made his way downstairs, his limbs now loose and his body moving in an exhausted, satisfied amble.

The second he heard the young tycoon's footsteps descending the stairs, Jake pulled off the condom, leapt from the bed, and opened up the Emirates ticket. Richard was booked on a flight to Beijing, leaving first thing in the morning. Something told Jake he had to be on the same flight.

Teasingly Richard answered the door naked and took from the blushing room attendant a champagne bucket and tray carrying two crystal flutes. By the time he returned to the master bedroom, Jake was once again lying flat on his back on the Egyptian cotton sheets, hands clasped behind his head, cock still swollen and resting on his licked belly.

Richard popped the champagne and filled their glasses with bubbles.

Bubbles filled the water outside the "submarine" as they submerged, gliding through a seascape so exquisite it was almost dreamlike. Jake wasn't sure whether he was being taken on an amusement park ride or entering the villain's lair in a Bond film. As they disembarked, the maitre d' of the Burj Al Arab's underwater-themed restaurant, Al Mahara, personally escorted Richard and his guest to their table beside a myriad of curious sea creatures all gliding, darting, and fluttering through the tropical waters that surrounded the restaurant.

No sooner had the maitre d' seated them than the headwaiter appeared with a smile and a mountain of menus. Richard waved them away.

"A bottle of your best New Zealand Sauvignon Blanc will do fine," he said.

"Very well, Mr. Conrad. And might I recommend the petit fish pot au feu for entrée tonight, followed by the Black Sea turbot with truffle oil."

"Thank you, Eduardo. That sounds delicious." He shot a mischievous glance in Jake's direction. "Almost as good as the dish I just had served to me in my suite."

Eduardo feigned a puzzled look, but knew all too well Mr. Conrad's reputation. The headwaiter promptly took his leave, letting Rich relish his little quip.

Before he was out of earshot, Rich added, "Oh, and Eduardo, is the harpist trying to sound aquatic or angelic? I feel like I'm about to enter the pearly gates."

"She's trying to sound a little of both, sir," was the diplomatic reply.

"Well, tell her this is a restaurant not a funeral parlor."

"Very well, sir," Eduardo bowed away.

"You come here often?" Jake asked as a large yellow-striped discus fish sailed by his head only inches away.

"I practically live here." Contrary to what Jake had

gleaned from Richard Conrad so far, the remark was said without any egotism. It was a simple fact. "Dubai and I have a lot in common. We both move fast, make things happen, seize an opportunity when we see one. Believe it or not, half a century ago Dubai was little more than a sleepy fishing village. Now it's a billionaire's playground. And if you hadn't already noticed,"—Rich leaned forward—"I like to play."

"Do you ever find time to work?"

Rich smiled. "I work smart, not hard, but please don't think I was born with a silver spoon in my mouth. It was more like a scrap-metal spoon. My father, that's how he built his meager fortune, out of scrap metal. He made enough money to get by, to raise a family, but not nearly as much as he could have made. You see, he lacked vision. He lacked daring. He never saw the fun in it."

"Sir?" Eduardo had returned, accompanied by a sommelier brandishing a bottle of wine. He poured a small amount into a tasting glass. Richard smiled as he swirled the wine in the glass, then briefly smelled the bouquet, tasted a sample, and nodded his approval. The sommelier poured their glasses and the waitstaff bowed and left.

Richard continued his story. "When my father died, I turned his money into millions, then into multimillions. I went from crushing scrap to creating skyscrapers. Did you know seventy-five percent of the world's cranes are currently leased to jobs in Dubai, Shanghai, and Beijing? At this very moment, only three cities on the entire planet account for three-quarters of the world's construction. Conrad Constructions is a major operator in this industry. I don't race dune buggies for a living, Mr. Stone. I race them to live life to the full. But let's cut to the chase, shall we? You're not here to talk about my hobbies; you're here to talk about my relationship with Sen. Are you part of the police investigation, or are you some private investigator Chad hired?

I'm not sure how much I should tell you without my lawyer being present."

"In case you say something that might incriminate you?"

"No, in case you twist things around."

"I'm not part of the police investigation. A dear friend of mine was kidnapped along with Sen. To be honest, I don't know Sen at all. All I really care about is getting the Professor back."

"Well, if you must know, I haven't seen Sen for months. He's been extremely busy assessing the potential of new mines in the U.S."

"Has he found anything?"

"Not yet. All the excavation machinery I've contracted to him is still up in Shandong. The mines there are still producing, so we're still digging."

"The diamonds you gambled on the race, where did you get them from?"

Richard smirked. "Mr. Stone, I'm a man of money and means. I don't have to steal to get what I want, if that's what you're implying."

"Excessive spending, illegal racing, questionable friends... You don't think you might be considered a suspect in all this?"

"My reputation and relationship with Sen and his employees is beyond measure. We've worked closely for many years, built empires together. I would never do anything to harm Sen. We're like family."

Just then, the food arrived. Large plates, small, elegant meals. As the waiter topped up their glasses, out of nowhere Richard asked Jake, "What or who is Eden?"

Jake stopped in mid-sip. "Why do you ask?"

"You said it. While we were fucking."

Richard timed the comment for maximum impact, playing one of his games, hoping to make Jake feel awkward in front of the waiter, who was now delicately wiping the lip of the wine bottle with a napkin. Jake refused to be intimidated, though he held back his reply until the waiter left the table.

"Eden is a friend. A good friend."

"A lover, perhaps."

"No," Jake took another sip of his wine.

"Although you'd like him to be," Richard drilled deeper.

Jake didn't respond. He began eating.

Taking the silence as victory in making Jake uncomfortable, Richard sat back with his glass of wine. "Don't lack the vision to take what you want in this life, Mr. Stone. Don't lack daring. Live your life to the full, otherwise it'll be over before you know it, and the one thing you could have had...will be gone."

IX

San Francisco General Hospital, California

ELSA SAT IN A CHAIR IN THE WAITING ROOM, CONSTANTLY praying and crossing herself while Sam paced the floor.

"This is stupid. I could be out there helping them." Sam mumbled his feelings to himself rather than announce them. Elsa heard nonetheless.

"Sam, you're better off here. Eden needs us."

"How? All we're doing is sittin' around waiting for news. Good or bad, there's nothin' you or me can do to change things."

"We can be here for him."

"I'd rather be over there. Helping them!"

"And give me one more thing to worry about? *Nein!*"

Elsa's patience was wearing thin and so was Sam's. "Forget it," he said with a dismissive wave of his hand. "I'm going for a walk."

Elsa let him go. She stood and returned to the window into the intensive care unit. Eden hadn't moved. Elsa thought to herself how much he would hate being connected to all those machines, a captive in a coma. Elsa knew what Eden was like—how clever and stubborn and kind he was—and the thought of that made her smile just a little. But her smile quickly gave way to silent tears as she realized Sam was right—there was nothing they could do to change the outcome of Eden's fate.

Sam burst through the emergency doors and spilled out of the hospital, an angry, tired, frustrated young man. He began walking the night.

Lately there was always frustration. Hell, things were supposed to be looking up. They were supposed to be getting better. He had left life on the streets of New York in an effort to take control of his life. And yet now, he had no control over anything whatsoever.

The Professor had been kidnapped, Eden's life was hanging in the balance, and Jake and the others had taken off and left him behind—to do what? Pace hospital halls? Watch Elsa pray? What good was that? The only person who had any control, any power to see Eden through, was the doctor.

He was Eden's only real hope. The only one with the answers.

Suddenly Sam stopped in his tracks and did an about-face. Suddenly he wanted to talk to Dr. Dante, one to one, find out exactly what Eden's chances were. He needed to know unquestionably what the truth was. He told himself he wanted to know for Elsa's sake. But deep down, he wanted to know for himself, to protect his own emotions—emotions he had unwittingly laid on the line when he decided to join the Professor's "family." Like all street kids, he was used to taking risks with his life—but not with his heart.

He returned and found Dr. Dante's office on the third floor of the hospital. He knocked on the closed door. When there was no answer, he knocked again and called through the door, "Doctor, are you there? I want to talk to you about your patient, Eden Santiago."

When there was still no answer, Sam tried the doorknob. It was unlocked, and so—he entered the office.

There was nobody inside the small, tidy room. Since Angelo Dante was a visiting doctor, this was not his permanent office. Yet the Italian doctor had quickly surrounded himself with his own possessions. Medical texts and numerous bound notebooks neatly lined the shelves. Several small organs sat solemnly in the bottom of preservative-filled jars. Degrees and honors hung on the wall. Sam tried to read them, but most were written in Italian. He quickly decided he was wasting his time here, and felt his frustration levels rise once more.

He was about to go when he decided to leave Dr. Dante a note, telling him he wanted to see him as soon as he could spare a minute. Sam walked over to the doctor's desk, sat down, and searched the desktop and the drawers for a piece of paper and a pen. The first drawer contained only an array of medical equipment. In the second drawer he found several pens in a tidy stationery tray. He grabbed one, and in the third drawer he found a notepad. He pulled it out and began to write when he noticed something was paper-clipped to the pad, several pages down. Sam flicked through the blank pages until he found the paper clip.

A donation check was attached to the page, from an anonymous source, made out to San Francisco General Hospital in the sum of $250,000. Sam's eyes lit up at the sight of all those zeroes and for a moment his survival instincts kicked in. Pocketing the check and getting the hell out of Dodge seemed like easy money. He'd find someone who could cash it, no problem; he knew plenty of people in the fraud and laundering game who could pull off a trick like that for a cut of the profits. He started to slide the check loose. But then he thought about Elsa and the Professor and Eden and Jake, and with clenched teeth Sam reluctantly bit back the urge to grab and run.

Then something else caught his eye. Something written on the pad.

He thumbed the check over, and there on the page, circled in heavy pen, was the name *Eden Santiago*, followed by the words *Sone Sher Ka Ashru*.

"Can I help you?" The words were short and firm, clipped with an accent and filled with annoyance.

Sam slapped the pad closed and looked up to see Dr. Dante in the doorway. "I was just...I wanted to see you...I couldn't find you...I was looking for a piece of paper, to leave you a note."

Dr. Dante stepped up to the desk, took the pad from Sam's hands, and eyed him sternly. "This office is full of confidential patient files. I suggest next time you want to see me, rather than invite yourself in, you simply ask to have me paged."

"The door was unlocked," Sam said with a shrug.

"That's because the previous occupant still has the key. Now please leave, I have work to—"

Like an alarm sounding, the pager clipped to Dr. Dante's belt started frantically beeping. The doctor snatched it in his hand and read the message, his expression switching from anger to alarm in a heartbeat.

"It's your friend," he said, his voice rushed, his tall frame already turning for the door. "He's gone into cardiac arrest."

The heart rate monitor let out a piercing wail as the flatline spilled across the screen. Three nurses raced around the room, one yanking the tiny electrodes off Eden's chest, one administering an injection of epinephrine, while the third hurriedly pulled the defibrillator unit to the side of the bed and flicked several switches. The soft whine of the charge competed with the sound of the flatline.

As Dr. Dante ran into the room, he seized the defibrillator paddles and ordered the first nurse to close the curtains, shutting out the sight of the nearly hysterical Elsa on the other side of the glass.

Dr. Dante shouted, *"Clear!"*

Eden's body jolted violently.

"Elsa!"

With more strength than he realized, Sam pulled Elsa back from the window, hauling her into a tight embrace.

X

Hong Kong, China

WILL STIRRED GROGGILY, A SMILE ON HIS FACE. HE HAD woken up like this before: a splitting headache, a raging hard-on, and the flesh of a seriously hot guy pressed against him.

But as his eyes slowly opened he heard an urgent whisper close to his ear. "Will, wake up! You have to wake up now!"

Alarm set in instantly. He blinked back the pain, blinked away his blurred vision, and tried to make sense of his disfigured surroundings, realizing at the same time that he couldn't move his arms or legs. All he could do was wriggle and squirm.

He surmised that he was lying down. No, he was lying *on top* of someone.

"Will, wake up!" It was Bradley.

As he squinted and finally managed to focus, Will saw that he was in the boardroom of the Zhang Diamond Corporation. Or more precisely, he was in the boardroom, on top of the boardroom table, with Bradley writhing naked and nervous beneath him. The two men were facing each other, arms wrapped tightly around each other, both tied securely together but not with ropes—with their own clothes. Their clothes had been coiled tightly and were now looped and knotted around their torsos, wrists, and ankles, binding them together in a captive embrace.

"What the hell's going on?" Will asked, their faces so close that their noses touched.

"I think they plan on killing us."

"They?"

Will cocked his head and saw Mya, Xi, and Chad standing around the table, grinning disdainfully. Beyond the panoramic boardroom window, Will noticed night had fallen and Hong Kong's skyline glittered and sparkled. The light in the boardroom, however, was dim.

And flickering—with the flames of dozens of candles.

"Romantic, isn't it," Chad said, lighting another tall wax stem with a lit taper. He made his way from one end of the boardroom table to the other, kicking Will's and Bradley's discarded shoes out of the way, setting candles aglow as he walked.

"Chad, what are you doing?" Will demanded in a level voice.

"I'm setting the mood," was the lyrical reply. "Candles. Two naked men. A forbidden romance."—Suddenly his fingers tipped one of the candles over—"And an accidental blaze that killed them both."

The candle fell from the table and hit the carpet of the boardroom. A small pool of wax and fire spread outward.

Instantly, Will began tugging at the knotted clothes.

Bradley spoke sternly, alarm in his voice. "Chad, don't do this."

"Too late. It's as good as done. Not even the smoke

detectors and sprinkler system can save you, as, unfortunately, there's a glitch in the system." At that moment, Mya walked up to Chad with his laptop in her arms. She opened the computer for him, and he tapped a few keystrokes. "Or at least there is now. That's the privilege of rank. I know the manual override code for every one of the building's operating systems, including the fire protection system."

He hit ENTER, then looked up and smiled as the small red light on the smoke detector in the ceiling blinked and died.

"You're forgetting I'm the same rank," Bradley responded.

"And you're forgetting that your hands are tied," Chad smiled. "By the time you get out of those knots, every computer within reach will have been destroyed by the fire. Rest assured though, Xi tied you up nice and tight. We would have used rope, but the nylon fabric of your clothes will give the police something to puzzle over. I intend to eliminate both you—*and suspicion*."

Bradley watched with growing dread as the pool of small blue and yellow flames spat and crawled across the carpet, growing rapidly in size. "Chad, don't destroy something you've helped build. This is your home. It's Sen's home. It's our corporation's heart."

"Not anymore. After tonight, my heart belongs in San Francisco. We'll be focusing all of our efforts on the Montana Project and consolidating the entire North American market before selling into Europe and the rest of the world. As for China, well, once the Beijing Project is complete, I think the only efforts they'll be concentrating on will be disaster relief."

Will glanced from Mya to Chad, then said with grave certainty, "You're going to blow up Beijing. You've got a zidium device."

"As a matter of fact, we've got two," Chad said gleefully. "But we'll only need one to raze greater Beijing to the ground. The other one is for the Zhang diamond mines. We need to obliterate all evidence that the company's trade has all but dried up. You see, we've been covering it up for three years now, drip-feeding demand, staggering the last remaining exports to make it look like we still had a viable business. When in fact the Shandong mines are now little more than a facade."

"Facade?" Bradley's brow was creased with concern for the spreading flames and shock at what he was hearing.

"Yes, it's all just make-believe, I'm afraid. We've been playing happy families. The fact is, China's running out of diamonds. Our investigations in Montana have proved rather fortuitous. It seems the United States has an as yet undiscovered and untapped supply. We've managed to keep up appearances, hiding the numbers from everybody including yourself and the board. Conrad's cranes and bulldozers still make noise at the site when they need to, we hire peasants from the mountain villages to mill back and forth in filthy miners' uniforms. Hell, we even maintain the rail link. But it's all a show. And it's about to come to a spectacular end."

"A spectacular end?" Will spat in disgust. "Is that what you call blowing up Beijing? If there are no diamonds left in China, why don't you just leave? Start mining Montana and leave the people of China alone."

Chad shook his head impatiently. "You're not listening. Perhaps it's the crackling of the flames or the panic pounding in your ears. We need money to expand, to mine, to conquer. That money will be sourced from several insurance policies. As you know, Bradley, I've always been rather fond of your uncle. It's just a matter of timing, that's all. The world economy is hungry and desperate. We're at a crossroads. There can be only one world leader. We choose America. It has more diamonds." He shrugged casually. "I'm greedy, I know, but what can I do about it? It's a curse."

"So you're going to cripple the Chinese economy?" Will said. "Just like that?"

"Not cripple. Destroy. Terrorism's best-kept secret is to make the rich richer and the poor poorer. Blow up Beijing and a shocked world will turn to the United States for guidance, security, leadership. Every country in the world will hand financial control over to Uncle Sam in the hope that America will save the world economy from spiraling out of control. The most powerful business empires in America— including the new improved Zhang Diamond Corporation— will have the rest of the world eating out of their hands."

With a hiss the pool of flames slithered across the carpet in different directions. Chad, Mya, and Xi all took one or two steps back, making sure they still had time to make their exit.

On the boardroom table, Will struggled even harder, his flesh grinding against Bradley's, both bodies growing slippery with sweat as the temperature in the room began to rise. "Exactly how the hell do you expect to get away with all this?"

"You mean the fire? Well, that will be your fault. Of course, when the police discover the cindered remains of two naked men, twisted and charred in the clothes they tried to wrench from each other's bodies in an act of sodomy, I'll be the first to advise the board of discretion. Such a scandal would bring shame to a company that's already in the headlines. I'll see to it that the whole matter is suppressed as quickly as possible."

"And Beijing?" Will grunted through his locked jaw. "Who's gonna take the blame for that?"

Chad laughed a genuine, hearty laugh. "Oh, come on, what terrorist organization in the world wouldn't want that on their resume? Every man on the CIA's Ten Most Wanted List will have his hand up, desperately claiming this was his own ingenious plan."

His laughter turned to a cough as the air in the room began to turn into a toxic haze. Smoke completely concealed the ceiling now, swirling and churning.

"Ingenious plan!" This time it was Bradley's turn to offer a spluttered laugh of disbelief. "This isn't a plan. This is insanity! It's a scam from a man who is completely deranged!"

"Deranged!" Chad stepped up to the boardroom table and slammed his hand down beside Bradley's head. The flames were now leaping up from the carpet beneath the table. "Who the hell are you to insult anyone else's ambition? Who are you to call my hard work deranged? Your fate was always written. You came from money. Your family was always going to pay your way—until now. Someone like me, on the other hand, came from nothing. I put myself through school working three jobs. Do you have any idea how many years I spent at Harvard busting my ass, knowing there had to be a smarter way—a *faster* way—to becoming one of the world's richest men? This 'scam' as you call it entails an insurance portfolio worth more money than you can imagine, starting with Sen's life insurance and risk management, which includes a hefty payout for kidnapping, ransom, *and* murder. Add to that the payout on the Eye of Fucanglong, not to mention the entire network of Shandong mines, and we're talking in excess of—" He turned to Mya and asked in fiery jest, "Mya, what comes after millions?"

"Billions," she answered arrogantly.

"And after that?"

"Trillions," she purred.

"And after that?"

She smiled. "Us."

Chad sneered at Bradley, his vicious smile so full of rage and greed that there was no room left for happiness. "Make no mistake. *This—is genius.* And while China smolders and digs through its ashes and the world weeps and panics, we'll emerge as the new saviors of Wall Street. We'll ensure that the United States will remain the dominant force in the world's economy. We'll create jobs, opportunities, wealth, the likes of which America has never known before!"

"By annihilating China!?" Will fumed.

"By neutralizing the competition. Minimizing the strength of the opponent."

"Minimizing? You're talking about killing hundreds of thousands of innocent people!"

"Actually, given the area of the impact zone and the strength of the device, we've put our estimated body count at around four million," Chad said with a shrug. He checked the spreading flames, which were now crackling up the walls, and decided it was time to leave. "Actually, make that four million and two."

Chad took his laptop from Mya and shot a nod to his accomplices. Mya and Xi swiftly exited through the board-room doors, a curtain of flames on either side of it now. Chad tucked his laptop under one arm, then gave a confident, cool farewell salute. "I'd like to say no hard feelings," he said with a smirk, glancing down between Will's and Bradley's legs, "but by the looks of it that's going to be your one last pleasure."

Despite the growing sounds of the fire, Chad's snicker was distinctly audible above it all as he fled the room in a smoky wake.

"My back's burning." Bradley sucked in his breath, then coughed with the smoke he inhaled.

Will watched Bradley grimace beneath him and noticed the surface of the table begin to smolder and pop. "We have to get off this table."

"And go where? Roll onto the carpet? It's on fire!"

As if his answer was a yes, Will began to roll from side to side, his now drenched naked body slipping against Bradley's, their chests and stomachs and groins sliding together.

"Will, what the hell are you doing!"

"My jeans," he grunted, picking up the momentum, rolling left, then right, pulling back just before each edge of the table. "The pocket of my jeans is somewhere under you, near my hands. If we can just put enough weight on it to—"

Suddenly over the intensity of the blaze he heard a muffled *chink* and stopped.

"What was that?"

Will's hands were already trying to wriggle and squirm toward the pocket, feeling their way down Bradley's hot, tensed back until he managed to pry a small, broken shard of glass out of the pocket. "It's a mirror. At least it was a mirror. Now if I can just—"

Clutching the sharp piece of glass between two contorted fingers, he blindly positioned it against the shirt that had been used to bind his hands and began sawing away at the material.

"Ah, shit!" Bradley winced from the glass that stabbed into his back.

"Sorry!"

"Careful!"

"I'm trying!"

Part of a sleeve gave a little. Will kept cutting, his forearms flexing and biceps bulging, squeezing Bradley tighter and tighter in their bound embrace before the material gave way another inch, then another. Will could feel his hands pulling apart, his shirt ripping, and then—

"I'm loose!"

As the flames reached and grabbed for them over the edges of the table, Will pulled his arms free and used the glass and his bare hands to cut and tear the rest of the knotted clothes until Bradley was free as well.

Will hauled him to his feet and the two stood naked atop the table as they scanned the room for a way out. Will was the first to make a go of it, reaching over the edge of the table, through the biting flames, grabbing one of the boardroom chairs. He lifted it up, swung it back over one shoulder, then hurled it with all his might at the floor-to-ceiling windows.

"No, Will, it's shatterproo—" was all Bradley managed to shout before the leather and steel chair hit the glass and ricocheted straight off it.

From behind them they heard a popping, cracking sound and turned in time to see the glass doors to the boardroom surrender to the intense heat and erupt in a shower of tiny shards, followed by the shattering of the display cases along the wall. The only way out had now turned into a corridor of glass.

"How far are the emergency stairs?" Will shouted.

"Down the corridor. Next to the elevators. Do you think we can make it?"

As Bradley asked the question, the ceiling above the boardroom doorway came crashing down in an avalanche of burning plaster and red-hot beams.

Will stared at the roaring wreck now blocking the doorway and shook his head. "Not anymore, I don't." He grabbed Bradley by the arm. "Come on, think. There's gotta be another way outta here."

"Wait, there is," Bradley yelled, pointing to the far wall opposite the doorway. "There's a panic room through that door!"

"A secret door?!" Will smiled. "Cool!"

"You have no idea. It was built as an escape route in case of emergency."

"I think this qualifies as an emergency."

"It's small, but once we're in, the entire room acts like an express elevator and drops directly to the ground floor."

"What about the fire? Didn't your teachers ever tell you not to get in an elevator during a fire?"

"This one's different. The shaft is impervious to flames—theoretically."

"What do you mean, theoretically?"

Bradley shrugged. "It's never been used before."

With an ominous groan, the smoke-filled ceiling bowed as the flames began to eat their way across the panels above their heads.

"I think it's time to put the theory to the test," Will said. "How do we get inside?"

"There's a concealed square panel to the right of the door. A good push on the panel will trigger it open. Behind it there's a keypad."

As Bradley spoke, Will quickly snatched up his ripped and ragged jeans and slid them on, then threw Bradley's tattered trousers to him. He leaned over the edge of the burning table and saved their shoes from the flames, and the two of them covered their nearly scorched feet.

"To open the door you need to type in a ten-digit code," Bradley said.

"Which is?"

"*HongKongHQ*. No spaces." Bradley couldn't take his eyes off the fiery distance between the table and the wall. "But how do we get to it?"

Will winked. "Do you know how to surf?"

"No!"

"Don't sweat. There's nothin' to it. Just follow me."

Suddenly Will broke into a sprint.

He ran in a fast, straight line all the way down the length of the burning table, using it like a runway, before launching himself off the edge of it and onto one of the boardroom chairs. He landed with one boot on top of the chair's back to steer him, and one anchored on the chair's seat, his momentum setting the wheels of the chair in motion and sending him speeding across the blazing floor before slamming into the wall that concealed the secret door.

He looked for a small safe patch of carpet and pushed off the chair. He spun back to see Bradley sizing up the distance between himself and the end of the table with deep nervous breaths. Above him the ceiling panels were completely ablaze now. One chunk of burning debris fell and splattered on the table right beside his left foot. Hissing flames began to hail down on him. It was all he needed to launch him into a panicked dash down the length of the table.

He hurled himself through the air, hit one of the chairs in a standing position, just as Will had done, and careened crazily through the raging fire, trying desperately to maintain balance and direction until—

Bam!

Will stepped swiftly out of the way just before Bradley's out-of-control chair crashed into the wall. As the chair spun and swiveled backward into the flames, Will grabbed Bradley by both hands and yanked him to safety.

"See? No sweat!" Will grinned. "You okay?"

Bradley nodded. "Yeah. But I think I prefer skating."

Will turned to the wall. His fingers felt their way around until he located the small square panel. He pushed and it popped open to reveal a small keypad set into the wall. With care, he began typing in *HongKongHQ*, his brow furrowed in concentration, his eyes stinging with smoke.

Behind them, the ceiling collapsed completely onto the boardroom table with a crash. Glowing rubble tumbled across the room as the fire chewed its way through the story above. Will blinked beads of sweat out of his eyes and tried to stay focused on the keypad.

He finished typing.

Bradley waited for the door to swing open with an automated sigh of relief.

Nothing happened.

"Did you type it right?"

"Yes! I'm sure I did."

Bradley's fingers started dancing over the keypad. "*HongKongHQ*," he said as he typed.

The two men looked at the door.

There was no sign of movement whatsoever.

"Maybe the fire's disabled it," Will thought aloud.

"Impossible. This thing's built to withstand any disaster, natural or man-made. Someone's changed the password."

"No prizes for guessing who."

Outside the room they heard several small explosions. The fire was well on its way to destroying the entire tower.

"What would Chad change it to?" Will asked in a desperate rush. "Come on. Let's think!"

"It's not his name. The code has to be ten digits long. *ChadChambers* is—" Bradley quickly counted down his fingers "—it's twelve, it's too long."

"He talked about the Montana Project. What about that?"

"Too long."

"*Montana*?"

"Too short."

"*Beijing*?"

"No. They're all too short."

"*SanFrancisco*?"

"Too long! Can't you count?"

Another beam fell from the ceiling and shook the floor. "No! Not when the whole damn building's burning down around me!"

Bradley was ignoring him, still counting letters on his fingers as quickly as he could. "Not *Zhang Sen*. Not *Diamonds*. What about—"

"*Fucanglong*!" Will and Bradley both exclaimed together.

Bradley punched the word into the keypad.

Again nothing happened.

In the middle of the room, the charred carpet peeled

backward and the floor beneath the table began to buckle and drop. A fiery hole opened up. Half the boardroom table sank. Within seconds the entire table plunged through the burning floor.

"Wait a second," Will said. "He does everything in reverse."

"What are you talking about?"

"Chad. He does things *backward*."

"Seriously?!"

"Type *Fucanglong* backward!"

Bradley had to think. "God, how do you spell Fucanglong backward?"

Will started, "G-N-U—No!—O! G-N-O-C—No!"

"Shut up and let me concentrate!" Bradley's eyes darted around the keypad. He typed in *G*, then *N*, then *O*, then *L*, then—

Another massive section of the ceiling collapsed, hit what little was left of the center of the room, and sent it all plummeting into a blazing heap that consumed the level below, sucking burning chairs and shattered display cases into the burning chasm. Will stared, his eyes wide, his feet shuffling back against the wall as far as possible. He and Bradley were now standing mere inches from the giant flaming hole. "Shutting up. But please hurry!"

Hurrying was exactly what Bradley was doing.

G–N–A–C

The edges of the rest of the floor began to crumble.

U–

Will felt his left foot start to slide off the edge.

–F

There was an electronic hiss.

Bradley's hand shot out and hooked Will under the arm.

The fire-covered wall transformed into a thick metal door that breathed open beside them.

They both fell into the small panic room, the fire leaping and bounding, snatching at their shoes as they collapsed one on top of the other. Bradley gave the large red punch button on the wall a good kick. The steel door slammed shut behind them. Sealing *them* in, and the fire *out*, and then—

"Hold on!" Bradley told Will.

It was as though the bottom dropped out of the world as the small cubelike panic room went into a free fall, plunging from the 40th floor of the tower straight for ground level. It dropped so fast they actually lifted off the floor for several moments.

"We're gonna crash!" Will's voice slurred, his lips smearing with the sudden force of gravity.

Before Bradley could reply, they heard a series of detonations outside the panic room. With each blast, the rapidly descending cell shot grips into the walls of the shaft, like hooks, slamming on the brakes until the small cube came grinding to a halt on the ground floor.

The door opened automatically.

Will and Bradley scrambled out the exit and spilled across the lobby floor so fast it looked like the wall just opened up and spewed them out.

Startled, George, the security guard, pulled his gun.

Shirtless and singed, Bradley and Will both held up their hands.

"Don't shoot! George, it's me, Bradley! Call the fire department!"

"The fire department? I didn't hear any alarms!"

"George, listen to me. Did you see Chad leave here?"

George nodded, flustered and confused. "Yes, sir. He left with Ms. Chan and a white-haired man. They seemed to be in a hurry. Headed straight for the harbor."

"Thank you. Please, call the fire department. Then get out of the building as fast as you can. Do you hear me?"

"Yes, sir!"

As George phoned for help, Will and Bradley burst from the lobby doors and without breaking pace bolted into the night, heading straight for the nearby harbor. Their smoking shoes slapped against the Hong Kong streets and onto the wharf packed with tourists and locals getting in and out of bobbing sampans.

The lights of a thousand vessels flickered and flashed across the surface of the hectic harbor in all directions. Boats of all shapes and sizes rocked and lurched through the melee.

"Jesus, it's worse than the L.A. freeway!" Will gawked, skidding to a halt at the edge of the wharf.

All around them, people were already stopping and staring at the two soot-covered and topless men. But Will and Bradley were oblivious to them all. Bradley recognized the sleek white cruiser heading out across the crowded harbor and into the bustling night.

"That's them. That's my uncle's boat."

Behind him, Will turned at the sound of fire truck sirens filling the Hong Kong streets. From here he could see the Zhang Diamond Tower, its top burning in a silent blaze slowly consuming each floor until the shatterproof glass finally gave way as the pent-up fire exploded outward, shaking the ground and shattering windows throughout the building. Everyone on the wharf suddenly gasped and ducked in terror.

"Come on," Will said, seizing Bradley by the hand and pushing him aboard the nearest unmanned sampan. The young American unhooked the line, ripped the cord on the outboard motor, and twisted the throttle to full.

As the bow of the long, narrow boat tilted into the air, Bradley rolled down the length of the leaky, cluttered vessel and smashed awkwardly into Will at the stern.

"Get up front!" Will yelled over the buzz-saw drone of

the motor. "I can't see where I'm going! I need you to weigh down the bow and navigate!"

Hand over hand, Bradley pulled his way up to the bow, tilting the nose of the narrow craft lower as the bow dipped with his weight. He looked out over the chaotically busy Hong Kong Harbor and screamed, "Starboard! Turn starboard now!"

Mere feet in front of them, a Chinese junk was sailing sluggishly across their bow, moving directly into their path.

Will jerked the outboard to veer hard right.

"No! Starboard!" Bradley yelled. "You're going the wrong way!"

"You said starboard!" Will shouted back. "This is starboard!"

The panicked passengers on the junk all screamed and waved in vain to avert disaster.

"That's the way they're going!" Bradley screamed. "Go the other way! Go left!"

"That's not starboard!" Will screamed back.

"Then don't go starboard! Anything *but* starboard!"

Will turned the boat hard port. Like a torpedo suddenly changing course, the sampan ditched and veered as the underside of the bow splintered the side of the junk and bounced off.

"You're supposed to be watching!" Will shouted.

"I am!" Bradley screamed back.

"Starboard is right! Port is left! There's no port *left* in the bottle, you got it! You tell me port, I turn left; you tell me starboard, I turn right! Understood?"

"What's straight ahead?" Bradley shouted.

"Straight ahead is straight ahead!" Will yelled with a roll of his eyes.

"Then floor it, because if you don't we're either gonna get hit by the ferry coming up on port or the ocean liner on starboard!"

"Jesus," Will whispered to himself with sudden alarm.

As the tiny sampan skimmed across the choppy water, the blast of the packed passenger ferry's horn and the blaring lights of the ocean liner illuminating the water came from both sides.

Will twisted the throttle as hard as he could.

The little sampan reared up even higher in the water and cut a line as fast as it could across the waves.

The passenger ferry's horn filled the night again. Smaller boats broke tack and spun about, seeing the angry ferry approach. Amid it all, the tiny sampan cut right, only to veer directly into the path of *The Duchess of Hong Kong*, one of the largest liners ever to sail the Orient.

At the stern of the little sampan, Will shot a glance to starboard to see the cruiser carrying Chad, Mya, and Xi skim across the water, seconds before the almighty bow of *The Duchess* loomed large before them, threatening to rip them to shreds.

"We'll never make it!" Bradley shouted from the nose of the boat.

But Will knew if they didn't try, they'd lose the cruiser altogether. "Hang on! And keep your head down!" was all the warning he gave.

With a quick turn to port, Will saw the swell from the ferry's wake rise up behind them. He knew *The Duchess* would cut the wave like a knife, but not before the sampan had a chance to ride the wave clear across the bow of the ocean liner—hopefully. He gave it all the outboard had to reach the tip of the wave, then steered the tiny boat to ride the crest straight toward the bow of the ocean liner.

"Will?! What are you doing?!"

"Stay down!"

The wave swept them toward the oncoming ship.

Its 14-story-high bow sliced the water.

The little sampan sailed the wave, its motor buzzing furiously, its nose about to smash directly into the hull of the ocean liner—until, seconds before impact, Will steered the tiny boat just a fraction to port.

Still riding the wave, the sampan edged slightly ahead of the point of impact.

At the bow, Bradley gasped and ducked as low as possible.

The mighty ocean liner gobbled up the wave.

Will held the throttle locked at full speed, clenching the old rubber grip so tight he thought his hand would bleed.

The ship's razor-sharp bow shaved off the nose of the sampan, cutting the bow off the little boat with such force that it didn't even splinter—it just cleaved it clean off.

Bradley gasped again, the bow having been sliced off only millimeters from his head.

Will cut sharp, veering port again even harder, hoping the momentum of the sampan would carry the now bowless boat out of harm's way.

It did—almost.

The liner clipped off the outboard motor, sending the sampan into a powerless pirouette, floundering and flailing in the dangerous waters as it was dragged down the ocean liner's starboard side. Water began gushing up through the rapidly sinking craft. At the same time the sampan slammed into the mighty hull several times as it threatened to pull the crippled boat down at any moment.

Bradley scrambled back toward the stern as the harbor drank in the bow of the boat.

Will heard the stern of the ocean liner approaching, knowing that the real danger was yet to come. With no motor, they had no hope of escaping the drag of the ship's propellers. They were too close. It was only a matter of seconds before it pulled them down and churned them out. Even if they jumped overboard, there was nothing they could do now to save them.

Just then, the cruiser sped up alongside them. It scraped along the sampan, but not with the intention to sink it—that fate seemed already at hand. No, the cruiser was there out of reluctant necessity.

Chad glared over the side of the cruiser, his face fuming. "Xi, pull them aboard! I can't afford to have their bodies floating in the fucking harbor, not when they were supposed to burn alive."

"What are we going to do with them?" Mya appeared beside Chad.

"We'll just have to make them disappear altogether. Let's see them outsmart the zidium. Until then, get them out—"

Everyone on the sampan and the cruiser turned as the powerful *chomp-chomp-chomp* of the liner's submerged propellers approached.

"—*Now!*" Chad screamed.

XI

The Zhang Diamond Express, Central Beijing, China

"MAX, WAKE UP! MAX! WAKE UP—*NOW!*"

The desperate voice in his ear was the first thing the Professor registered. The second thing was the immense pain. In his stomach, in his sides, in his pounding head. His eyelids fluttered open, although his blind eyes could see nothing. "Sen?" was all his parched, cracked lips could utter.

"I'm here, Max. Are you all right?"

The Professor nodded, although he wasn't all right at all. The slightest move sent a wave of agony through his body. He realized quickly he was sitting up, in a chair—no, *tied* to a chair, his wrists fastened to its wooden arms. His torso was sticky and wet. He felt the constriction of bandages wrapped around his waist, adding severe discomfort to the pain. He was bound so tight he was certain the bandages had broken several ribs. Then he remembered.

"They cut me open, didn't they."

"Oh, Max, I tried to stop them. There was so much blood I was certain you would die. But they kept you alive. They were determined to keep you alive. And just as determined to find that thing inside you and get it out."

"The tracking device. It's gone?"

"Yes. The doctor pulled it out of you with his bare fingers and crushed it on the floor of that filthy apartment." Sen paused a moment, then said defeatedly, "Nobody will ever be able to find us now, will they."

The Professor didn't answer. Instead he took a deep breath for courage, then winced at the pain. "Sen, are you blindfolded? Are we alone?"

"No, I'm not blindfolded, and yes, we're alone. But not for long. That crazy doctor is supposed to be guarding us, but he left to get some alcohol. He's already drunk everything in here."

"Here? Where's here?"

"We're on board the Zhang Diamond Express."

The Professor looked puzzled. "We're on a train? We're not moving though, are we?"

"No. At least not yet. Max, I think they're planning something terrible."

"Why?"

"There's something else in here with us. Two open crates. There's something round and silver inside each one." Sen swallowed nervously and his dry throat clicked. "Max, I think they're bombs."

The Professor remained calm. He said nothing for a moment, thinking carefully about their situation, about what had happened. Eventually he said, "Sen, breathe deep. I need you to start describing where we are. Tell me everything you can see."

Sen chuckled a moment, feeling a hint of comfort through his fear. "You were always so good at that, Max. Back at Oxford. I remember how good you were at calming friends down the night before an exam, how logical you were about making people feel relaxed when they were as nervous as hell. You've always had such clarity, such purity of mind. I loved that about you."

"Sen, concentrate. Where are we?"

Sen blinked back his fear and nodded at the instruction. "Okay. We're in the master carriage."

"You know this place?"

"Very well. The Express has been in my family since 1947. This car is in the third position on the train, behind the engine and the coal car. It was made for comfort and business—that was my grandfather's instruction to the engineers who refurbished the train. My family conducted all their dealings in this car, as well as entertained. It's about thirty feet long, carpet from Persia, red velvet curtains, all drawn. Two meeting tables and my desk. There's a cell phone sitting on it now. There are several lounges from Paris, footstools from Italy. Two chandeliers with diamond-tipped crystals. You and I are tied to two original Louis the Sixteenth parlor chairs—"

"And the crates?"

"They're at the other end of the car. Next to—" Sen stopped. He failed to mention that the crates were beside a life-sized bronze statue of himself shaking hands with one of his employees, a miner. A symbol of equality, respect, opportunity. Right now, it seemed inappropriately self-righteous.

"Next to what?" the Professor asked.

"Next to the door that leads to the car behind us."

"And the train. Tell me about the train. Where does it go?"

"From here, straight up to the mines in Shandong. Like I said, it's an express. It's a showpiece, built for business, to take investors on a scenic tour up to the mines and back. It runs on a private railroad line my grandfather purchased."

"How many cars?"

"Six cars in total. The engine and the coal car, then this, the master carriage. That's followed by the exhibition carriage, where diamonds are displayed, followed by the sleeping carriage, then finally a flatbed freight car which I added a few years ago to transport the company helicopter up and down from the mountains. We don't use the train very often anymore. It's a symbol of days gone by, a museum piece, although it still runs."

"And the others. Did they say where they were going?"

"I have no idea. Mya was stressed, that's all I know. She left us in the care of that crazy doctor back in his apartment. Her plans, whatever they are, seemed to be going wrong, I can guess that much." He paused another moment. "They're going to kill us, aren't they, Max." It wasn't a question.

The Professor didn't respond. Instead he asked another question. "How long ago did the doctor bring us here?"

"It's hard to say. Hours? Maybe a day? Maybe more. I don't even think I've been conscious the entire time. Everything's a blur. Max, I'm afraid."

"It's all right," the Professor said in a quiet voice. "I'll get us out of here."

"How?"

Again, the Professor didn't answer.

Sen sighed. "I've never told you this before, but I suppose if there was ever a time to say it, it's now. I loved you all those years ago. Back at Oxford. Before your accident. But I realized it was all for nothing."

"Why?" the Professor asked, his blind eyes fixed on Sen now, as though he was looking deeply into him. "Why was it all for nothing?"

"Because you were in love with *him*."

The Professor shook his head. "I was never in love with him. He fascinated me."

"He was no good, he never was. You were blind to that,

you were blind to how much I loved you, even before you lost your sight."

The Professor said nothing for a long time, then quietly, genuinely, uttered, "I'm sorry Sen. It seems that foolish young man has grown into a foolish old man."

"You're not a fool. You're the smartest, kindest person I know, you always were. But I had to move on, I had to let you go. I threw myself into the family business. I became obsessed with diamonds. It was easier than being obsessed with you. Diamonds don't break hearts."

The Professor took a deep breath, clearly uncomfortable both physically and emotionally, then said, "Sen, there's something I need to ask you—"

Suddenly the door to the car burst open. The Professor could smell Doctor Cyclops before his heavy, drunk footsteps even staggered into the car. Unsteadily he stomped up to the Professor and through a pungent cloud of anger shouted, "Stop talking! Shut up! Both of you! You're not here to talk, you're here to *diiiiiiieeee!*" he cackled. He gave the Professor a backhanded slap across the face, sending him back down into a black, dizzy spin. He tried to fight against unconsciousness, but it was sucking him down into a whirlpool of darkness too fast.

"Sen," he slurred, "I have to know—"

But his head rolled.

And his eyes slid shut.

And once again the Professor passed out.

XII

Beijing, China

THEY FOLLOWED THE SIGNAL, BEING WHISKED THROUGH
the *hutongs*—the tight, labyrinthine lanes of Old Beijing—in
a cramped and dilapidated pedicab. Their driver was a tiny,
toothless man who appeared to be as old as the neighbor-
hood through which he recklessly steered them. He giggled
at every chicken he narrowly missed and shouted friendly
abuse at the children in the street.

"Are you sure this is the fastest way?" Shane shouted to
the chuckling driver.

Emphatically the driver nodded and smiled and chatted
back in Mandarin as though Shane knew exactly what he
was saying. He tapped Luca's watch, which he had clipped to
the steering wheel, and every now and then said in midsen-
tence, "Beijing Betty!"

"That's a sweet name," Shane remarked.

The driver cackled even more.

It was midafternoon, but time meant nothing at Beijing

Betty's. As the pedicab rounded a tight corner, Luca and Shane peered out the window, their eyes catching sight of the rickety, run-down, four-story building before them.

"That's Beijing Betty's?" Shane asked, adjusting the cowboy hat on his head.

The thumping, frenzied beat of Asian electronica escaped from several broken windows, along with a pulsating strobed light. Drunk Chinese businessmen with their knotted ties at half mast and their shirts untucked lingered in the doorway, cigarettes bobbing up and down between their lips as they shouted jokes at one another and laughed raucously. A young male hooker, lean and pale and dizzy, staggered through the doorway and received a good hard slap on the ass from one of the drunk businessmen.

"Not so sweet!" said the driver of the pedicab, laughing through his toothless grin as he turned back to Shane and Luca.

"Come on," Luca said, paying the driver, who gave him back his watch. Luca and Shane hurried to the door of Beijing Betty's, pushing past the drunk businessmen and into the bowels of the dark, decrepit building.

Inside, the smell of scotch and sweat mingled with the pungent scent of opium. The music thudded while the drunk and stoned men barked drink orders at the topless male waiters. A young male stripper danced on the badly lit stage, swaying slowly, completely out of time with the fast-pounding music, while several men sitting on stools at the foot of the stage leered and rubbed their own laps.

Suddenly the crowd began to whoop and hoot. From behind the stage, pushing past the dirty, cigarette-singed curtains, the only woman in the room came strutting out, shouting like a crazed banshee and screaming with laughter. She was short and thickset, her stout frame strapped snugly into a pink-satin-and-lace corset, her hair a shiny black bob and her round face caked in too much makeup.

As a barrage of abuse and laughter poured from her loud pink lips, she stopped at the edge of the stage and pulled out a leather whip that was hitched to the side of her corset.

She turned to the male stripper and cracked her whip.

"Dance!" she ordered in English before shoving her hand down his crotch and taking the fistful of money nesting there. She rammed it down her corset and continued snapping her whip.

Luca and Shane turned to stare at each other, then looked back at the scene on the stage.

Shane muttered, "I'm guessing that's Betty."

"You distract her," Luca said. "I'll go look for the Professor."

"What?! Are you crazy! How the hell do you expect me to distract that?"

Luca didn't say a word. Instead he simply snatched the cowboy hat off Shane's head and hurled it across the room. It whirled through the air like a flying saucer, cutting through the smoke and haze to make a perfect landing right in the middle of the stage.

Betty stopped whipping.

The music stopped thumping.

The crowd stopped hooting.

Every head in the room turned to see who had thrown the hat.

"Luca!" Shane gasped, horrified.

But Luca had already vanished, leaving Shane standing in the middle of the room, stunned, all eyes on him. He smiled nervously and waved. "Ah, hi everyone."

"Who are you?!" Betty demanded from high on the stage, her piercing voice as cutting as her whip.

"Ah, my name's Shane. Shane Houston. I'm ah, new in town. Nice place you have here—"

"Shut your filthy mouth, Shane Houston, and get your dirty, sexy ass up here now!"

Shane gulped and stood doe-eyed, terrified, hesitating a moment.

Betty snapped her whip. "I said *now*, you cowboy slut!"

Several hands began pushing Shane from behind; several more pulled him forward as the crowd bellowed and boomed. By the time the tall cowboy reached the front of the room, the enthusiastic drunks practically threw him onto the stage. He slid across the grimy boards and came to a halt at Betty's fat stilettoed feet. He moved to grab his hat on the floor next to him, but the whip split the air inches from his hand.

"On your feet!" Betty ordered in her thick Chinese accent.

Nervously Shane did as he was told, standing almost twice as tall as Betty once he straightened up—but then again, he wasn't the one holding the whip.

Taking four or five steps back, Betty eyed Shane's tall, muscular form from top to toe, then with a sweep of her arm the whip sliced the air and bit off the top button of Shane's shirt.

Completely motionless but for his gulping throat, Shane saw the button shoot across the bar just before Betty worked her whip again.

The second button was plucked clean off.

Snap! Pop!

The third, then the fourth button of Shane's shirt shot across the room like bullets.

With each flying button the crowd roared, watching with sheer drunken delight as Shane's shirt fell open further and further, revealing his large swollen chest, his lungs full of trapped air; he was too terrified to do anything but hold his breath.

Another crack of the whip and the last button took to the air.

The shirt fell open.

Nervous sweat trickled down Shane's abs.

Betty looked on approvingly, then shouted to the crowd, "More?"

Arms and empty glasses flew into the air as the cheer went up. "More! More!"

Betty grinned. The tongue of her whip struck the button at the top of Shane's jeans and spat it across the floor.

Shane finally let out a whimper.

"Your dick likes danger!" Betty observed, eyeing the bulge in Shane's jeans.

Shane swallowed hard. "And I like my dick, so please don't—"

"Silence!" she ordered, and then with a wicked grin on her face declared, "The highest bidder joins me and the cowboy slut in Betty's Den of Iniquity!"

At that point, to say that Beijing Betty's bar went into a state of hysteria would be an understatement. Money flittered through the air like a ticker-tape parade. Men cursed and screamed at one another. Punches were thrown.

And all Shane could do was bite his lip and whisper to himself, "Den of Iniquity? Oh, that sounds bad!"

After tossing Shane's hat, Luca vanished swiftly through the crowd. He slipped his way past the bar and into the stinking garbage room and found an unsteady staircase leading upward. He began kicking rats out of his way as he quickly ascended, until he realized the rats were licking at something on the stairs: solid black pools of dried blood.

With a furious squeak, another rat went flying off the end of Luca's boot. The young Italian knelt down low and stuck his finger in a coagulated pool. It was blood, all right, spilled within the last few hours.

Hastily Luca followed the trail up the stairs, beyond the second floor and up to the third. The spatter trail led down a corridor and disappeared beneath a splintered door with bloody fingerprints on the handle. Luca checked his watch.

The red dot on the grid was still flashing, still indicating he was within the vicinity of the Professor. He tried the handle—locked—then didn't hesitate putting his shoulder into the door.

It popped open, sending the old rusted lock rattling across the blood-soaked floor inside.

Luca had to hold on to his stomach. The scene was deserted—and grisly. A table in the middle of the room looked as though it had been used to slaughter an animal, filling Luca with dread. Then a flash caught his eye and he saw it, shimmering in a groove between the floorboards: the tiepin.

The tiny tracking device had been cut out of Professor Fathom's gut—but not crushed under Doctor Cyclops's boot as everyone had thought. He had simply wedged it in a crack between the floorboards and not bothered to check. That was the first mistake Doctor Cyclops had made after the operation.

The second mistake was forgetting to take the map to the Zhang Diamond Express train terminal with him. It was a map Mya had given Cyclops after the operation, just before she and Xi had departed for Hong Kong, with strict instructions to deliver Professor Fathom and Zhang Sen to the train and wait for her arrival. In his drunken haste and his excitement Doctor Cyclops had left the map lying on the tattered mattress in the corner.

Luca slipped the Professor's bloodstained tracking device into his pocket and made his way over to the mattress, having spotted the unfolded map.

He squatted and looked at it. It was a large-scale map of central Beijing. There was an *X* marked at the center of the map, and next to it in red pencil was something in Chinese, something Luca couldn't read. From this central *X* a wide circle had been drawn, capturing what looked like a large portion of Beijing. More Chinese symbols were noted inside the circle.

Luca's heart sank with fear.

He grabbed the map and quickly raced out of the dank room and down the corridor and began pounding on doors. He tried doorknobs. "Hello! Hello? I need help!"

A young Chinese woman peeked out her door, a baby in her arms. She looked frightened.

"Don't be afraid," Luca insisted, although his desperation made her all the more wary of him. "Do you speak English?"

The woman nodded cautiously. "Yes. A little."

Luca thrust the map at her with such a flap it made the woman jump.

"It's okay, it's just a map. I need to know what this says."

Luca pointed to the X in the middle of the map. The woman squinted at the scribbled handwriting next to it. "Zhang Terminal," she read.

"And this?" Luca pointed to the words scratched next to the wide circle.

The woman looked at it, then looked at the young man at her door with grave concern and said, "Blast radius."

Luca swallowed hard, then pointed from one side of the circle to the other. "How far is it from here to here?"

"I don't know. Five miles. Perhaps more."

Luca looked from the map to the woman. "Are we in this circle?"

The woman nodded fearfully. "Yes."

"Pack. Get anything you need now!" He raced back down the corridor and began banging on the other doors again. "Get out! Everyone get out of here! Now!"

The highest bidder was an obese investment broker from Shanghai whose body consumed a squeaky vinyl sofa. He stared humorlessly into space, stoned out of his brain, as he guzzled down his scotch.

Betty didn't care. She could barely even see. The Den of

Iniquity was a room made opaque by a fog of opium smoke and illuminated only by candles. A lot of candles. Burning dangerously close to the plush curtains surrounding them.

She was standing beside a large silver bowl. In it was an enormous cake of white opium; underneath was a single candle, heating the opium enough to send up tendrils of smoke that filled the whole room.

Betty took a deep breath and waved the smoke into her lungs. Then she looked at Shane and giggled and waved the smoke in his direction. "You like, cowboy slut?"

Shane couldn't answer, on account of the black leather gag in his mouth. Instead he just grunted, half angry, half high, his hands cuffed in front of him and ankle cuffs binding his feet.

Betty took the grunt as defiance and quickly pulled out her whip. "You have problem, slave? Then you demand discipline! Now dance, bitch!" she hissed as she cracked the whip at Shane.

He was naked but for his cowboy hat, his crocodile tooth necklace, and a leather-studded codpiece courtesy of his captor. As the whip snapped again near his left shoulder, he growled. Then the opium haze made him giggle. "Op ee," he muttered through the gag in an attempt to say "Stop it."

"Not until you dance!" ordered Betty. She turned back to the highest bidder, swaying. "You like my new slave?"

The fat bidder just continued to stare into space.

Betty turned back to Shane. "He like you! Everyone gonna like you! Now, dance!" She flicked the whip again.

This time Shane giggled less. "Ah! At urt!"

"Then move your feet, bitch boy!" *Snap!*

This time the whip nicked into Shane's side. "Uck!" he shouted, the opium no longer able to make him laugh at the situation.

"You not like?" Betty sneered. "Bad luck for you! Welcome to my world of pain!"

Betty cracked her whip at him once more, but this time Shane held up his cuffed hands and let the tip of the whip latch on to the chain binding his hands together. The leather looped fast and locked hard around the chain links. Between Betty and Shane the whip held taut for one surprised moment. Then with a swift jerk Shane snapped his hands back and yanked the handle of the whip clean out of Betty's grasp.

The tail of the whip flicked across the room and smashed into a candelabra, knocking one of the candles off its perch and into the silver bowl, setting the opium cake alight and sending a giant puff into the air like a smoke bomb.

The candelabra tipped over, spilling its other candles across the floor, igniting everything like a bonfire.

Betty screamed.

The fat bidder didn't move from his sofa, staring at the flames as though he was watching a movie.

Shane looked on wide-eyed and muttered through his gag, "Oh, uck!"

As the clouds of opium churned through the room, the flames shredded the curtains and snaked quickly across the carpet.

Shane tried to make his way over to the stoned bidder on the sofa, but the shackles around his ankles sent him tumbling flat on his face. With great effort, Shane got himself back onto his feet, using his cuffed hands and every muscle in his bare torso and legs to right himself. With several long, high hops he bounded over the flames that crisscrossed the floor, seized the bidder's tie in two cuffed hands, and screamed through his gag, "et up!!"

The desperate command shocked the stoned businessman into action, and with a petrified squeal he launched himself off the sofa and through the blazing curtains. His squeal was like a siren. Every drunk patron began to fumble and shout as they caught sight of the fire and smoke billowing from the Den of Iniquity. Panic instantly swept the club as men trampled for the exit.

Inside the den, Betty was still screaming. Shane quickly hopped through the flames to her and seized her by the corset.

"eeee! Where's da eeeee!"

Betty just stared at him, terrified. Shane rolled his eyes, then shook Betty on her stilettos until he heard something jangle. His fingers followed the sound of the tinkling keys to an anklet on her left foot.

As the flames intensified, Shane's fumbling fingers tried one key at a time in the handcuff lock until eventually they snapped open. He did the same thing again with the ankle cuffs until—*ching!* He was free.

In one quick movement he scooped the screaming Betty up in his arms, leapt under the threshold of fire, jumped clear of the burning carpet, and launched himself into the mayhem of the bar. Once there, he plonked Betty down and she hit the ground running, tearing patrons out of her way to get to the exit first.

As the fire began to gnaw its way through the club, Shane saw Luca come clambering down a staircase behind the bar with a woman and a baby.

"uca!" Shane suddenly realized he still had the gag on, and his fingers tore it from his mouth. "Luca!"

"What the hell are you wearing?" Luca shouted to Shane over the top of several panicked heads as he and Shane brought up the rear, shoving everyone toward the exit.

"I was keeping Betty distracted, no thanks to you! What did you find?"

"This," Luca said, holding up the bloody tracking device, then producing a folded piece of paper. "And a map!"

The last patrons and residents stumbled out of the now blazing Beijing Betty's, followed by Shane and Luca. Everyone pulled back from the inferno as far as they could, coughing and spluttering, watching the fire dance and the opium cloud billow into the night.

Shane turned to Luca and shouted over the roaring fire, "A map to where?"

"Hopefully, to the Professor," Luca shouted back. He then turned to the crowd and tracked down the young woman with the baby, grabbing her by the elbow. "Get out of here. Tell as many people as you can. Get out of central Beijing!"

At that moment, the shrill, angry voice of Betty could be heard piercing the crowd. She was cursing furiously in Mandarin, pointing at Shane, angrily rallying her patrons.

"Oh, dear," Shane uttered to Luca. "I think Betty's pissed!"

The crowd began to turn on them. The bleary eyes of drunk, enraged patrons flickered with fire. But, just then, Luca and Shane heard the clownish horn of a pedicab as it pulled up behind them.

"Jump in! Jump in, my friends!"

Luca and Shane turned to see the cackling, toothless grin of their pedicab driver. "Jump! Jump!" he told them. "Now! Now!" he warned.

Luca and a scantily clad Shane needed no further coaxing. They leapt into the pedicab, and with a clown-car honk, the cab whizzed off into the night, leaving Betty to howl and clutch at the cash still stuffed in her corset as her filthy firetrap burned to the ground.

XIII

Somewhere over Mainland China

SNOW CLOUDS HAD MOVED IN OVER THE MOUNTAINS OF Shandong. The lakes along the ranges had already frozen over and a blizzard warning had been issued. So the black Bombardier Learjet tilted its wings and altered course, heading east before circling Beijing and approaching from the north to avoid the bad weather in the south.

Xi sat at the flight deck controls. Mya sat in one of the white leather passenger seats in the main cabin, facing backward, her back to the cockpit, her eyes fixed on Will and Bradley. The two captives sat facing forward, directly opposite Mya, their hands tied behind their backs. Mya trained her small, diamond-studded pistol on Will, her hand steady even through the occasional turbulence caused by the cloud bank building up outside.

Suddenly there was a loud *pop!*

Will and Bradley both flinched, then realized it wasn't the gun going off, but the cork of a bottle of Moët unleashing a gentle fizz of tiny bubbles. In the galley behind them, Chad began to pour two glasses of champagne.

"I hope you don't mind, but I'll be damned if I let the two of you stand in the way of us celebrating." At that moment the jet hit a pocket of air, and Chad spilled some champagne from the bottle. "Xi!" he screamed at his pilot.

"I'm sorry, Mr. Chambers," was Xi's obsequious response.

"Just keep the damn plane steady and get us there in one piece."

"And where is there?" Will asked, not taking his gaze off Mya.

"Beijing, of course. Where the second bomb will be detonated. But first, we're all going to take a train ride up through the mountains and bid a fond farewell to the Zhang diamond mines—as well as the two of you, Sen, and that interfering old Professor of yours."

Chad set the bottle down on the galley counter and returned with two glasses of champagne, handing one to Mya.

"The others will find us," Will said confidently.

Chad laughed. "The others won't find anything. Sorry to disappoint you, Mr. Hunter, but we've removed the tracking device from inside the old man. If you could see your watch you'd know this, but of course your hands are tied on the matter."

Will struggled in vain at his ropes and Chad laughed more, then calmed himself down with a sip of bubbles. "As I was saying, the others won't find anything. Not a single piece. Eventually the investigators will uncover a shadow of DNA left in the rubble, once they excavate the entire mine. But by then you'll be a distant memory. Along with all the other shadows they'll discover lost in the ruins of Beijing. You have no idea the power of zidium."

"Then tell us," Will pressed.

Chad hesitated a moment, reluctant to divulge. But there

was little Will and Bradley could do to stop things now, so where was the harm? "Mya, would you like to explain?"

"My absolute pleasure," Mya said, then swallowed a sip and smiled. "The zidium device is a fission design, made up of two separate cylinders of zinc and iridium, contained within a plutonium core, housed in a titanium sphere. The device is activated with a four-digit code and a countdown timer set to a designated time. Ten minutes from the end of the countdown, the cylinders inside the sphere break open. When mixed together, zinc and iridium are two of the most volatile, unpredictable substances on the planet. Once the device goes supercritical and the plutonium shell compresses, however, the results are assured: utter destruction. When the first bomb goes off in the mines it will implode the entire center of the mountain. Every shaft, every tunnel, every pick and mine car left lying around will be completely destroyed. The second bomb will be sent back to Beijing on the train, a one-way trip to annihilation, timed to go off as the train arrives in Central Beijing."

"Of course we'll be long gone by then," Chad added. "Our colleague is bringing the chopper, and somewhere between the Zhang mines and the soon-to-be-destroyed Beijing, while the train steams its way to disaster, we'll fly away into the night headed toward a new world order."

"By the way," Mya smiled. "The zidium comes with its own built-in fail-safe device. A defense mechanism. If somebody tries to interfere with the bomb, whether or not the countdown has been activated, the device automatically triggers the ten-minute destruction timer. The cylinders inside will crack open, the zinc and iridium will mix, and nothing will stop it from destroying everything within five miles. Tampering with the bomb is simple suicide."

Will eyed the gun in Mya's hand, then switched his angry stare from Chad to Mya and back again. "You'll never get away with this."

"So you said back in Hong Kong," Mya snapped.

"When you tried to kill us and failed," Will snapped back.

"Don't tempt me!"

Mya cocked the hammer on the glittering petite pistol. "Mya," Chad said with a warning tone in his voice. "I don't want bullet holes in the leather if we can help it. Or the fuselage, for that matter! It'll be a lot more fun blowing these boys to kingdom come in the mines, don't you agree?"

Mya and Chad looked at each other, and Mya's anger melted into delight. The two stole a moment to chink glasses and giggle, then suddenly—

—the jet hit another pocket of air and dropped sharply.

The bottle of Moët fell from the galley counter and rolled down the aisle, gushing its contents on the carpet. Mya's and Chad's champagne launched from their glasses. In a reflex reaction they tried to avoid the spillage, juggling their slender champagne flutes.

As champagne splashed everywhere, Chad gripped the arm of his seat with his free hand.

Mya lost focus on the pistol.

Will noticed.

With a sharp snap of his leg, Will's foot flew into the air in front of him, connecting with the pistol in Mya's hand. She gasped as she felt it leave her grip and fling into the air.

Xi regained control of the jet, which leveled out, a little too quickly. Mya leapt into the air to catch her gun, trying to push her weight up as gravity forced her down with the leveling jet. But Will was already up, hands tied behind his back, putting his shoulder into Mya's stomach. He knocked Mya against Chad's seat. She bounced off and collapsed in the aisle, winded.

Meanwhile, the momentum of Will's tackle sent him sprawling toward the cockpit, collapsing on the threshold. The gun came down. Chad reached for it in midair.

Bradley jumped out of his seat and rammed his shoulder into Chad's chest, pinning him back down. Chad's fingers missed the gun by an inch. It bounced and skipped down the aisle toward Mya.

Will clambered to his knees. Mya snatched the gun. She pointed recklessly and pumped off two shots in Will's direction. Will dropped instantly to the floor.

The first bullet whizzed past him and shot straight through the windshield of the jet, punching a hole in the glass. It didn't crack, but sucked the pressure clean out of the aircraft.

The second bullet hit even lower, smashing into the controls of the cockpit in a shower of sparks before ricocheting off and slicing a divot out of Xi's temple, deep enough for his eyes to roll, his consciousness to slip away, and his cast-iron frame to slump against the steering column.

The jet swooned into a nosedive.

Mya hit the deck. The pistol rattled down the aisle. She made a grab for it again, but Bradley kicked it under a seat. Mya grabbed the next best thing, the Moët bottle rolling along the floor. She seized it by the neck, like a bat, and with all her angry strength made a swing for Bradley.

Bradley ducked. The bottle swung wide and hard—

—and slammed directly into Chad's forehead with a heavy dull *THUNK!*

Chad's head wobbled, eyes stunned and staring blankly at the ceiling before he passed out, slumping forward in his chair.

The jet continued to dive, a deafening drone of doom filling the fuselage.

Mya glared at Bradley, her face red with rage, and made a lunge at him with bottle in hand. But Will was on his feet now and threw himself on top of her in mid-lunge. Bradley sidestepped and fell against a seat as Will and Mya went crashing to the floor. One of the champagne flutes smashed under their weight.

Her face pressed against the carpet, Mya opened her eyes and saw her diamond-handled pistol wedged under a seat.

Will looked behind him, back toward the flight deck. Through the windshield he saw the peaks of mountains fast approaching. "Bradley! The controls! Get to the controls!"

Bradley jumped into action. "But I don't know how to fly," was all he could mumble, let alone the fact that his hands were still tied behind his back. But it didn't stop him from stumbling through the cockpit door and dropping down into the copilot seat beside the unconscious Xi. A powerful arrow of air pierced the hole in the windshield, turning the entire jet into a wind tunnel. Papers flew through the air. Bradley stared uncomprehendingly at the control panel, sizzling and sparking from the bullet wound it had received. Computer screens blinked on and off madly, filled with a scramble of digits and readings that made no sense to Bradley, with the exception of one screen. "Altitude," Bradley read. The numbers on the screen were dropping faster than he could read them.

Bradley blinked away his fear and stared straight ahead at the ever-shrinking distance between himself and the jagged mountains below. He struggled with the ropes behind his back, but he couldn't get his hands free. Instead he hoisted his legs up, hooking his right leg around the right handle of the controls and locking his left leg around the left hand side of the steering column. Then, in his best contortionist act, he pushed down with both legs, trying to pull the plane out of its deadly dive.

In the cabin behind him, Mya pushed Will off her and tried desperately to reach for the gun. It was stuck tight and even her small hands had trouble getting under the seat.

With a thud Will landed on his bare back and felt daggers of shattered glass cut into him as the second champagne glass broke beneath him. He felt a razor-sharp shard at his fingertips. Quickly he gripped it, twisted it in his hands, and started slashing at his ropes.

From the flight deck he heard Bradley shout, "Will, I need help here!"

Entwined around the wheel, Bradley's legs trembled and throbbed as the entire jet began to shudder violently. "We're falling too fast! I can't pull up!"

Mya's fingers touched the tip of the gun.

Will cut frantically through the rope, slashing his fingers and wrists in the process. The glass began to cut through the twine.

Through the windshield, over the ridge of a fast-approaching mountain, Bradley caught sight of something long and serpentine, dipping and climbing across the landscape.

Mya managed to hook the handle of the pistol in her fingers, got a firm grip on it, and pulled the gun out from under the seat.

The rope broke. Will's hands pulled free. He grabbed the first thing he saw.

Mya sat up and turned to face Will, bringing the gun up in one swift move.

And suddenly—

WHACK!

The wide heavy base of the champagne bottle slammed into Mya's cheek. She folded instantly, flopping to the floor, limp and unconscious.

Will dropped the bottle and turned to the cockpit, clambering to the front of the shuddering plane. "We have to try to land," he said desperately, unbuckling Xi's belt and hauling the heavy henchman out of the pilot's seat. Will took the chair and seized the controls in both hands, pulling back as hard as he could.

"Land?" Bradley gasped. "Where?"

Will gestured dead ahead with a dip of his chin. "There!"

As the plane slowly began to pull out of its dive, a long, straight landing strip appeared before them. Only it wasn't a landing strip at all.

"The Great Wall! Will, are you crazy?!"

"Pretend it's a runway." Will glanced at the craggy slopes of the mountains on either side of the ancient slender wall. "Besides, we ain't got much choice!"

Terrified, Bradley took a deep breath. This far north, the sections of the wall were deserted, crumbling and crippled by centuries of erosion, making it unsuitable for tourists—but perfect for jets with nowhere else to crash-land.

Will tilted the wheel left, then swung right, trying to level the craft, pull out of the dive, and line up the narrow wall all at the same time, aiming for a long section of wall between two fortresslike watchtowers. The nose began to tilt upward, but he had to get it higher. His fists quaked but didn't let go of the shaking controls.

Through the windshield, the wall zoomed toward them.

Will's eyes skimmed the control panel. He found the button for the landing gear and punched it, hoping the wheels of the jet might buffer the landing. A red light flashed on a screen, along with the word *Malfunction*.

"Hold on to something. This is gonna get rocky."

"I can't," Bradley said, hands still tied behind his back. He fixed his feet against the control panel instead.

The jet sliced the air, low and fast. It cleared the first watchtower by mere feet.

Will tilted the nose up as hard as he could. The tail of the plane hit the walkway of the wall first. The craft jolted and slammed down on its belly—hard.

On both sides, the wings tore centuries-old bricks off the high walls on either side of the walkway before the wings snapped off completely, flinging into the air and crashing down the mountain slopes to the left and right.

With the wings gone, the fuselage of the jet torpedoed

along the section of the wall like an unstoppable missile. The nose of the plane tore up stone and debris and sent it flying into the air, smashing through the windshield. Will and Bradley ducked. A large chunk of brick shot into the left tail jet, which exploded in a puff of black smoke.

The nose of the plane slammed into a small stepped section of the walkway, destroying the steps and the nose of the jet, sending the plane bouncing in the air, heading straight for the second watchtower at the end of the strip.

Stealing a glance through the shattered windshield, Will saw the watchtower approaching fast. There was no point in steering anymore. Quickly he grabbed Bradley and pulled them both out of their seats.

He threw Bradley into the cabin. Bradley landed on top of the unconscious Mya. Will threw himself on top of Bradley, just as the jet slammed into the solid watchtower.

The nose and cockpit caved in completely in an eruption of smashed glass, twisted metal, and flying bricks, bringing the jet to a halt with a high-impact jolt. Instantly the cabin began to fill with smoke.

As the battered plane gave one last groan, Will pulled himself to his feet and was about to help Bradley up when he saw the gun in his face.

Chad was conscious and holding Mya's pistol, aimed directly at Will's head.

"Open the door!" Chad ordered. "Get everyone out! Now! And don't try anything stupid or I will kill you. And this time I mean it!"

Slowly, Will raised both hands in the air, then backed toward the jet's exit. He put his shoulder into it, coughing through the smoke, and pushed open the door. As the smoke poured out, Chad waved Will out of the way so he could be the first out of the smoldering wreck.

Outside, it was freezing. The mountain wind was howling. Chad kept the tiny weapon trained on Will and

Bradley as they removed the unconscious Mya and Xi from the jet. Then he pulled his cell phone from his pocket and made a single call.

"Richard. Change of plans—again! Bring the chopper here....No, I don't know where the hell 'here' is, somewhere along the Great Wall! Just follow it north and look for the fucking smoke!"

XIV

Beijing, China

JAKE HAD KEPT A LOW PROFILE AT THE AIRPORT IN DUBAI.
All the gumshoe tricks were clichéd, but they worked.
Hiding behind newspapers. Sidestepping to browse a duty-
free stand. Turning away at just the right moment to take
a pretend phone call. All to avoid the distracted, impatient
glances of Richard Conrad, who treated everyone from
the check-in assistant to the smiling purser as his own
personal servant, there to attend his needs and otherwise
be ignored.

Richard was seated at the very front of the plane. Jake
asked for a seat in the very back row. Upon arriving at
Beijing Capital International Airport, he had to make haste
through the terminal so as not to lose sight of Richard, who
was the first person off the plane.

With only a single carry-on bag, Richard bypassed the
baggage claim and breezed through customs. Jake got his
passport stamped and raced to catch up. He saw Richard

talking on his cell phone and making a beeline not for the main exit, but toward another door with a sign above it that read: "Private Connections. Cargo. Charters."

Richard approached the uniformed guard at the door and spoke to him, producing his passport and several other papers. The guard scrutinized them, spoke into a two-way radio clipped to his lapel, waited for a response, then nodded and waved Richard through the door.

Jake pulled his passport from his pocket and made his way through the crowd.

"I'm with him," he said matter-of-factly to the guard, flashing his passport, not breaking his stride.

The guard broke it for him. Barking sternly in Chinese, the uniformed man stepped swiftly in front of Jake, halting him immediately and placing a hand on his holster. Jake backed up right away, hands raised. "Whoa—it's okay. Wrong door, my mistake."

Rather than push the lie and cause a scene, Jake turned and quickly slipped outside, away from the guard's suspicious gaze. He briskly made his away from the terminal building and followed a chain link security fence that enclosed a number of giant hangars. Through the wire he caught a glimpse of Richard being escorted across the tarmac by three airport guards toward one of the hangars. Several ground staff were already hauling open the hangar bay doors to reveal a black helicopter waiting inside.

Jake sized up the fence as well as the decision whether or not to pursue Richard. He glanced at his watch, the tracking device blinking red on his wrist. The grid indicated that the signal was here in Beijing and moving fast through the maze of streets.

As Richard signed several clearance forms and stepped aboard the chopper alone, taking the pilot's seat, Jake turned away from the fence and back to the streets, hailing the first cab he saw.

*   *   *

The pedicab carrying Luca and Shane sped through the streets in a beeping blur and turned down a narrow deserted road, the driver laughing all the way. "Beijing Betty gone bye-bye!"

"Are you sure you know where you're going?" Luca asked, leaning over from the backseat and trying to draw the driver's attention to the map.

Without even looking, the driver pointed ahead and said, "Zhang!" At that moment he pulled up in front of a high steel gate. Above the gate was a sign that read "Zhang Terminal."

As they thanked their trusty driver and stepped out of the pedicab, Luca eyed the seemingly impervious gate while Shane looked left and right, scanning the high concrete wall that stretched far into the distance on either side of the gate.

"How the hell do we get in?" Luca asked.

"I'm not so sure we even want to. This place looks like a prison. Or an insane asylum."

"So what are we gonna do now?"

"Stop the bomb, that's what."

"Great plan. If only we knew where it was, *what* it is, and *how* to stop it!"

But Luca was already staring down the nearly empty street. Something else had caught his eye. "Perhaps *he* does."

Shane turned to see a thin, swaggering figure stumbling down the pavement toward them. In his hand was a brown paper bag, into which he reached and pulled out a bottle. With his one eye, the man had to focus hard on the open neck of the bottle to get it to his lips.

Luca realized quickly that the drunk with the eye patch hadn't seen them yet, but it wouldn't take long. Grabbing Shane by the arm, Luca hauled him swiftly across the street and crouched behind a mound of garbage covered in flies.

They watched as the drunkard made his way to the gate and juggled the brown paper bag while rummaging through his coat pocket for a key. Instead of a key his fingers found a large serrated knife, which he pulled out, stared at intently, decided it wasn't what he was looking for, and chuckled to himself before replacing it. Eventually he found a long, rusty skeleton key and after several attempts slid it into the lock on the gate. He turned it and pushed the heavy old gate open, but as he did so he lost his grip on the bottle in the paper bag. He dropped the key but caught the bottle inches before it smashed on the ground.

He laughed again. Then he stumbled through the gate. It slammed shut behind him with a heavy clang.

Luca and Shane both stood and stared at the key still lying on the ground in front of the gate. And both of them smiled.

XV

The Great Wall of China, North of Beijing

CHAD TOOK CARE OF THE KNOTS HIMSELF THIS TIME, FIRST tightening the ones binding Bradley's hands, then retying the rope behind Will's back, securing it tightly around Will's slippery, bloody wrists. Then he noticed something red and flashing.

Chad seized Will's wrist, bringing up his forearm so hard and fast that Will grimaced at the armlock Chad put him in.

"Mya!" Chad screamed, anger now ever-present in his voice. "Why the fuck is the tracking device still flashing? And why is it now located at the Zhang Express Terminal?"

Mya shook her head. "It's impossible. We cut it out of him."

"Well, somehow it's managed to find its way home!" Chad bellowed. He snapped up his phone once more. "What the fuck is that psychopath's number?! We need to tell him he's got company!"

Unable to stop himself, Will let out a relieved laugh.

Furious, Chad tightened the ropes even more and leaned in close from behind, breathing in his ear. "I wouldn't be so amused if I were you. If your friends have come looking for you and the Professor, then the body count just went up!"

In the distance the sound of chopper blades filled the sky as Chad made his call.

The sun began to sink into the mountains as Richard spotted the trail of smoke that twirled and looped in the cold wind. He followed the wall to the plane wreck and with confident, reckless care he set the chopper down on top of the watchtower.

Richard stepped out of the chopper, its blades still whirring. He looked down at the shattered jet on the wall at the foot of the tower. "Chad! Did you do that? One of these days you'll take up my offer to teach you how to fly!" he said mockingly.

As the others made their way up the watchtower, Richard opened the rear cabin door and Mya and Xi shoved Will and Bradley into the helicopter. Xi strapped the captives into place, then took a seat next to Mya, who nursed a bloody bruise on her face with one hand and kept her gun in the fierce grip of the other.

As a stern and humorless Chad climbed into the front passenger seat of the chopper, he glared at Richard, who was now strapping himself back into the pilot's seat. "I don't fly. I'm flown. Which is exactly what you're gonna do if you still want your piece of the pie. Now get us to Beijing!"

Richard smirked. "I never thought I'd say this, but when there's this much money at stake, you're the boss."

With a slight pitch, then an adjustment, the chopper lifted off the unsteady, ancient surface of the Great Wall, swooping left into the sky as it headed back for Beijing.

XVI

San Francisco General Hospital, California

ELSA HAD STOPPED CRYING LONG AGO. A STOIC RESOLVE
had set in once again, and the headstrong German was
making up a list of things that the Professor needed to fix
around the house on San Sebastián to make it more livable
and safe. Elsa needed something to keep her mind occupied.

"There's a squeaky step on the porch, I'm certain of it,"
she told Sam, noting it down with a pad and pen. "It could
be rotten. If someone falls through it, they could break a
leg! Or twist an ankle! And if I'm not there, who else knows
how to set a splint or pop a knee back into place?"

"Elsa, Eden's going to be fine," Sam said, trying to calm
her down, though his own stress levels were rising with
every hour.

"I'm not talking about Eden! I'm talking about the house!
And those trees! So many palm trees around the house!
What if there's a storm? Coconuts could come crashing
down on our heads!"

"Elsa, that's enough, okay?" Sam began pacing once more.

Elsa shook her head, furiously making notes. "No, Sam, you don't understand. Accidents happen."

"Not to Eden, they don't! Don't you get it? This wasn't an accident at all. This was planned. It was premeditated! This was terrorism!"

Suddenly Elsa screamed at him and jumped out of her chair. "I know it was! But what can I do if you all keep putting yourselves in front of it, trying to save everyone else, trying to protect everyone else? What can I do but make sure you're fed and hope that you're safe and fix the damn step and pray for sunny days with no storms?!" She flopped back into the uncomfortable chair, her stoic resolve gone again. "If you boys want to stop the bad guys, then let me try to stop the accidents. That's all I ask."

Suddenly she started crying again.

Sam dropped into the seat next to her and squeezed her tight.

Elsa picked up the hem of her generous dress and wiped her tears away. "The same thing happened to the Professor," she said in a reflective voice. "It happened all those years ago, before I even met him. He doesn't talk about it. He only mentioned it once—that he lost his sight in a fall. A very bad fall." She whimpered. "Just like Eden's fall. Only I fear Eden may lose more than just his sight."

She put her head on Sam's shoulder and a cascade of tears soaked up his shirt. He hugged her even tighter as a sweat-soaked Dr. Dante emerged from intensive care. The Italian surgeon slipped off his mask and looked from Sam to Elsa.

"I'm afraid we tried everything..."

XVII

Beijing, China

THE PROFESSOR WAS STILL SLUMPED IN HIS CHAIR, unconscious, when Doctor Cyclops staggered back into the master carriage. Sen was awake, tied to his chair, and sneered at Cyclops as he stumbled past. Suddenly courageous, Sen shouted abuse at the drunk man in Chinese.

The one-eyed doctor simply ignored him. As he set his bottle down hard on the desk—next to the empty ones—the cell phone on the desk rang as though the slam had set it off. Doctor Cyclops jumped, then found himself amused by his own surprise. He picked up the phone. His amusement was short-lived.

"You fucking fool, you've been followed! Show me their bodies when I arrive." It was Chad's voice, short and furious. And suddenly the phone call was over.

The Zhang Express Terminal looked even more like a prison on the inside: a vast concrete yard, square in shape, surrounded by four high walls and dotted by tall weeds here and there. The moon was rising, illuminating several rail lines that crisscrossed the yard, slipping away under another enormous gate at the far end of the terminal.

In the center of the yard, positioned on the tracks and facing the exit gate, was a six-car steam train. The curtains were drawn in the third car, the one directly behind the coal car, but Shane and Luca could see the lights on inside.

Then suddenly the lights went off.

In the shadows along the wall, Shane turned to Luca. "I think someone knows we're here."

Luca glanced left and right. "Let's split up. You start at the front of the train, I'll take the rear and work forward." As the moon crept higher, the two of them bolted across the yard in separate directions, leaving the gate ajar behind them, ready for a quick getaway.

The last car of the train was not a carriage at all, but a long flatbed platform. Climbing onto it, Luca saw several chains secured along the length of the platform. Then he turned to the second-to-last car and stepped across the large steel coupling—the linchpin that connected the two cars together—and climbed over the railing to stand on the back landing. There was a door leading into the darkened car. Luca tried the ornate gold handle. It was unlocked.

He pushed it open enough to peer inside, but could see nothing through the darkness. He thought about taking a step inside, but paused, trying to allow his eyes to adjust. Soon he could make out the shape of what appeared to be a large bed in the center of the car. On the walls around the room he picked up glints and glimmers here and there, random reflections of the moonlight outside bouncing off unknown objects. There seemed to be no other signs of life. It gave Luca the confidence to push the door open a little wider. He planned to give himself just enough space to slip through, find out whether or not there was somebody hiding behind the door, then explore further.

He never got that far.

As Luca edged the door open, a thin arm seized him around the throat, bracing him in a headlock. The arm was certainly feeble enough that Luca would be able to fight off his attacker, were it not for the thick syringe that plunged into his neck.

As the needle sank into his flesh, Luca instantly felt his knees buckle and his entire weight give way. Within seconds, his limp, unconscious body melted out of the headlock and fell inside the door of the bedroom carriage.

Rather than pull the needle out, Doctor Cyclops simply let Luca's body slide away from the syringe. With the back of his hand he wiped the drool from his bottom lip and ogled the beautiful, unconscious body slumped in front of him. With every muscle in his wiry frame, the doctor dragged Luca inside the car and kicked the door shut behind him.

The engine of the train was a large black beast, a classic locomotive engine with a pointed grill at the front like a giant spearhead, a huge cylindrical body, four large piston-driven wheels on each side, and a tall smokestack. Wisps of steam were already escaping from the stack.

Stealthily, Shane pulled himself up into the driver's compartment. The back of it was open-ended, for easy access to the coal car. At the front of the driver's compartment was a round sealed furnace door, perhaps five feet in diameter. Shane took an oily rag off a rail to one side and used it to spin the cast-iron wheel-handle in the middle of the furnace door. He could feel the heat seep through the rag, then felt the glow on his face as he opened the door and saw the long bed of bright orange embers inside the furnace. The engine was fed and the train ready to travel.

Suddenly Shane heard a footstep outside the driver's compartment. He ducked low, crouching silently.

A hand appeared on the ladder railing leading up into the compartment. Someone was boarding the engine, and Shane wasn't banking on a friendly greeting.

A second hand gripped the railing. Before the visitor could climb any higher, Shane leapt to his bare feet, swung around, and threw a kick, aiming for the head of whoever was on the ladder.

But the intruder was on the alert. One hand let go of the railing and grabbed Shane's foot before it could make contact, then twisted it up and around, managing to knock Shane off balance and send him crashing to the compartment floor. He landed on his face with a grunt and a clang.

Instantly his hand went for the shovel next to his head. He heard the intruder jump up into the compartment. Shane seized the shovel, pulled himself to his feet, turned, and cut the air with the blunt flat blade.

Jake reeled backward, the shovel missing him by an inch. "Shane! It's me! What the fuck are you trying to do, kill me?"

Shane dropped the shovel. "Jake! Jesus, you scared the shit outta me! What the hell are you doin' creepin' up on me like that?"

"What the hell are you wearing, is more the question!" Jake was looking Shane up and down, taking in the studded-leather codpiece and cowboy hat combo with a bemused look on his face.

"Ask Luca," Shane said.

"Where is he?"

"Searchin' the other end of the train. How did you find us?"

"I followed the Professor's tracking device."

"It's not inside the Professor anymore. The bastards cut it out of him. You were following me and Luca. Jake, there's a bomb. They're gonna blow up Beijing."

Out of the night, the *whump-whump-whump* of an

incoming chopper filled the sky. Shane quickly looked outside and saw the light of a helicopter approaching. He turned to Jake. "I think we have company."

Jake saw the chopper too. "You and me need to find a place to hide. Now."

As they flew through the night over the squat concrete blocks and *hutongs* of Beijing and neared the terminal, Richard looked out the pilot's side window and saw something unexpected. People were running through the streets, suitcases and children in hand. At first he thought it was some sort of street festival or parade, but it was happening in more than one street. And as he took the chopper lower he could see on the faces of the people not joy and excitement, but fear and panic.

He leaned over to the passenger seat of the chopper. "Chad, I think we need to pick up the pace."

Richard gestured through the window and Chad peered out. "Get us down" was his only order. "Now!"

The tall weeds in the concrete yard were whipped and slashed by gusts of air as the chopper circled the Zhang Terminal before lining itself up for a perfect, if hurried, landing on the flatbed car of the Zhang Diamond Express.

"Out!" Chad ordered. "Everyone out! Xi, tie her down, then get this train moving!"

While the blades were still whirling, Mya unloaded the captives from the back of the chopper as Chad and Richard disembarked from the front. With her pistol in hand, Mya waved Will and Bradley off the flatbed car and onto the concrete ground of the terminal yard.

"Take them to the exhibition carriage," Chad barked. He pointed directly at Will. "I want him kept separate from the old man. At least until we're on our way."

Mya climbed the short ladder leading up to the landing at the rear of the fourth car and opened the door, waving

Will and Bradley inside with her pistol. Once inside, she quickly paced the room, lighting several antique gas lanterns attached to the walls. Soon they were bathed in the plush red of the carriage. Red carpets, red wallpaper, red curtains. Even the many diamond-filled glass-topped display cabinets around the carriage were a rich red oak. In the middle of the room, in a glass display case all to itself—

"The Eye of Fucanglong," Bradley breathed.

For a moment he stared at the giant, bedazzling jewel. Then he quickly tore his eyes away.

Mya saw him and began laughing. "You superstitious fool! You honestly believe the curse is real?"

"Look what it's done to you," Bradley replied calmly. "All of you."

Mya pouted mockingly. "Poor little Bradley. Always the honest one. Always so naïve. Always the last to catch on. Chad was right: when it comes to business, a gay boy is no match for a real man. You should have stayed out of the boardroom. You never should have hung up your pretty white skates. Look where it's got you now."

"I gave up skating because I wanted to make my uncle proud."

"By bringing shame upon his name with your perverted desires? By making him feel obliged to hand you a career, a future, when all you did was embarrass and disappoint him?"

"I never once did anything to shame him. I am who I am. I worked as hard as I could to bring him honor."

"Obviously you didn't work hard enough."

Will suddenly interjected in a low, serious tone, "Don't listen to her, Bradley."

The butt of the diamond-studded gun struck Will hard across the face. Will's head reeled from the blow, then returned to face front. Giddy-eyed, he licked at the fresh blood on his bottom lip. "Jesus, you're a bitch," he said.

"Consider it payback for the Moët bottle."

Mya turned and stepped up to the display case in the center of the room. The anger and cruelty in her eyes slowly slipped away, making way for a sort of spellbound awe as she set her gaze upon the Eye of Fucanglong. "If you want to believe in childish tales of witches and dragons, then go ahead. All I believe in is money. This diamond is worth more than a fortune. It's the price of the future. It will bring about chaos, then herald a new world." Her gaze became more trancelike at the thought, her eyes unblinking, locked on the diamond. "I suppose one part of the legend is true, though. When the first zidium device detonates, Fucanglong will indeed burst from the mountain in a terrible explosion of fire and smoke. And after that—" Mya finished her sentence with a smile.

Once Xi had secured the chopper, he made his way promptly to the engine of the train.

At the same time, Richard and Chad boarded the third car, the master carriage. They stepped inside and saw Sen and the Professor tied to their chairs, the Professor now waking and wincing.

"Where the fuck is Cyclops?" Chad demanded of his captives, his eyes scanning the car.

"How should we know?" Sen answered angrily, glancing back and forth between the slowly rousing Professor and Chad.

"Watch them!" Chad said to Richard. He stormed through the car, departed through the rear door, and crossed a connecting walkway into the exhibition carriage.

"Your doctor's gone missing," he hissed at Mya, walking straight past the gun-packing woman and her two captives. He exited through the rear door of the exhibition carriage, crossed another connecting walkway, and pushed open the door to the fifth car, the bedroom carriage.

He stopped in his stride.

The bedroom carriage was precisely that, a large suite with a four-poster bed in the middle of it. Plush, pristine, elegant. At least it was—until the drunk, psychotic Doctor Cyclops had taken the liberty of transforming the car into his own private chamber. A torture chamber.

Like a handyman's toolshed, the car was adorned with the tools of the doctor's trade. A dozen or more large instruments were now hanging from hooks where centuries-old works of Chinese art had, until an hour or so ago, been hanging.

Spread-eagled on the bed, completely naked and face up, his wrists and ankles tied to the bedposts, was an unconscious Luca, the most beautiful specimen Doctor Cyclops had ever laid his eye on, at least on the outside; he suspected the inside was even more heavenly.

On the bedspread between Luca's bare legs were several syringes of different sizes filled with different colored fluids: blood thinners, pain killers, numbing agents, all to keep the victim alive and conscious so the doctor could extend the torture for as long as possible.

The one-eyed drunk was holding a syringe in his shaky hand, squirting a jet or two of liquid into the air, when Chad entered the room.

"What the fuck are you doing, you goddamn psycho!"

Doctor Cyclops turned sharply, surprised but not enough to lose the grin. "I'm going to take his life from him. Inch by beautiful inch. I'm going to find out what's underneath."

"Jesus Christ! Who else is here? How many of them followed you here?"

"Just him." Cyclops said, shrugging unconvincingly.

Chad fumed. "Kill him. Kill him now and be done with it! There's too much at stake now, there're already too many loose ends!"

"Let me have this one, just this one. He's so—" a foamy

trickle slipped from the doctor's cracked bottom lip "—perfect. Keep your money, you don't have to pay me. All I want is—"

"I said kill him now! Before he wakes up, dammit!"

As Chad pushed his way through the door leading out of the bedroom and stormed across the walkway back to the exhibition carriage, he heard the *choof* of the engine. Looking up, he saw the first cloud of steam fill the night sky.

Then a lurch. Then another loud *choof!* The wheels of the train began to grind against the tracks, rolling slowly at first, then building up momentum with every huff of the steam engine.

Automatically the gates of the compound opened to release the train, and despite his rage and frustration at Doctor Cyclops, Chad couldn't help but smile, knowing that the train's return trip to Beijing would end in one of history's greatest catastrophes.

A chuckle escaped him as he entered the exhibition carriage.

Mya, her gun still trained on Will and Bradley, turned to him.

"We're on our way," Chad said with a grin. "I think it's safe to reunite these two with the Professor and Sen now. I'm looking forward to this."

XVIII

The Mountains of Shandong Province, China

THE TRAIN BILLOWED CLOUDS OF STEAM, WHITE-RIMMED in the light of the moon, as it powered its way up through the mountains, leaving the glow of Beijing far behind. As the locomotive curved and climbed higher and higher, the temperature dropped lower and lower.

In the engine compartment, however, Xi had worked up a sweat. He climbed on top of the mountain of coal and dug his shovel into the black nuggets, scooping a load into the basket.

Beneath the coal, something shifted. But the blanket of coal was so black, Xi didn't notice.

Buried as deep as they could manage in their haste to hide, Jake and Shane tried desperately to move their legs to avoid Xi's stabbing spade. They had trouble breathing, the coal dust thick in their lungs, but as Xi dug deeper into the mound, the greater danger came not from suffocating but from losing a limb to Xi's shovel and being discovered.

Xi had a weapon already in hand. Jake and Shane were unarmed. Right now, remaining undetected was their best chance of staying alive and trying to rescue the others.

Crunch! The shovel's blade missed Shane's foot by an inch.

Stab! Jake forced his leg a fraction to the left and barely missed having his thigh severed.

Slice! Shane bunched up his fingers and managed to keep them.

Then the coal basket was full. Leaving a black smear across his sweaty forehead, Xi wiped his brow, threw the shovel on top of the basket, and picked up his coal before laboring with it back to the locomotive's engine.

Through the coal heap, a single sooty finger appeared, pushing the loose nuggets aside before a blackened face broke the surface, gasping for air. A second charcoal-covered face burst free next to the first. Jake and Shane pulled their arms loose and wiped desperately at their eyes, taking in lungfuls of frigid mountain air.

"You okay?" Jake asked.

Shane nodded. "You?"

"Yeah." Jake was already taking in their surroundings. Ahead of them he could see the raging furnace and the silhouette of Xi in front of it, tirelessly fueling the fire. Above, the trail of steam clouds puffed into the night. Beside the tracks, excited villagers and their children ran to see the train, carrying lanterns and waving, thrilled at the rare sight of a train passing through the night.

"Look at them," Shane said. "They have no idea what's about to happen. We have to find that bomb."

He began digging himself out of the coal, but Jake held him back. "Not yet. We're outnumbered."

"We can take him," Shane said, gesturing to Xi.

"Then what? We try to take control of the train and risk everyone's life? That's not a plan."

Shane shook his head. "Since when does Jake Stone care about plans? I thought you were supposed to be the reckless one."

He tried to pull away, but Jake grabbed Shane even harder, his voice burdened with guilt and regret and responsibility. "That was before Eden ended up in a coma."

Shane stopped pulling.

Even before he opened his eyes, Luca could feel the tickling sensation running up his side. He groaned groggily and tried to open his eyes, but his lids were made of lead. When he did manage to open them slightly, his sight was smeared.

Then a figure moved across his field of vision.

Despite the tickling on Luca's side, it was the blurred, giggling figure in front of him that triggered an alarm inside Luca's brain. Suddenly he forced his eyes wide open, trying to snap his arms and legs into motion. But his limbs simply tugged against their ropes.

His vision cleared and he realized quickly he was a captive and naked.

Strapped to a bed at the mercy of a spidery man with a patch over one eye and a broken-piano-key grin.

Luca felt the rock and pitch of the car now and realized the train was moving. "Where are we going? What are you doing?" he spat through clenched teeth, his Italian accent strong in his panic.

Doctor Cyclops chuckled excitedly. "I'm going to cut you open." The doctor buzzed. "I want to see how perfect you are. Outside…and in." He held up a leaky fountain pen, his fingers dripping with black ink. Luca glanced down over his naked body and saw intricate dissection marks crisscrossing his entire frame, as though the young model's body had been turned into a crazed work of art. He pulled at his ropes even harder, straining, trying in vain to work himself free. "You're the one who cut open the Professor, aren't you. Is he alive?"

216

"Oh, yes," the doctor answered, concentrating on his drawing once more. "But not for much longer. You, on the other hand, I intend to keep alive for as long as possible. I'll take my time. I'll make every incision slow. I'll lift and fold your skin like silk. And I'll let you watch it all."

In his excitement he pressed too hard on the pen and the sharp nib broke, puncturing Luca's torso. The young Italian winced as ink and blood ran down his side. Doctor Cyclops panted with delight. "You'll see just how pretty pain can be."

They were seated in a semicircle in the master carriage, tied to armchairs—Will, Bradley, Sen, and the Professor. Mya stood before them, gun still in hand. Richard was admiring the bronze, life-sized statue of Sen and the nameless mine worker. "Immortality," he mused. "Nice to know it's one of the things money can still buy."

He wandered over to one of the plush Parisian lounges, sat down, and pulled the curtain aside to peer at his own image in the glass. He caught sight of conditions outside. "It's started snowing. Rather fiercely too. It'll be cold at the mines."

"Only for a short while," Chad said, walking over to the desk, opening the top drawer, and pulling out a gun for himself. "I'm sure the zidium will warm things up."

"You'll end up killing yourselves," the Professor cautioned. "You can't expect to dabble with this sort of danger without ramifications." He flinched then as a sharp pain shot through him.

"Professor, are you all right?" Will struggled against his ropes, then turned angrily to Chad. "He's losing too much blood. Let me check his wounds."

Chad stepped up to the Professor and looked down into the old man's blind eyes. His eyelids were heavy, his head rolling from one side to the other. The carpet had grown sticky and squishy with blood under Chad's Italian shoes.

"I'm not touching him. And I'm not carrying a corpse all the way down to the mines," Richard muttered from his seat on the lounge.

Chad drew an agitated breath. "Shut up!"

"Dammit, let me help him!" Will shouted.

"No!" Chad shouted back. He looked from Will to Bradley and said, "*He* can do it." Chad glanced at Mya, and a sharp nod of his head told her to untie Bradley's hands.

She did so, then stood behind Bradley with her diamond-handled gun trained on the back of his head as he knelt before the Professor, one knee in the pool of blood, gently unbuttoning the Professor's shirt to reveal the filthy, hastily applied bandages around the old man's torso.

Chad stepped back, moving behind Sen.

Richard grimaced from his place on the lounge, his tongue clicking against the roof of his mouth as though he might be sick.

Mya pressed the snout of her gun against the back of Bradley's head impatiently. "Check him. Make it quick."

Bradley looked at the Professor's face apologetically and said softly, "This might hurt." Then tenderly he touched his fingers to the bloodiest of the old man's wounds. The bandage taped to the Professor's abdomen made a sucking sound as Bradley peeled it away. A gush of blood flowed from the sticky wound.

"The stitches have all come loose," Bradley said urgently. "He needs help."

Chad groaned with annoyance and looked at Richard. "Go get that fucking psycho of a doctor. He's in the bedroom carriage. Tell him he needs to do his job. Properly, for once." Then he muttered, "And for the last time."

Richard grumbled, then agreed reluctantly and exited the car.

As the door shut behind him, Bradley shot a look at Will,

who returned the same look. A look that said, *I'm game if you are. Now's our chance.*

Mya had the gun against Bradley's head. Will knew he needed to somehow get that gun pointed somewhere else. He needed to distract her, enough for Bradley to try to make a move. Will's hands were tied to the arms of the chair. But his feet weren't.

Slowly he began to inch his boots across the carpet toward Mya's high spiked heels. His intention was to get close enough to try to trip her up, but Mya was no fool. She spotted him out of the corner of her eye and quickly veered the gun toward him, pointing straight at his crotch.

"One more inch and I'll put a bullet right between your—"

But before she could finish, Bradley's strong skater's legs launched him backward, onto his feet. He jerked his head back and the top of his skull butted Mya square in the forehead.

The gun went off.

Will's legs spread wide, his body shifting back in the chair as far as he could as the bullet split the upholstery, missing his crotch by a millimeter.

Bradley spun on Mya, snatching the gun clean out of her hand, then twisting around behind her and using her as a shield, jamming the pistol into her temple.

"Let us all go or I'll kill her," he demanded, immediately facing off opposite Chad.

But Chad had already made his own move. Standing behind Sen, he seized the old man in headlock, lifted him out of his chair as high as his ropes would allow, and pointed his own pistol at the crown of Sen's skull. "Go ahead. Kill her. Kill her and your uncle dies too."

"I mean it!" Bradley shouted, cocking the pistol's hammer, looking on desperately as Sen struggled.

Chad laughed. "Don't be stupid. Are you really willing to sacrifice your own uncle? Now, drop the gun!"

"Don't do it," came the groggy voice of the Professor. All eyes turned to him as he sat up as best he could, straightening his head, his blind eyes pointed toward the sound of Bradley's voice. "Don't do it," he repeated. "Don't let go of the gun."

Bradley looked at him, stunned. Mya wrestled in his arms. Bradley tightened his grip on her and on the pistol. "But my uncle—"

"Trust me," the Professor said. "Don't surrender the weapon."

"Max!" Sen suddenly pleaded, his face turning red as Chad tightened the headlock. "Max, what are you doing! Don't let him kill me, please!"

The Professor didn't take his blind gaze off Bradley. "Kill her. Kill her or we'll all die."

Chad laughed and cocked his weapon. "Fine. Do it. We can count to three and do it together."

Will turned to the Professor, shocked at his words. "Professor?"

"Shoot her now," was all the Professor could say.

Chad began counting determinedly. "One!"

Bradley squirmed. "Professor?"

Chad raised his voice. "Two!"

In a calm, exhausted tone, the Professor said, "Don't let go of that gun, Bradley."

"Three!" Chad cried. He made a move to squeeze the trigger.

Sen begged, "No!"

Bradley threw the gun on the floor. "Don't shoot him!"

He released Mya and stepped backward quickly, unarmed, at which point Mya turned to face him and struck him with a left hook that knocked him to the floor. She picked up her gun and pointed it at him.

Chad eased his grip on Sen, who gasped with relief, "I'm sorry. I'm sorry, Bradley."

"Don't be," Bradley replied, not taking his eyes off the barrel of Mya's gun pointed straight in his face. "I'll never let them hurt you."

Sen's gasps turned to laughter. A weak chuckle at first. Then something louder. Something stronger. Something more than stress or exhaustion. This was genuine amusement. "Thank you, nephew," he said with a smile. "Unfortunately I can't say the same of you."

Will turned to Sen as the grim realization of what he'd just heard set in.

Bradley looked from the barrel of the gun to his uncle, confused, bewildered, fighting off the sense of betrayal that began to flood his heart.

Sen continued to laugh. "As I was saying, I'm sorry. I'm sorry, but you should have listened to the Professor."

Chad removed his gun and began to untie Sen. "I hope I didn't hurt you," Chad remarked as he released Sen's hands.

Bradley stared, uncomprehending at first. Then the hurt and anger slowly seeped in. "Uncle?"

Doctor Cyclops's fingers rattled like the needle on a Richter scale. He had decided to start with the inner thighs. High up Luca's leg. Right beside the scrotum. He could smell the scent of fear, of sweat. He watched with one eye as the young Italian's balls writhed inside their sack, squirming, trying to escape the knife.

"Don't do this," Luca tried to negotiate desperately. But the doctor had been a little too generous with the dosage he'd given Luca, and soon his eyelids grew weary and settled shut.

"Dammit," cursed the doctor. He had wanted Luca to watch. Nevertheless, with fingers trembling, Doctor Cyclops pressed the rusty scalpel to his specimen's inner right thigh. He pushed deep and popped the skin. A thick drop of blood appeared and drew a red line down to the bedspread.

His fingers shaking, the doctor tried to follow his inked blueprint down the inside of Luca's leg, managing to follow his mark no more than two inches before the door to the car burst open.

Richard entered, took one look around, and said, "What the—?"

He saw the doctor stand up stiffly from between the now unconscious Luca's thighs. In one hand he held his scalpel, shiny with blood.

"Jesus Christ," Richard tut-tutted in his British accent. "You really are one sick bastard, aren't you."

"What do you want?" the doctor snapped.

"Chad needs you in the master carriage. The old man's making a bloody mess."

"The old man?" the doctor uttered fearfully.

Richard shook his head. "Not *our* old man. The other old man. The Professor. Now put down your toys and follow me."

In the master carriage, Sen laughed at his nephew as the young man stared back in astonishment and anger. "Oh, Bradley, you have no idea how pathetic you are. So honest. So naïve. Your parents would be proud of you. Be sure to give them my regards, you'll be seeing them again sooner than you think. I'm sure you'll have a lot to talk about."

Bradley shook his head in disbelief. "What are you saying?"

Sen shrugged. "I'm saying that sometimes accidents happen, and sometimes, well—sometimes there just aren't enough diamonds to go around. Of course there was a time when I would have shared my life happily with those I loved. Isn't that right, Max? But those days are long gone."

Sen was standing now. He shot a commanding look at Mya and ordered, "Get my nephew back in his chair." Mya promptly acted, hoisting Bradley to his feet and shoving him onto a chair. Chad kept his gun on Bradley while Mya secured Bradley's ropes.

Sen made his way almost casually over to the window and peered outside. He saw the white tips of the forest trees capped with snow, and beyond them a large expanse of white. "Ah, the Lake of a Thousand Stars," he commented, almost sentimentally. "This was always my favorite part of the journey, even as a child—watching the lake go by as the train curved its way around its shores. The water was always such a deep, bottomless blue in summer. And at night, a perfect mirror of the stars. A thousand stars, just like its name. Except, of course, now, with the coming of winter, when its surface is frozen solid."

At that moment the door between the cars opened. Richard and Doctor Cyclops entered the room, and in an instant Sen's look of fondness turned to controlled rage. He stormed up to Doctor Cyclops and slapped him across the face.

"That's for being too enthusiastic with the acting," Sen scolded.

"I'm sorry I touched you," Cyclops replied, trembling.

Sen turned to Mya sternly. "Are you sure this fool can do the job?"

Mya nodded, though the deep breath she took made her own doubts evident.

"What more can he do?" Will demanded. "Look at the Professor! Haven't you butchered him enough?"

"Not quite," answered Sen. "We need to cover our tracks. We need to make allowances for the scientific investigations that will no doubt ensue over the following months, years, decades. In case they uncover molecules of DNA in the devastation we'll leave behind. And for that, we need the Professor's body. Not all of it, you understand. We'll be taking the head with us and disposing of it elsewhere, in case forensics does manage to recover any trace of skull or teeth in the ruins of the mines; they're always a dead give-away. Which is why we need the doctor." Sen shot Doctor Cyclops another angry glare, and Cyclops cowered backward fearful of a second slap, or worse. Sen turned back to his captives and continued. "As for the rest of the Professor, however, if there's so much as an atom left at the scene for the investigating authorities, they'll trace the DNA back to me. Zhang Sen. I'll be the one they confirm as dead."

"How can the Professor's DNA match yours?" Will contested. "That's impossible."

"You're absolutely right. Unless of course you alter the information at the source."

"The blood," the Professor panted, recalling his long journey to China. "The blood Mya took on the Learjet. You've switched it with yours."

"Very good, Max," Sen said with a smile.

"I don't understand." Will strained against his ropes, frustrated, confused, impatient.

The Professor explained drowsily, "Before they operated on me, before they drugged me full of opium and cut the tracking device out, Mya took a sample of my blood."

"Which I switched with the sample in the security vault in the laboratories run by the insurance firm in Beijing," Mya put in, adding her part to the puzzle. "Which was why I arrived late for the meeting in Hong Kong—just in time to find you snooping through the files on Chad's computer."

"That's not entirely true, is it, Mya," the Professor challenged weakly. "You were in fact scheduled to deposit the sample the following day, but you were forced to make an early rendezvous with Doctor Cyclops for one reason. The tracking device. You had to get rid of it. You didn't know about it until we were all on the plane. In fact, nobody knew about it, except myself and my men—and Sen."

Slowly Sen started to applaud. "I was wondering when you started to piece everything together. Always so sure of yourself, aren't you, Max. Let me remind you, you've made mistakes before. Even you've been guilty of trusting the wrong person in the past. What if you had been wrong this time? What if Chad had shot me?"

"You were the only one who knew about the tracking device. Only, by the time we told you, in the boardroom back in San Francisco, there was no time, no opportunity to tell the others. Not until we were on the jet and Mya escorted you to the bathroom. That's when you told her. That's when she changed plans. That's when she took my blood—"

"—and made it into mine," Sen said with satisfaction.

The Professor took a breath. A short breath, his chest tight, his heart heavy inside. "But why? You could have taken anyone's blood, you could have used the body of any man your age. Instead you risked everything to get me involved."

Sen stopped in front of the Professor and looked down at him, his face full of nothing but tortured hate. "Don't you see, Max? You turned my heart to ice and you didn't even know it. All my life, all I wanted was revenge."

But as Sen looked into Max's blind eyes, all he could see was the reflection of his own hate in the Professor's sightless gaze. Angrily he pulled himself away and walked over to the desk, where he unlocked the second drawer down. From it he took an old envelope, still sealed. On the front, handwritten in faded ink, was the name *Max*.

Sen took a daggerlike letter opener from the drawer and said, "I could open it, but whose heart would I be cutting out?"

Then he placed the letter opener down on the desk and pulled a lighter from the drawer instead. He triggered it with his thumb and a flame ignited. He held it to a corner of the envelope, then placed it gracefully, almost ritualistically, down on the desktop. The flaming envelope and its contents burned bright, charring the marble top.

Maximilian Fathom could smell the flames, he could smell the black smoke. And he knew then the damage he had done. That there was not a fire on earth that could melt the icy heart of Zhang Sen now.

It was far too late. And Max knew there was nobody to blame. Nobody but himself.

XIX

The Zhang Diamond Mines, Mountains of Shandong

SPARKLING CRYSTALLINE FLAKES OF SNOW DANCED AND drifted in the spherical silvery reflection of the orb. To Will, the sight seemed almost magical, something straight out of a small-town Christmas parade or a wondrous winter festival.

But the orb was not filled with magic or wonder. It was filled with zinc, iridium, and plutonium. It was filled with wires and a fail-safe timer. It was filled with death and the promise of mass destruction.

After rounding the ridge surrounding the frozen lake, the steam train had journeyed further south, heading higher into the mountains, passing more lantern-lit shacks and villages. At one point it passed a track switch where the railway line divided into two parallel tracks before merging into a single track again several miles up the line.

Eventually, with an exhausted puff and a sigh of steam

from the undercarriage of the engine, the train had arrived on the turntable terminal of the Zhang diamond mines near a mountain summit.

Sweating despite the freezing night air, Xi had slipped his shirt back on, shut off the vent to the furnace, and opened a small metal trunk near the rear of the engine compartment. Out of it he took a utility belt lined with small cylindrical grenade explosives. He strapped the belt around his waist before joining the others in the master carriage.

Will, Bradley, and the Professor were untied. Will and Bradley were ordered at gunpoint to help the Professor up and take him out into the cold and dark.

Mya alighted from the car first. Will and Bradley followed her, easing the badly injured Professor out of the car and into the falling snow.

Chad stayed close behind them, followed by Doctor Cyclops, who had by now retrieved his large cutting shears from the bedroom carriage, reluctantly leaving the unconscious Luca still strapped naked to the bed.

Xi carefully lifted one of the zidium devices out of its crate and carried it out into the drifting, dancing snow. It looked like a giant bauble on his arms, a perfect shining sphere, with the exception of the timer panel set into the curved surface, its small rectangular screen black and unactivated.

Richard watched Xi carry the bomb from the car and said, "I think I'll stay right here." He began sifting through a box of Cuban cigars sitting on the antique side table beside his lounge. "Don't get me wrong, you all know I love a little reckless adventure. But someone has to cover up the evidence if you lot blow yourselves to kingdom come."

"Perhaps you could make yourself useful by rotating the turntable track," Sen told him. "We want the train to be ready to return to Beijing as soon as we're done with the mines."

"Will do." Richard sighed, clipping the end off his chosen

cigar. "Once I'm through with this Cuban. Seems a shame to waste it, don't you think?"

Sen shook his head impatiently, then stopped in the doorway of the car and looked outside. From the higher vantage point he took in the sight of the mines—the source of his family's fortune for generations—one last time.

Mya had already entered the shedlike, snow-covered generator room located just beyond the circular turntable, and with a loud *Puumph* several dozen stadium-style lights ignited, drenching the area in bright white light.

To the right of the small circular rail yard Sen looked upon the main entrance to the mines, a massive opening carved into the mountain, at least six stories high. The round man-made entrance was constructed from cement and steel, but several meters inside the tunnel the cement work stopped. Beyond that the walls and ceiling of the mine were blasted rock and earth, supported at regular intervals by metal beams. A single track for mine cars was laid into the floor of the tunnel, with spotlights on either side like a nighttime runway. It disappeared into a luminous glow deep inside the mountain.

To the left, a quarry road led down to a second mine entrance that had been abandoned since the diamonds had all but dried up. The second mine was nothing but a half-excavated entryway that led directly to a deep and treacherous vertical shaft—a bottomless sinkhole that had opened up when the digging had begun. The sinkhole had now been cordoned off with planking and warning signs, while the Conrad Construction vehicles that had been used to unearth the mine were left scattered throughout the quarry.

A temporary portable office still remained at one end of the quarry, sitting on stacks of bricks, ready to be packed up, picked up, and shipped away at a moment's notice. Because the facade of an operational mine was the one thing

Sen, Chad, Mya, and Richard had wanted to maintain this entire time, the office remained. To keep their lies—and plans—a secret.

Sen looked at all this now, as well as the others:

He saw Xi holding the zidium device;

Chad and Mya each holding their guns;

Will and Bradley half naked and shivering, holding up the Professor.

Then with a great sense of peace, of accomplishment, he said: "Let's get richer!"

Jake blinked coal dust out of his eyes and cautiously lifted his head out of the heap. Beside him, Shane did the same, sending several chunks of coal rolling away. Beneath the bright, humming glow of the industrial lights they saw Will, Bradley, and the Professor being escorted toward the massive mine entrance. Without exchanging a word, both men knew that the chances of their friends returning from the mines were slim. But as Shane began to dig his way out of the black heap, Jake quickly caught his arm once again. "Someone's missing," he told Shane, counting heads. "Richard. Richard Conrad's still here somewhere."

On cue, the British billionaire jumped down from the master carriage, a satisfied smile on his face as he puffed on his Cuban. Shane hastily dropped back into the heap and half buried himself, staying low as he and Jake watched Richard strut across the circular turntable platform toward the generator shed.

As Richard opened the door to the small shed, several lumps of coal next to Shane's shivering, scantily clad ass rolled loose, clattering and bouncing down the heap and setting off a small avalanche that clanged loudly against the steel-sided coal car.

Richard heard the noise. He stopped and turned, slightly, eyes scanning the brightly lit yard, the embers of his cigar glowing. He did not linger. He already knew he wasn't alone. He remained composed and entered the shed—knowing there was a rifle inside.

As soon as Richard disappeared into the shed, Jake and Shane quickly scrambled, pulling themselves out of the coal and climbing down the side of the car.

Inside the shed, Richard took hold of the turntable controller that hung from the ceiling. It was a rectangular device, a brick with a key and two large punch buttons on it, one green, one red. He twisted the key to unlock the control and thumbed the green button. Then he reached for the cabinet where the rifle was stowed, a security measure to keep away wolves and other predators. Or in this case, intruders.

The ground outside hissed and groaned and the enormous turntable rumbled to life, slowly spinning counterclockwise, turning the train 180 degrees to face the way it had come, ready to deliver untold destruction to the people of Beijing.

As Jake and Shane jumped down from the coal car the ground beneath them began to move. But that proved to be the least of their problems. Between the twisting platform on which they stood and the main entrance to the mine was the generator shed. Or more accurately, Richard, standing outside the generator shed, holding a rifle.

BLAM!

Jake and Shane dropped as a bullet shell put a two-inch dent in the side of the coal car behind them, ricocheted, then rattled across the ground, quivering on the rumbling, turning platform where it lay.

"Shit!" Jake immediately scrambled under the coal car, followed by Shane.

From where he stood outside the stationary shed, Richard laughed and fired off another shot, missing Shane's scurrying bare ass by inches.

Hurriedly, Jake got behind one of the wheels and sat against it, pressing his back hard up to it, using it as a shield. Shane did the same with the wheel at the far end of the car. He peered around the rim of it, trying to gauge the growing distance between themselves and Richard as the platform turned, trying to guess the speed of rotation, when suddenly another bullet *ding*ed against the outer side of the wheel next to his head.

"Can you see him?" Jake called to Shane over the rumbling of the rotating turntable.

"Not without getting my damn head blown off!"

"Well, we can't stay here. We're just spinning around in one place."

"We could make a break for the mine?" Shane said it with a shrug. It was more a question than a suggestion.

Jake didn't have an answer. He peered around the curve of the wheel behind him and tried to cock his head enough to see the shed. It was gone from view. He turned and looked the other way, to the left of the car, to see if the shed was coming into view there as they continued to rotate. No sign of it.

"We're at ninety degrees," Shane said as the realization dawned.

"Which means?"

"Which means if Richard stayed where he was, it's impossible for us to see where he is. Unless of course—"

At precisely the same time, Shane and Jake both looked down the length of the undercarriages, all the way down the track, to see a smiling Richard come into view at the end of the train, squatting low, with his rifle in hand.

"Hello, Jake," he called down the length of the train. "What a surprise to see you here." Then, with cigar clenched between his teeth, he pumped off one, two, three shots straight down the barrel.

Sparks flew as the bullets scraped and pinged their way

down the narrow course between the tracks and the under-carriages. Shane bolted left, springing out from under the train. Jake launched himself right, somersaulting backward into the bright light. He leapt to his feet and saw the mine entrance in the distance.

Suddenly another bullet exploded in a starburst on the side of the coal car, just behind his head. "Jake!" he heard Shane shout from the other side of the car.

Jake glanced down toward the tail of the train and saw Richard emptying spent cartridges and reloading. He looked ahead of him, at the mine entrance, and knew he'd never make it.

The turntable was still rumbling, rotating. The mine was slipping away.

"Jake, get out of there! Now!"

Another blast from Richard's rifle was all Jake needed. He threw himself back under the coal car and scrambled to the other side, kicking his way free. Shane's hands had him by the shirt, dragging him out as fast as he could. "This way, hurry!"

As Jake pitched and stumbled to his feet the two of them sprinted for the far side of the yard, heading not for the mine entrance but in the opposite direction, their only escape—the quarry.

With a loud thud the rotating platform jolted to a halt. The train was now facing back toward Beijing. Jake and Shane stumbled away, disappearing quickly down the icy road that descended into the quarry.

At the rear of the train, Richard saw them vanish down the slope. The daredevil tycoon threw his rifle and Cuban away, grinning at the thought of a much more fun challenge in the pit below.

Against all expectation, the tunnel didn't slope down-ward into the mine but rather *ascended* into the heart of the mountain on a gentle gradient. The group followed the mine car tracks along the well-lit upward slope.

Carrying the Professor on either side were Will and Bradley. As they made their way toward the end of the tunnel, the old man wheezed and coughed and a thin line of blood ran from his lips. Will lovingly wiped it away with his thumb and fingers.

"Just make sure he doesn't die before he gets to the bottom," Chad muttered, observing the blood. "Otherwise you two will be carrying the dead weight."

The bottom, Will assumed, was at the base of the elevator shaft he could now see at the end of the tunnel. A large square mine car stood stationary at the end of the tracks that led them to the shaft, its sides dented and scraped by the millions of rocks it had carted back and forth over the years. Beyond that was a large elevator cage suspended above the vertical shaft.

Burning white bulbs fixed into the wall of the shaft illuminated the drop, which disappeared into a well of light.

Mya hauled open the cage door while Chad pushed Will, Bradley, and the Professor onto the steel grate of the elevator platform. Sen followed behind with Doctor Cyclops, who giggled as he clicked his shears in the air, and Xi, cradling the zidium device in his arms.

"Whatever you do, don't let go of that bomb," Chad warned Xi, triggering a button on the control box on one wall of the cage. With an ear-piercing whir and the grinding of winch gears the elevator sank clunkily down into the shaft.

Jake and Shane laced their way swiftly around the abandoned quarry machinery, scanning the area, looking for another way into the mines, all the while glancing behind them for any sign of Richard and his rifle.

Shane stopped Jake and pointed. "Over there."

Jake looked to see the massive, roughly excavated entry to the sinkhole, boarded up with planks and warning signs. "I don't like the look of that. What about there?" he said, gesturing to the small portable office perched on bricks at the opposite end of the quarry. "There must be blueprints or some kinda map to the mines inside. Come on."

The two hurriedly weaved their way through the vast array of machines and found the portable office unlocked. They slipped inside, Jake glancing back once more before closing the door and locking it behind him.

Inside, Shane closed the horizontal blinds and clicked on a small desk lamp. Jake had been right, the place was covered in blueprints and maps spread across several desks, along with mountains of construction equipment strewn across the floor. Back in Texas, cartography had been Shane's forte. He knew he could find a way into the mines if he could just get his hands on the right map. He started at a desk at one end of the small office and began rifling quickly through large sheets of paper. "Jake, help me here."

Jake, however, was at the other end of the office, peering suspiciously through the thin horizontal blinds, scanning for Richard in the dormant equipment outside. "Where the hell did he go?"

Shane didn't have an answer. He was too busy sliding sheets left and right, looking for a master blueprint. Then he found it. He turned to Jake excitedly.

But Jake was still staring through the blinds, eyes suddenly wide with horror.

Shane heard a rumble outside.

All Jake had time to do was turn and say, "Shane, hold on to something. Now!"

But before Shane could so much as move, the head of one of the excavators smashed through the side of the office with a deafening blow.

The entire office lurched. Shane was thrown to one end

of the building, Jake to the other, as the excavator's teeth shredded the thin aluminum wall, smashed the windows apart, and pulverized a desk in the middle of the office. The head reared left, taking out the entire wall and ripping through several filing cabinets, then pulled itself out of the wreckage before coming in for another swing, even harder than the first. This time its jaws clamped down on the roof and got hold of the small building, lifting it clear off its bricks and hurling it into the air.

The office twirled slowly as it sailed, then landed with an almighty crash that split it clean in two, sending each half rolling and spinning into pieces, spitting chairs, desks, tables, and Shane and Jake in different directions.

Shane hit the ground, bounced, then landed facedown. Instantly he felt the vibrations of an oncoming vehicle sending tremors through his torso, now pressed against the earth. He heard the grind and squeal of the excavator's caterpillar tracks grow louder and louder. He opened his eyes and leapt out of the way seconds before the churning tracks of the excavator had a chance to mince him into the ground.

Stumbling and slipping through the snow, Shane caught sight of a laughing Richard Conrad in the cab of the excavator. Richard rotated the cab now to face Shane, before sliding the machine into a turn and lining the cowboy up in his sights once more.

Shane looked around desperately. He knew he was no match for the excavator rumbling toward him at top speed, its neck craning high, open jaws ready to swoop. He needed a hiding place. Or better still—a beast of his own.

Ahead of him was a bulldozer, stout and built for defense. He made a bolt for it.

Jumping into the cab, he saw the key in the ignition. He turned it, and the bulldozer chugged into life just as the entire vehicle jolted. Shane shielded himself from the glass as the cab's windshield exploded inward. The head of Richard's excavator tried to claw at him through the broken opening, but the cab's frame was too narrow for the excavator's jaws.

Shane grabbed the nearest gearshift and yanked the bulldozer into reverse. At the same time he pulled hard on the blade lever. The bulldozer's front blade plate swung upward, knocking the excavator's head away from the smashed windshield and up into the air.

The excavator groaned, the front of its caterpillar tracks leaving the ground momentarily. It landed with a heavy thump, instantly regaining its sturdy, powerful stance.

The bulldozer retreated so rapidly Shane didn't see the drill rig behind him until it was too late. He backed into it, crumpling and fracturing the rear of his bulldozer until it became twisted in the thick hydraulic cables and chains of the vertical drill shaft.

Shane lowered the blade and saw the excavator coming for him once more. He ripped through the gears, trying to pull free of the drill rig. The bulldozer's mighty engine revved and whined, tracks spinning in the muddy snow. But the beast was locked in the web of the drill lines, now taut and straining.

Richard's excavator was tearing across the quarry toward Shane now, jaws snapping hungrily.

The bulldozer's gears began to burn, smoke billowing from its undercarriage as it tried to free itself. But it was a sitting duck. Shane tried to raise the blade again in an attempt to defend himself, but sparks burst from the blade lever as the vehicle's hydraulics blew under the strain.

The excavator had a clear run for its target. Richard cranked into top speed, sending two massive jets of mud soaring into the air behind the excavator's churning caterpillar tracks. Nothing would stop him from destroying Shane and the bulldozer now.

Nothing but the second excavator he couldn't see that attacked from the side—

—the one driven by Jake, smashing headlong into the side of Richard's excavator, crashing into it with all its force and knocking it off course, seconds before it could plow into Shane's bulldozer.

The two excavators slid and skidded through the icy sludge, pirouetting together through the dancing snow before they sailed apart and slid to a halt, facing one another.

Richard shook the dizziness from his head, a cut on his temple. He dabbed at it with the palm of his hand.

In the second excavator Jake eyeballed him. Through their cracked windshields their eyes locked. "Let's play," Jake challenged over the roar of their rumbling beasts.

Richard simply smiled. "Winner takes all."

Their hands gripped their gears and levers, and the two mechanical dinosaurs roared into life.

The temperature dropped as the elevator descended deeper and deeper into the mines. Will and Bradley shivered, but the chill they felt was nothing compared with that of the Professor, whose loss of blood had turned him a deathly pale. Will and Bradley held him close and tight between them, trying to share what little body heat they had left.

As the elevator continued to rattle and clang its way downward, the shaft opened out to reveal a vast excavated cavern lit by brightly burning floodlights generated from the mine's power grid.

The Professor's teeth chattered as he feebly lifted his head. "Sen, don't do this. You still have time to stop it. You still have a chance to do what's right."

"Don't lecture me on what's right, Max. At least I'm not under the delusion that I'm a good person."

"But you are. At least you were."

"And you changed all that. How ironic that the day you

lost your sight was the day I found my vision. My dream. I'm a different man now."

"You're a terrorist, that's what you are," Will interjected angrily.

Sen shook his head. "Terrorists do things for stupid reasons. For religion. For politics. Me? I'm doing it for the money. In today's world that makes me a businessman. An entrepreneur. A futurist!"

Suddenly the elevator thumped to a halt at the foot of the shaft.

Mya pulled open the cage door and Sen gestured to the vast cavern. "Welcome to the heart of the Zhang diamond mines. And your final resting place."

"From this location, the blast from the bomb will bring down every tunnel in the entire network," Chad added, motioning Will, Bradley, and the Professor out of the elevator with a flick of his gun. "This section of the mountain will literally vanish. By which time we'll be on our way back to Beijing to deliver the second bomb."

Sen saw Will shoot a wary look backward over his right shoulder at the device in Xi's arms. He couldn't help but laugh. "Oh, don't worry, Mr. Hunter, you won't feel a thing. When the device detonates you'll already be dead, lying here on the ground with a bullet in the head. Except of course you, Max. We're taking your head with us. Just to be sure. Loose ends make for bad beginnings."

Doctor Cyclops giggled deliriously.

Chad marched the captives toward the far end of the cavern. With a hard shove from behind the Professor grimaced in pain, his frail knees struggling. Will and Bradley did their best to prop him up.

"You'll be okay, Professor," Will assured him. "We'll get you outta here."

Mya's gloss-red lips shimmered in a smirk. "And how exactly do you plan on doing that?"

"With a bang" was Will's short, sharp answer.

Suddenly he left Bradley holding the Professor and spun quickly to face a startled Xi head on. He reached down with both hands. He ripped the pins from two of the small cylindrical grenades tucked into Xi's belt, one on his left, one on his right.

Xi gasped, still holding the zidium device in his arms.

Chad fired a hasty shot at Will and missed completely.

Mya pointed her pistol but couldn't get a clear shot with Chad in the way.

Doctor Cyclops screamed, dropped his shears, and ran as fast as he could in the other direction—toward the elevator.

Sen's eyes bulged with panic as he tried to stumble away from Xi. He ran forward, crashing straight into Bradley, who, still holding up the wounded Professor, lost his balance. All three men crashed to the floor of the cavern.

In the midst of the chaos, all Xi could do was drop the bomb. Literally. The zidium device fell from his arms like a payload falling from the bomb bay of a plane. Only instead of dropping 10,000 feet to its intended target, this shiny round payload fell a mere four feet from Xi's arms to the rocky floor of the cavern.

It hit the ground with a *clunk* and bounced.

With a beep, red digits appeared in the bomb's small display panel.

10:00:00

Ten minutes.

With another beep, the fail-safe mechanism kicked in, irreversibly.

The seconds began to tick away.

And the first of the two zidium devices began its countdown to disaster.

The excavators collided head on and bounced off each other, the thunder of the clash echoing through the quarry. Jake rocked in his seat. Chunks of metal were flung through the air. Snapped cables hissed.

Suddenly the cab of Richard's excavator twirled around, followed by the powerful swing of the beast's head. It slammed into the neck of Jake's excavator, knocking the entire machine into a spin across the muddy ice.

Jake pushed through the gears—forward, reverse—trying desperately to find some traction in the snow. But as his machine spun helplessly, Richard's monster attacked once more, its head swooping down from above. It sank its huge teeth deep into the top of the driver's cab as Jake's out-of-control machine continued to spin, and Richard's beast ripped the roof right off the cab like a giant can opener.

Just then, the tracks on Jake's excavator took hold, gripping the earth and churning up snow. But it was too late.

The head of Richard's machine came plunging down through the ripped-open roof of the cab, jaws chomping and thrashing. The upper jaw smashed against Jake's shoulder, breaking the bone. Jake screamed in pain as the head pinned him low against the back of the driver's seat. His arm was wrenched away from the gears and control levers, which vibrated just out of reach.

Richard snapped the beast's jaws again, trying to bite Jake in half. He missed by mere inches, the space inside the cab too small and the angle of the head unable to snag Jake's low-lying body.

Through his cracked windshield Richard watched and laughed. He looked beyond Jake's excavator then to see the boarded entrance to the bottomless sinkhole 50 or so feet away, directly behind Jake's machine. "Time to finish this," he said determinedly. He jerked the gears and his machine shoved forward, pushing Jake's machine backward, toward the sinkhole.

As the jaws continued to open wide and clamp shut above him, Jake pressed himself lower into the driver's seat.

The fingertips of his uninjured arm reached desperately for the control lever. They brushed the top of it, but he couldn't get a grip.

Snap! Snap! He felt the air rush through his hair with every chomp of the ravenous jaws.

Push! Richard's machine forced Jake's excavator another 10 feet toward the abandoned shaft, the tracks of his machine turning up gray sludge like a snowplow.

Jake managed to lift his head a fraction, enough to see through the broken rear panel of the cab; enough to see he was being nudged toward the boarded sinkhole entrance.

He grimaced with the pain. "Oh, this is not good."

The countdown had begun.

As the timer on the zidium device activated itself, Xi reached desperately for the two unpinned grenades in his belt.

His left hand snatched one of the explosives as though he was a gunfighter in a quick draw. He flicked the live grenade across the cavern floor, straight toward the fallen heap that was Sen, Bradley, and the Professor.

Will watched it scuttle across the ground toward them. He launched himself into a dive, sliding painfully across the rocky ground, far enough to give the grenade a backhanded hit that knocked it a few feet further away.

Xi fumbled for the second grenade, juggling it loose and hurtling it into the air before joining Mya, Chad, and Doctor Cyclops in the sprint for the elevator.

The second grenade landed square in Bradley's lap as he sat up from the fall.

"Oh, shit!" He scooped it out recklessly with both hands.

It sailed through the air—

—hit the still-bouncing zidium device—

—then ricocheted straight back at them.

"Get down!" Will shouted, not thinking about the fact that they already were down. He covered Bradley and the Professor, one arm shielding each of them.

Tink-tink-tink!

The grenade hit the ground and trickled toward them, then—

Boom!

Followed closely by—

KA-Boom!

The first grenade exploded, followed instantly by the second.

The cavern trembled. Rock, rubble, and dust blasted into the air.

Mya, Chad, Xi, and Cyclops bent down and covered their heads momentarily before continuing their desperate dash for the elevator, none of them looking back.

As Will tried to shake the ringing out of his ears, he slowly lifted his head and peered through his eyelids a fraction, trying to look through the veil of dust. A split second later his eyes shot open in panic.

"Get up!"

He tried to pull Bradley and the Professor to their feet, but he was too late. The two grenades had set off two mini-quakes, one on either side of the men, each opening up a crevasse that quickly ate its way in a wide arc, encircling them until the entire crust of earth beneath them fell away like a giant china plate falling to the floor.

Into the darkness below.

Taking Will, Bradley, Sen, the Professor, and the zidium bomb with it.

Cruuuuunnch!

The ice and snow continued to compact against the tracks of Jake's excavator with another long heave from Richard's machine.

Chomp! The huge steel teeth of the machine clanged sharply together, trying to get to Jake.

Push! Jake's machine backed through the boards and planks crisscrossing the entrance to the short tunnel that led to the sinkhole. The wood broke apart easily, the warning signs flipping to the ground before smashing apart under the weight of the excavator.

Jake peered once more through the rear panel of the cab. Across the rocky floor of the unfinished tunnel he could make out the massive black chasm of the sinkhole only 10 feet or so away. Frantically he looked for something to hold on to, knowing one more shove would be enough to—

Shove! The tracks of the excavator slid across the tunnel floor and over the edge of the sinkhole. The machine came to a stop halfway over the edge of the black hole.

For a moment it teetered on the brink. Jake felt the entire vehicle seesaw, dipping over the hole, then correcting itself, and then—

With a loud groan Jake's excavator tipped into the hole, its tracks sliding down the edge, sending a rockfall into the chasm with the excavator behind it.

Jake had no way out. He glanced through the smashed glass at the laughing face of Richard Conrad, who jerked his control levers, about to shut the jaws of the excavator and pull the head free of Jake's doomed machine.

But in the second before Richard managed to clamp the jaws shut and lift the head clear, Jake shot a glance upward into the gaping jaws of the excavator. He saw the dangling tendrils of the hydraulics.

He reached up with his good arm, as high as he could, up into the mouth of the beast, and snatched a handful of squirming cables. Then he pulled as hard as he could, severing the hydraulics with a hiss and a howl.

Instead of closing, the jaws snapped apart, locking themselves wide open. Too wide for Richard to lift the head of the beast out of the shattered cab and free himself.

"Oh, shit," Richard breathed, wrestling with the levers.

Jake glared at him through the shards of glass. "If I'm goin' down, *you're* comin' with me."

As the weight of Jake's machine slid backward into the chasm, it began pulling Richard's machine with it.

Richard stood on the brakes but the tracks of his excavator simply rattled and bounced across the rocky surface, crushing stones and tearing two wide gutters in the earth; gravity was simply too powerful to stop him from following Jake's beast over the edge.

With a jolt, Jake's vehicle twisted and tipped into a vertical position, metal moaning, accelerating Richard's approach to the chasm.

Jake fell against the broken back panel of the cab, nothing but blackness and a long plunge beneath him. The cracked glass splintered even more beneath his weight.

Richard tried to jam his own vehicle in reverse, unwilling to let go of the brake. The gears shrieked, the engine revved, but the edge was approaching too fast.

He had to jump. And jump now.

The tracks of his machine were dragged over the edge.

He knew as soon as he took both feet off the brake the chasm would instantly suck both machines down. He pushed open his door, still standing on the brake, ready to launch himself out of the cab and away from the hole as far and as fast as he could.

The machine tilted downward with a fierce jerk.

Richard lifted his feet off the brake, ready to send Jake plummeting alone to his death. He turned for the door. And in the same moment, he heard something whip through the air.

A giant hook punctured the roof of his cab. The line twanged taut. Twisting the sliding excavator. Knocking Richard back into his seat just as the machine toppled over the edge.

"Gotcha!" Shane cried, grinning determinedly. He had roared toward the tunnel entrance inside a giant mobile crane, swung the 60-foot latticed boom of the crane as far back as he could, then hurled it forward, letting the line go at just the right moment.

But the catch was heavier than the cowboy had bargained for. As the hefty combined weight of Jake's and Richard's excavators dropped into a free fall, the line of the crane snapped tight, metal buckled, and the pull of the excavators yanked the entire boom of the straining crane flat to the ground before dragging the long-necked machine at full speed toward the tunnel as well.

Inside the cab of his falling excavator, Jake's weight shattered the last of the glass. He dropped through it but managed to grab on to the twisted rim of the cab with his good arm.

At the same time, Richard fell toward the open doorway of his own cab, trying to grab on to something, anything, before tumbling out. His hands hooked the edge of the door. The hinges twisted, threatening to break altogether as the door swung wide and bent the wrong way. It slammed against the side of the excavator, barely clinging to the cab while Richard barely managed to cling to *it*.

As the two machines continued to fall, Shane's crane cut through the snow toward the tunnel. The 60-foot boom snaked inside, then bent and buckled and twisted downward into the sinkhole, following the plunging excavators, pulling the cabin of the crane after it with Shane inside.

Shane's eyes widened at the sight of the approaching black hole. He held on even tighter. With a moan, the cabin of the crane was pulled over the edge of the sinkhole.

Shane put his bare feet on either side of the wide dash in front of him as the cabin fell forward. The entire view in front of him tipped downward, into the bottomless black chasm.

Shane shut his eyes.

And then—

—with the screech of rock chewing into metal and a gigantic jolt—

—the wide base of the outrigger wedged itself in the opening of the sinkhole.

The crane and the two excavators snapped to a halt.

Shane fell with a grunt against the windshield of the crane's cab and heard the cracking of glass.

A hundred feet below him, the jolt broke the hinges off Richard's dangling door, sending both Richard and the door plummeting 15 feet before crashing onto Jake's excavator.

At the same time, Jake held on to the shattered rim of his cab with his one good arm, three of his fingers sliding loose, with nothing between him and the abyss below. He glanced up and saw Richard on the front of the cab, still clinging to the dislodged door.

Richard in turn glanced down and saw Jake dangling helplessly.

An eerie groan of metal echoed up and down the shaft as the two excavators swung gently, like a broken pendulum waiting to drop.

High above them, Shane tried to lift himself off the windshield, but as soon as he did so the pressure of his weight sent more cracks trickling across the glass. He shot a look over his shoulder and saw the retraction switch for the boom. He needed to get to it before the glass shattered so he could try to winch Jake up to safety.

"Jake? You down there?" Shane's voice traveled down the abyss.

It gave Jake hope. Just enough for him to hook one of the fingers that had slipped back onto the rim of the mutilated cab. "Yeah, I'm here!" he called back, then whispered to himself, "just barely."

Then came Shane's reply, bouncing down the walls of

the sinkhole. "I suggest you grab hold of something. I'm pullin' you up!"

"Oh, Jesus, I'm trying," Jake muttered. Ignoring the daggers in his bad shoulder, he quickly lifted his other arm up, knowing that when Shane said hold on, he meant it!

Suddenly Shane launched himself for the retraction switch. The glass beneath the cowboy broke. His finger hit the button.

Jake's injured arm reached up and hooked the rim of the cab just as the excavators lurched into motion once more, this time being pulled upward.

As his finger slipped from the switch, gravity sent Shane through the cracked windshield. He tried to grab levers and gearshifts as he fell, missing them all before knocking the wind out of himself as his torso slammed into the boom below. He grabbed desperately, his arms catching on the latticed neck of the crane, hands hooking the beam, bare legs swinging out from under him, then slamming back against the boom.

As the automatic retractor began to haul the twisted, conjoined excavators upward, the pull on the crane sent rocks tumbling from the sides of the sinkhole as the strain on the wedged outrigger increased.

Richard let go of the door and gripped the cab of Jake's excavator with both hands.

The door slid from his grasp and fell over the edge, flipping and twirling through the air, narrowly missing Jake before spinning into the dark depths. Jake and Richard stared into the blackness below, waiting to hear the door crash on the bottom. They stared unnervingly long. When the sound of impact finally came, it was faint and far below.

Jake glanced back up. He knew he had to get past Richard before the whole thing came crashing down.

But Richard was already climbing. He too knew the only way was up—and fast!

More rocks showered down around them from the crumbling walls of the sinkhole as the crane's outrigger dropped a few more feet, slowly surrendering to the drag from the ascending excavators.

Shane began to spider the boom down toward Jake. "Jake! You might wanna hurry, pal!" Another shudder and another short drop put even more urgency in Shane's descent.

"Would you quit stating the damn obvious!" Jake shouted back, annoyed and panicked, pulling himself up painfully by his good arm and his badly wounded one. Peering up, he saw Richard clamber up the side of his own excavator cab, pulling his way past the opening where the cab door had once been. Richard grabbed the giant hook jutting out of the cab's roof, then took a firm hold of the retractor cable with both hands. It sent vibrations down his arms as it pulled the two excavators swiftly toward the boom above.

Richard glanced downward with glee, watching Jake straddle the neck of Richard's excavator with great effort and begin to pull himself up.

Then, suddenly—*CRUNCH!* The retractor cable ran out. The excavators' ascent slammed to a halt at the point of the crane's boom.

The impact was accompanied by a bloodcurdling scream: Richard had been looking down at Jake when his hands, still gripping the cable, were pulverized in the collision, his forearms now wedged between the giant hook and the point of the boom.

The impact rocked all three of the huge, precariously placed machines.

The outrigger of the crane screeched another 10 feet down the sides of the sinkhole, triggering another small avalanche.

The rocks pelted Richard's excavator and one of the wheel tracks unraveled, sending a string of muddy, ice-caked steel treads raining down on Jake's excavator. The hammering caused the locked-open jaws of Richard's excavator to finally dislodge, sending Jake's dented, twisted machine plunging silently into the darkness below.

At the same time, Jake—still clinging to the steely neck of Richard's excavator—lost his grip and slid all the way down till he thumped against the creature's head, catching one of its huge rusted teeth just in time to stop himself.

Almost at the bottom of the crane's boom now, Shane watched in horror as Jake swung from the open jaws of the remaining excavator, once again with nothing between him and certain death.

Swiftly Shane reached the tip of the vertical boom and only now got a good look at where the screams were coming from. At first it looked like Richard was hugging the end of the boom, legs buckled, head pressed against the cold steel. Then Shane saw the blood running down his pinned forearms, flowing from the now red metal connection between hook and boom. Shane swung from the boom and landed deftly, lightly, on the dangling excavator.

"Help me!" Richard spat demandingly through his foaming agony.

Without hesitating, Shane sized up the situation and took hold of the retractor cable, pulling down on it with all his might, trying in vain to ease the pressure.

High above, the crane's outrigger gave another rumble, this time carving out 10, 20 feet of rock from the sides of the walls, dropping fast, then stopping, threatening to give way altogether at any moment.

"Hurry, you fucking fool!" Richard screamed at Shane. "Get me out of here now!"

Shane saw the pain in Richard's glazed eyes. But he also saw the slippery glint of self-preservation as well. He let go of the cable and glanced down to see Jake, his friend, desperately holding on to the excavator's teeth below.

With no time to lose, Shane made a choice.

He straddled the neck of the excavator and slid down its length, then held out his hand and said to Jake, "Let's get the fuck out of here! Now!"

Jake's palm slapped against Shane's. Together they clambered up the neck of the excavator and onto the cab.

Richard shot an enraged glare at the Texas cowboy, then a desperate one at Jake.

"Jake, help me! Get me out of here! I'll give you anything you want. Money, jewels, men!"

"Like I said before," Jake told him, "I don't want your damn prizes."

The crane groaned, gave a few more feet, and the three men jolted.

"Then tell me, what do you want?" Richard bargained frantically. "Name it, it's yours!"

Nursing his injured shoulder, Jake simply leaned into Richard's face and said, "I wanna stop that bomb!"

Then he turned away, and with Shane's help the two climbed as fast as they could up the boom, hand over hand, one foot up at a time, swiftly maneuvering through the metal lattice, leaving behind the echoing cries of Richard Conrad.

"You come back! I'll kill you! I'll kill you both with my own—"

Then, suddenly, a quake rippled down the boom as the outrigger began to give way completely.

Rocks fell away from the sides of the sinkhole. The entire shaft trembled with the weight of the crane sliding down into it. The sinkhole itself seemed to let out a roar with the thunderous echoes of falling rocks and grinding metal, opening its throat wide to swallow the descending crane.

Shane and Jake hauled ass.

They reached the cabin of the capsized crane, climbed up onto the underside of the outrigger, and with one quick glance at each other the two men sprang from the free-falling crane and latched on to the walls of the sinkhole.

As their feet left the outrigger—

—as their fingers clawed the rock wall and held on for dear life—

—they heard the last screams of Richard Conrad, along with the final moans of his machines, twisting and writhing into the darkness below.

Shane and Jake shut their eyes and waited for the sound of the crash, deep within the earth.

When it came, it echoed slowly, all the way up the sinkhole.

After a moment, Jake turned to Shane.

"Thanks, cowboy."

Shane tried to smile, then glanced upward, a little daunted. "Thank me when we get to the top."

"Well, if it's any consolation, it's a longer way down than it is up."

And with that, the two started climbing as fast as they could.

As the two grenades went off, sending a section of the cavern floor into the unknown along with Will, Bradley, Sen, the Professor, and the zidium device, Doctor Cyclops knew, as did Mya, Chad, and Xi, that the countdown to the bomb's detonation was ticking down, and nothing in the universe would stop it now.

With his one wide eye he saw the elevator almost within reach. Then Xi, Mya, and Chad bolted past him.

"You're work here is no longer needed," Chad told him as he sprinted past. "Consider your contract terminated!"

Doctor Cyclops shrieked and raced after the others. "Wait! Don't leave me here!"

Chad, Mya, and Xi had every intention of doing so, but as the three of them jumped into the elevator cage, the doctor scrambled on board with them. Xi seized him in an effort to try to evict him, but Doctor Cyclops kicked and screamed like a cat. Chad pulled Xi away. "No time. We'll figure out what to do with him later." He quickly nodded to Mya, who slammed the elevator cage door shut and punched the large green button in the control box.

"Mya, time check!" Chad snapped. "We have a new schedule."

Mya guessed that the zidium device had activated its destruct mechanism no longer than a minute earlier. As the elevator began to ascend with a whine and a clatter of cables, she clicked her watch to set its timer. "Nine minutes. And counting."

The rocky plate of earth crashed to the floor of a deeper, never-explored subcave of the main cavern. Will, Bradley, Sen, and the Professor all tumbled and rolled as the section of rock broke apart on the uneven ground of the hidden cave.

Registering the *ding-ding-ding* of the zidium device through his ringing ears, Will picked himself up instantly. Shimmering glints of silver, illuminated by the rays of light that shone down from the cavern above, pinpointed the path of the zidium as it bounced further into the darkness, eventually rolling to a halt a few feet away.

And all Will could see was the red digits on its display panel.

8 minutes.

34 seconds.

Beside that was a blur of numbers counting down the fractions of each second.

Will knew they couldn't afford to let a single red digit slip away.

"We have to get out of the mine! Now!"

Trying to be gentle in his haste, Will pulled the Professor to his feeble feet and began stumbling toward the wall of the newly formed well. It was shallow, and the floor of the cavern had collapsed in a way that made the wall not so much a vertical face, but rather a steep yet climbable rocky staircase. "Bradley! Come on!"

But Bradley had caught sight of his uncle, who had managed to rise to his feet and was staring into the darkness of the cave. The old man was now staring not at the zidium, but at something else altogether. Something he wasn't expecting to see. Not now.

"It's beautiful," he whispered.

"Uncle?" Bradley shot a glance between his mesmerized uncle and Will, who was struggling to get the Professor up the huge broken boulders leading to the cavern above.

"Bradley! Hurry, we have to go now!" Will shouted.

"Uncle? You have to come with us!"

Through his pain, the Professor could hear Bradley plead with his uncle. "Will, stop for a moment."

"We don't have a moment!" Will argued.

The Professor placed a hand on Will's chest. "Please. For me."

Will sucked in a deep, restrained breath, then turned the Professor around. "Sen," the Professor called with all the volume he could muster. "Listen to your nephew. You have to come with us. Whatever you've done, whatever *I've* done, let it be. Come with us, now."

"I can't, Max. Don't you see? It's beautiful!" Sen called back, not taking his eyes off the darkness.

The Professor simply shook his head. "No, Sen, I can't see. You were one of the last things I ever saw in my life. Remember? Come with us!"

Bradley had by now made his way down to his uncle and took him by the shoulder. He noticed blood trickling from the old man's forehead, a blow from the fall. "Uncle Sen, come with me now. You've hit your head, you're seeing things—"

"No!" Sen said, shaking Bradley off. "Look at them all! Like a thousand stars! Look at the diamonds! There *are* more diamonds here, after all! More than I could have imagined!"

He took Bradley's jaw in his hand then and turned his face toward the darkness. After a while, Bradley saw them too. After his uncle held his jaw tightly in place for a moment. After his eyes adjusted to the pitch black.

A sparkle. Small at first. Then glimmering brightly before spreading into the black.

Five sparkles. Six. 20. A hundred.

Then thousands upon thousands of diamonds appeared, swirling along the walls of the undiscovered cave, forming shimmering veins and brilliant new constellations within the rock.

Sen laughed excitedly, greedily. "It's mine. It's mine!"

Then Bradley's eye caught sight of something not sparkling and white, but red and very man-made. The digits of the bomb. "Uncle, we have to go."

"No!" Sen snapped. He turned aggressively and slapped his nephew before tugging himself free of his grip once more, stumbling further into the glittering cave.

"Uncle!"

"Bradley! We have to go!" Will shouted. "Right now!" He looked to the Professor then, holding on tight to the elder man's arm hoisted over his shoulders, and said softly, "We have to go, Professor. I'm sorry."

All the Professor could do was nod. Reluctantly. Regretfully. "I know. I'm sorry too. More than he'll ever know."

"Bradley!" Will called.

Bradley hesitated for a long, agonizing moment. He recalled moments in his childhood when his uncle would tell him stories down by the pond where the goldfish popped bubbles on the lily-filled surface. He remembered the day his parents died in the car accident, and he remembered the man who held him in his arms and promised that he would protect him forever. He recalled being told that the stars were his, so long as he followed in his uncle's footsteps, so long as he trusted the family dream and not his own. At that moment Bradley understood that the man trying to reach for the stars was no longer his uncle.

With a tear-filled sigh Bradley Zhang turned away, and against the cavern's lights above he saw the silhouette of Will and the Professor.

"I'm coming!"

Mya hauled open the cage door moments before the elevator slammed to an abrupt halt at the top of the shaft. She, Chad, and Doctor Cyclops began the dash down the sloped tunnel toward the exit, where the train awaited them. Only Xi remained at the elevator shaft a moment longer, unclipping two more of the grenades from his belt.

He jammed one into the cable winch at the top of the elevator's cage and another into the control box on the wall of the elevator, then pulled both pins and ran.

Xi made it 50 feet down the incline of the tunnel before the explosives sent a short, sharp *boom* down the mine.

The next sound he heard as he continued his sprint, quickly catching up with the others, was something like a missile plummeting toward earth as the elevator behind him plunged to the bottom of the shaft.

Will got to the last busted boulder at the edge of the hole in the cavern when the Professor finally floundered and lost his step.

But Bradley was there to catch him.

With Will's help, the two young men eased the Professor out of the darkness and up into the light, where Will and Bradley took an arm each and, lifting his feet literally off the ground, carried the Professor between them, hurrying him toward the elevator shaft. They got to within 10 feet of it before Will hesitated.

"Do you hear that?"

Before Bradley could even answer, the elevator cage came hurtling down the shaft and crumpled on impact in front of them, knocking all three men clear off their feet.

In the wake of a wave of dust and rolling nuts and broken bolts, Will sat up and whispered to himself, "Holy shit, we're screwed!"

Chad jumped up into the master carriage as fast as he could, allowing Mya to follow him but stopping Xi on the steps by placing a boot firmly on the snow-haired man's chest. "For fuck's sake, get to the engine now! Start this train and get us the fuck out of here!"

"Seven minutes, fifteen seconds," Mya reported without being prompted.

As Xi peeled away toward the engine, Doctor Cyclops caught up to them, howling in panic. Chad grabbed the front of his scruffy jacket and hauled his frail, rickety ass aboard. "You! Come with me! If there's one of the old man's boys still aboard this train, he better be dead. Otherwise, you will be!"

Doctor Cyclops whimpered and fell limp, blubbering, as Chad dragged him toward the back exit of the car. Chad juggled his gun and the doorknob with one hand, holding on to the doctor with the other, then turned to Mya. "Get the diamonds, activate the zidium device, and set the timer for Beijing. I'll get the chopper started, then let's get the hell off this continent. I'm so damn sick of Chinese food."

Mya took her orders and set her sights on the second silver bomb still sitting in its crate.

Chad left the car with Doctor Cyclops in tow. He hauled him into the car where Luca remained strapped to the bed.

The soft groans Luca uttered indicated that not only was he still alive, he was slowly waking from one of the good doctor's nasty concoctions.

Chad threw Doctor Cyclops to the floor, where he landed in a cowering heap. "Jesus Christ! Finish the job! Or would you prefer I did it for you?" With a sharp snap Chad cocked the hammer on his gun and marched over to the bed.

"No!" Doctor Cyclops begged.

But Chad ignored him. He reached the bed, pushed his gun against Luca's temple, put his finger on the trigger, then—

Choof!

Outside, the sound of the first puff of steam erupted from the engine's stack.

The train gave a small restless lurch, getting ready for its departure. Which was exactly what Chad wanted to do—depart. Time was running out. Getting the chopper ready to leave was more important than a man strapped to a bed on a train that was doomed anyway.

He pulled his gun away and decided to save the bullet. "Fine. Do it yourself." Turning away, he headed for the door to the flatbed car carrying the chopper. Out of sight and earshot of the doctor, he smiled and said, "Take your time. At least it'll keep you entertained on your return trip to Beijing. I'm sure you'll have a blast."

Through the wreckage of the construction machinery graveyard, Jake and Shane bolted, heading up the quarry road just in time to see the first white burst of steam mushroom into the snow-filled air and cloud the moon.

Choof!

"The others. They wouldn't leave without us," Shane reasoned.

"Which means they're still in the mines," Jake said. "Come on."

They skidded, slid, sprinted across the snow and charged into the massive entrance of the main mine, running uphill, following the mine car track to the peak of the elevator shaft before coming to a halt at the sight of the blasted winch gears.

"Will!" Jake shouted, hurrying to the edge of the shaft. "Professor!?"

At the bottom of the shaft, Will was trying to pull the bent, twisted metal of the smashed elevator cage out of the way to assess the damage when the three of them heard Jake's voice echo down the shaft. Will quickly pulled himself inside the warped cage and shouted upward. "Jake! We're okay, but the elevator's history! And I hate to tell you this, but there's a ticking bomb down here! We're talkin' minutes!!"

Shane was already sizing up the situation, eyeing the pulley cradle that had held the cables, attached to the roof of the tunnel directly above the shaft. He began pulling at cranks and busted wheels in the winch gears. "Jake, this thing's gone to God."

"I think we're all about to join it."

Shane grabbed a broken metal rod. "Maybe I could figure out a way we could lever it up. If we could find a cable maybe we could winch it ourselves."

"We don't have time!" Jake's shoulder ached and he held it tight, trying to think, trying to figure out—

Choof! Choof!

The sound of the train building momentum echoed up the tunnel, infuriating him even more. And then—

—enlightening him.

"Wait a minute. What did you just say?"

"Maybe we could lever it up."

"After that."

Shane shrugged. "If we had a cable maybe—"

"Shut up and run!"

Jake was already bolting back down the tunnel, away from the elevator shaft. Shane didn't ask why. He simply bolted after him.

In the engine compartment of the train, Xi frantically shoveled coal into the furnace, building up as much heat as the steam engine could take. Gauges and dials flicked and climbed rapidly.

In the master carriage, Mya knelt beside the second zidium device and began entering numbers into the activation panel. The panel flashed; the bomb was ready for its instructions. Mya instinctively checked her watch for an estimated arrival time to Beijing, and caught a glimpse of the first zidium's remaining time. Five minutes, 37 seconds. She gave a shiny bloodred smile, then began to punch in the Beijing bomb's countdown.

In the bedroom carriage, Doctor Cyclops rifled through his medical bag for a small bottle of multicolored pills, emptied a random amount into his trembling hand, and tipped them down his cracked dry throat, chewing on the last few that refused to slide down. His nerves seemed to calm instantly. He snatched up his rusty scalpel, then smiled as the handsome Italian on the bed stirred. It seemed Luca would be awake for his own dissection after all.

On the flatbed car, in the freezing wind and snow, Chad gripped one of the chains holding the chopper in place as the train finally lurched into motion. He glanced at the mine entrance and grinned. "See you later, Sen. Don't take it personally—it's business. I'm sure you understand." Then, as the wheels of the train began to rumble slowly into motion, he started unclasping the belts and chains that restrained his getaway helicopter.

Out of the corner of his eye, Jake saw the train let out another puff of steam. He heard the icy wheels finally find traction. Metal groaned and the couplings between the cars clanged and jolted as the Zhang Diamond Express rolled slowly into motion. He poured on the speed, racing not toward the train, but back down the quarry road, down into the graveyard of cranes and bulldozers.

Behind him, Shane wondered where the hell Jake was going. The mine was about to blow! The train was about to go! So why the hell were they headed back down to the—?

Suddenly Shane realized exactly what Jake was doing. He shot a sideways glance at the train as it slowly gained momentum. He sized up the distances in his head. And he too sprinted faster than he had ever sprinted in his life.

Jake practically crashed into the wreckage of the shredded portable office, its contents scattered across the ice. He saw coils of cables, long steel cables. He scooped one of them up just as Shane came sliding to a halt in the snow.

"Wait! That's not enough! We need two." Shane snatched up a second heavy looped coil, then the two bolted side by side back up the quarry road to the rail yard.

"You get the train," Jake said, grabbing the large end clasp from his own cable and connecting it to Shane's.

"No, you get the train," Shane asserted as they reached the top of the road, still running. "The mine's too dangerous."

"And the goddamn train's getting away. We don't have time to argue!" And with that Jake shoved Shane in the direction of the train, at which point Shane had no choice. Every second, every inch of cable, mattered.

Jake ran for the mine entrance, carrying his coiled cable.

Shane raced after the rear of the train, carrying his.

Between them the two clasped cables began to unloop, growing longer and longer as the distance between the two men quickly grew.

The train was chugging, still finding its pace, picking up speed. Shane was running his heart out, allowing the cable to unspool behind him as he jumped onto the tracks and pursued the train with all he had.

But before Shane could reach it, the locomotive matched his pace, then began to really pick up speed as it started to descend around the mountain. Shane gave it even more, leaping over the crossties of the tracks. He took the remaining end of the cable in one hand, opening the clasp as the rest of it continued to rapidly unravel. He got to within 10 feet of the train, pushing himself closer inch by inch, pushing himself faster second by second, ready to hook the cable onto the rear car—

—if only he could reach it.

The grind and squeal of the wheels grew louder as the train picked up speed. And Shane knew this was the closest he was going to get. The train was gradually beginning to slip away from him.

"Not so fast, you son of a bitch!"

He skidded to a halt. He quickly looped the end of the cable into a ring. He circled it quickly above his head like a lasso and hurled the steel loop as hard as he could. It whipped through the air, the cable's end snagging the chopper's tail.

"Yee-hah!" Shane crowed, panting with exertion, then quickly turned and raced back up the tracks toward the mine.

At the other end of the still unraveling cable, Jake charged up the mine tunnel toward the elevator shaft, shouting at the top of his lungs.

"Will! Will, can you hear me!"

Jake's voice echoed down the shaft as Will was still desperately looking for another way out. "Jake! I can hear you! We're runnin' outta time down here!"

"There's a cable comin' your way! You get one shot!" The cable began to snap and whip loose from Jake's grip.

He saw the shaft coming up and the winch pulley on the ceiling. "Get everyone on the elevator now!"

Down below, Will shot an urgent glance at Bradley, who was already easing the fragile Professor onto the tangled elevator platform.

Above, Jake opened the clasp at the free end of the cable, ready for Will to grab and hook onto whatever he could, then swung it high as he continued to sprint. The cable cut into the air, hit the roof of the tunnel just above the pulley, then dropped in a fast, vertical fall down the shaft.

"Incoming!" Jake shouted.

Hurriedly Will pulled away a broken section of the top of the elevator cage and saw the cable snaking down the shaft at full velocity. Suddenly the open clasp of the cable smashed against the top of the cage, inches from Will's head.

Like lightning, his hand grabbed it. Will hooked the clasp onto a steel bar on the top of the cage. The cable whipped tight, all the way up the length of the shaft. Suddenly the elevator carrying Will, Bradley, and the Professor took off up the shaft like a rocket.

The chopper reared up, snapped against its chains, then slammed back down on the flatbed. Chad had yet to release the restraints holding down the landing skids of the helicopter, but the jolt was enough to knock him off his feet and onto the icy flatbed. "What the fuck?"

With the shock of the jolt he didn't hear the crunch and grind of the lasso cable tighten its lock on the tail's boom. Instead he turned his head to the squall that was building above them, thinking the chopper had been picked up and dropped back down by the wind.

Now more than ever, all he cared about was getting this bird in the air before heaven descended upon them and hell erupted from below.

Back in the dark cave below, Zhang suddenly stopped in his excited tracks.

At first he thought he'd approached the end of the cave. In the blackness it was impossible to tell, but that strange sixth sense, that inbuilt radar, told him that his path was blocked. And he realized he was no longer alone.

The old man stood for a moment, lost in this dazzling dark world, speckled with diamonds—*his* diamonds—all around him, feeling the drip of his own blood down his temple, and sensing—

Suddenly the old man gasped.

Directly in front of him, only a few feet away, a cluster of diamonds appeared in the shape of an eye.

No, they didn't just appear. They *opened*. The glittering, diamond-filled eye before him opened.

It looked into his soul.

Then another eye, made up of another thousand tiny diamonds, opened beside it.

"Fucanglong," the old man breathed in sheer terror.

His wounded head swirled. He tried to step back but tripped on a rock and fell. He shut his eyes tight, knowing that the last thing he would ever see was the eyes of the dragon god of the underworld. A god that would protect its treasures at any cost, and destroy all those who tried to steal them.

Sen began to whimper. As the seconds on the zidium device in the cave behind him ran out, the dragon god inhaled and let loose his mighty roar.

The red digits sped toward finality then suddenly froze on *00:00:00*, and for a moment the whole world seemed to stop. Then the silver ball gave off a buzz, like a magnetic drone that increased in volume, seeming to suck the very space and air from its surroundings.

The blast was so fierce it completely vaporized the cave

of diamonds. It pushed outward in all directions in a white wave of destruction, letting nothing stand in its way.

The ceiling of the cave lifted up into the cavern above, breaking apart, then consumed completely by the blast. Boulders were pushed into the air and shattered to smithereens. Walls disappeared before they even had a chance to collapse. The wave roared down every tunnel extending from the vast cavern, then gushed upward, tunneling its destruction up the elevator shaft.

Will looked down through the steel grate of the elevator platform as the cage rocketed upward. His eyes shone in the reflection of the blast wave rushing up beneath them, devouring the walls of the shaft. "Oh, *FUCK!*" he cried.

Outside, on the train tracks, Shane stopped running at the sound of a powerful *oomph!* deep inside the mountain, so low and resonant it sent a shudder through the earth, followed by a ripple that buckled the train tracks. He started running back to the mine as fast as he could.

In the engine compartment of the Zhang Diamond Express Xi felt the tremor, then heard the screech of the train's wheels as they scraped against the warping tracks. He started shoveling more and more coal through the large open door of the engine's furnace, feeding the hungry fire and pushing the train to go even faster.

In the master carriage, the diamond-tipped crystals dangling from the chandeliers tinkled in panic. Mya looked up and felt the tremor ripple through the room.

In the bedroom carriage, the walls, the floor, and the bed rumbled. It was enough to shake Luca out of his groggy state of semiconsciousness. He opened his eyes and saw Doctor Cyclops grinning over him with a scalpel in his hand. The psychotic surgeon raised his knife and giggled, "Wakey, wakey."

On the flatbed, Chad opened the door to the chopper and placed his gun safely on the passenger seat, then felt the entire chopper shudder and strain, unaware of the pull on the tail's boom. He stared down the mountainside as the earth began to implode in sections beneath them.

Will hauled on the cage door while the elevator continued to shoot up the shaft. He jerked the busted frame two or three times to get it open. He grabbed the Professor by the scruff of his shirt and pulled him to his feet, feeling the soaring blast begin to heat the soles of his boots as he shouted to Bradley, "The second we hit the top, jump!"

The elevator screamed up the shaft as the blast wave roared up beneath it.

Will shouted as loud as he could up through the top of the cage, "Jake, get ready to run!"

Jake kicked the brake lock on the mine car that had been sitting dormant on the tracks. "I can do better than run. How 'bout an armored getaway car." He hauled the old car to the top of the slope leading down the tunnel, ready to roll.

The steel grate on the floor of the elevator cage began to glow red.

"Get ready!" Will shouted.

Then suddenly the top of the shaft was racing toward them. The elevator slammed into the winch pulley and wedged itself into the pulley mechanism.

The cable connecting the elevator all the way to the train held tight for a second—and in that second Will hurled the Professor, then Bradley, clear of the cage before throwing himself out of it onto the rocky floor of the mine tunnel.

As he did so, somewhere out in the snow, the clasps connecting the two cables together could no longer bear the strain of the wedged elevator and the train speeding around the mountain's descending curves. The two cables snapped loose, sending the detached clasps spinning and whistling through the falling snow. Suddenly freed from one another, the cables shot off in opposite directions.

Jake caught the Professor as Will flung him from the cage, and as the old man held on tight Jake hoisted him over the edge of the mine car and dropped him clumsily inside. "Sorry, Max!"

Will pulled Bradley to his feet. Behind them, the released elevator cage plunged down the shaft and into the fiery blast wave.

"Get in!" Jake shouted over the deafening rumble shooting up the shaft.

Bradley leapt into the mine car.

Will slammed into the back of it, helping Jake set the wheels in motion as the car started squeaking and rolling down the tracks—

—just as the wave of the blast erupted from the shaft.

Hurriedly Jake and Will jumped from the tracks and climbed inside the rolling mine car as it dipped into its descent down the tunnel, quickly picking up speed as Jake and Will sank low into the car, covering Bradley and the Professor.

The car swooped into a roller-coaster run down the tracks. Behind it the blast brought the ceiling down and lifted the floor of the tunnel off the ground. The car shot along the rails as the blast rose from beneath and pursued from behind, pelting the car with stone and warped metal beams.

As the last of the Zhang diamond mines collapsed, the entire earth shook—

—and a tiny square missile of a mine car shot from the dust-gushing tunnel entrance just before the crumbling rocks sealed the mine shut forever.

The mine car hit the ice, bounced, then sailed clear across the rail yard, tipped on its side, and sent its occupants gliding across the slippery slope until they came to a halt in the snow.

The Professor gasped, disoriented and in terrible pain.

Then he felt the gentle hands of Shane on him. "Professor? Professor, are you okay?"

"Yes," the old man whispered feebly.

Shane could see the trail of blood. He quickly took the Professor gently in his arms, and Jake helped him sit the Professor upright.

Will and Bradley stumbled hurriedly through the sleet and snow to join them, heads and torsos bruised and scathed.

"We need to get him to shelter," Shane said.

"Over there." Bradley pointed toward the rail yard's still intact generator shed.

Will and Shane aided the Professor to the shed while Jake, still nursing his wounded shoulder, kicked the door open.

"The second bomb," Will said urgently as they eased the Professor onto the cold floor of the shed. "We have to stop that train."

Jake glanced at his watch and saw the red dot moving away from them. "The bomb's not the only thing on that train. Luca's still aboard."

"But how can we catch it now?" Shane asked.

"I know a way," Bradley answered. "Over the mountain. The train has to go around it. We can cut it off on the other side. If we run—now!"

Instantly Bradley turned for the door and ran. Will bolted after him. Jake made a move but Shane pulled him back, shaking his head. "Not with that shoulder, Jake."

"I'm coming with you," Jake insisted. But then a bolt of pain shot through his arm and he caught his breath.

"No, you're not. Stay with the Professor. Keep him warm and keep him alive till we get back! You hear?"

Jake had listened to himself give the same speech to Sam on several occasions and knew it made sense for him to stay. He looked at the pale Professor and nodded reluctantly. "At least take these," he said to Shane, quickly kicking off his boots and handing them to the barefoot cowboy. Shane slid them on gratefully.

Jake watched him take off into the driving snow at breakneck speed, then he shut the door of the shed to keep the cold at bay and slid down onto the floor beside the Professor, wrapping both arms around him as tightly as possible, trying desperately to absorb the old man's shivering and suffering.

The earth literally moved under their feet as they ran. Icy chunks of ground sank and rose, potholes formed, and dangerous new sinkholes opened up as the mountain took on a new shape.

Will and Bradley leapt and sidestepped as they ran, narrowly missing the deadly gaps that appeared randomly in their path.

Shane was starting to gain ground a short distance behind them when the earth lurched and sent a giant snow-covered tree crashing down directly in his path. He stumbled to a halt as the mighty trunk thundered to the ground in front of him in a cloud of snowdust and shattered icicles.

Choof! Choof!

The train. It was close now, rounding the peak nearby.

Unable to go over the tree, Shane cut left and followed the newly defined landscape directly down to an embankment overlooking the train tracks. He saw the train cut around the corner fast. Further up the embankment he saw Will and Bradley reach the edge of the drop just as the train cleared the corner. Without hesitation they jumped, one at a time. Bradley landed and rolled on the roof of one of the middle cars, while Will was lucky to land on the flatbed at back.

Shane took a running leap and made a slippery landing on the coal heap behind the engine, sending a landslide of coal toppling off the side of the car, into the forest. He dug his boots into the loose coal and grabbed on to the sliding mound as best he could to stop himself from following over the edge. He soon slid to a stop, and suddenly felt eyes on him.

Looking left toward the engine, he saw Xi shoot him an ugly, angry snarl. Xi hoisted his shovel over his shoulder and rushed full force toward Shane.

There would be no more delays. No more distractions. At last the train was in motion and so was the plan. Mya's plan. It was Mya who planted the seed of destruction in Chad's head. It was Chad who convinced Richard to come on board. And it was all three of them who slowly, cunningly swayed an already sinister-minded Sen to risk everything for a financial reward greater than anything he or his predecessors could ever have imagined. Now it was just a matter of time and distance. Both of them were quickly diminishing.

Mya had already set the bomb ticking and left it in the cradle of the wooden crate on the floor of the master carriage. Then she quickly made her way into the next car. She locked the doors at each end and swiftly opened cabinets and drawers, sweeping hundreds of diamonds into small black velvet bags. When the sacks were full and the cabinets empty, she turned to the display in the center of the room. The large, spellbinding diamond inside—the Eye of Fucanglong—seemed to beckon to her. Each facet of its perfect surface picked up the light of the chandeliers and whispered to her softly, lovingly.

Everything you want, you shall have.

Everything you see through my eye, shall be yours to possess forever.

Your reward is coming.

Mya placed the velvet bags on the floor and stepped toward the bewitching diamond, her gaze transfixed on the giant jewel. Her hand was calm, slow, and confident as she reached for the door to the display cabinet. Her fingers rested lightly on the key sitting in the lock of the glass door, her eyes unblinking. With a soft click she turned the key.

Then, suddenly, her head snapped upward at a loud *thud-thump* on the roof of the car, her gaze broken. She took her hand off the key and pulled her pistol from the holster inside her knee-high boot.

On the roof of the car, Bradley had landed, leaping from the embankment. He crouched low and held on to the roof railings as tight as he could, then glanced back to see Will jump a second later, landing with a crash on the flatbed car carrying the chopper. Bradley pulled himself to his feet—

—just as a bullet shot up through the roof.

He panicked. Dropped. A thin beam of light shot up into the falling snow as a second bullet pierced the roof beside his head. Bradley stared at it for a stunned second, then rolled recklessly before the next bullet was fired. He tumbled clear off the side of the car, hooking his fingers onto the roof railing at the last second. His legs and body kept rolling as his fingers held on tight, his legs swinging wide, then snapping back, his shoes kicking straight through one of the windows of the exhibition carriage.

He let go of the roof railings as his legs and torso followed through the window, wrapping him tight in the curtain as he crashed inside, sprawling across the floor in a splash of red velvet. When he finally unraveled himself, all he saw was the snout of Mya's pistol. And beyond that, the smiling face of Mya herself.

"Get up!"

Doctor Cyclops held up the rusty scalpel and examined it. He decided he needed a more capable tool.

He staggered back to the operating utensils jingling on the wall of the bedroom carriage. Blinking hard in an effort to focus, he considered a jagged knife, then the saw, before finally settling on a set of rib-cutters. He smiled his cracked, rotted smile. "Yes. Let's cut you open and see what beautiful things you're hiding inside, shall we?"

It wasn't a question Luca needed to answer. All he needed to do right now was pull himself out of his drug-induced daze as fast as possible. All he could do was tug on the ropes. Harder and harder. The knots tightened around his wrists with every yank. But at the same time the ropes themselves stretched a little, giving him more length, more movement, inch by inch.

As Doctor Cyclops swayed his way over to the bed, he opened the rib-cutters wide. Taking an unsteady stance beside the bed, he used the tip to draw a line down Luca's naked torso. "I'll start here," he said, touching the two points of the open cutters against the base of Luca's throat. He traced a line down Luca's body to the base of his cock, pressing so deep he drew blood that trickled through Luca's pubic hair.

"You should thank me," the doctor said. "Not many people experience the pleasure of seeing their own death coming." With a giddy, satisfied smile, he brought the cutters back up to Luca's throat. "Although I should warn you: this is going to hurt. A lot."

Will landed with a crunch on the flatbed, knocking the wind out of his lungs. He gasped for air in the whirling, swirling snow and saw Chad spin around at the sound, immediately locking eyes on him. He was down to the last of the chains, unstrapping the landing skids of the chopper. Chad smiled and unclasped the second-to-last chain at the cleat, pulling it loose. Then he picked up one end of the chain, wrapping it around his hand and wrist, letting the rest dangle like a weapon.

Will coughed and struggled for breath, dragging himself up onto his hands and knees. But not fast enough.

Chad stepped confidently around the chopper, swung the chain in a circular motion, then brought it down as hard as he could across Will's back.

With a cry Will collapsed facedown on the rumbling floor of the car, his chin hitting the metal floor hard, his teeth biting down on his tongue.

"You think you can stop us now?" Chad shouted above the clatter of the wheels on the tracks. "When are you gonna give up, boy?"

Will spat blood from his mouth. "I was taught never ever give up."

"I know that lesson all too well. It's a hard class, but for some of us it actually pays off. For others, it's the last lesson they ever learn." Chad cracked the young man's ribs with another belt of the chain, and Will collapsed against the flatbed once more.

The train rounded a tight, icy bend, then veered away from the imploded mountain mines, snaking its way swiftly through the Shandong mountains toward Beijing.

On the coal car, trying to find his balance on the rolling, tumbling chunks of coal, Shane watched as Xi came for him with his shovel, climbing onto the coal heap and raising the spade high until he was within swinging distance.

Whoosh! He sliced the air with the shovel, aiming for Shane's head.

Shane ducked and lost his footing, sliding onto his back.

Xi plunged the sharp flat blade at him.

Shane rolled and the blade dug deep into the heap, splitting apart chunks of coal while Shane scrambled for the engine compartment, desperate to find a weapon of his own. He reached the front of the coal car and leapt into the engine with Xi clambering over the coal pile close behind him. The heat pumped out from the open furnace and

Shane's frozen skin instantly began to thaw, then perspire. He looked around frantically for a second shovel, a loose pipe, anything, but there was nothing but a few rocks of coal.

With a loud clomp Xi leapt from the coal car to the engine.

Shane looked quickly down at the coal on the ground, then down at his own body, or more precisely, the studded leather codpiece he was wearing. Quickly he pulled it off, stripping himself naked.

Xi charged with the shovel.

Shane snatched up a hunk of coal, stuffed it inside the codpiece, and then, holding on to the straps, swung the leather thong over his head like a slingshot, firing the chunk of coal straight at Xi.

The first rock hit Xi square in the nose, breaking it at the bridge and forcing him backward in a head-spinning stagger.

Shane took a step closer to the blazing furnace and grabbed another piece of coal.

Xi shook his head and returned for another charge.

Shane fired the second rock, this time hitting Xi directly in the throat, smack against his Adam's apple. Xi clutched at his neck with one hand, coughing and spluttering, then lunged at Shane with more speed and force than ever.

In front of the raging furnace Shane already had his third black rock at the ready. He twirled the sling.

But this time Xi was ready for him, swinging his shovel like a bat as the chunk of coal came at him.

Thunk! He hit it hard and head on, still in motion, charging at the naked cowboy and sending the rock firing straight back at him.

Shane dropped flat to the steel floor, ducking the flying piece of coal.

Xi did not stop, rushing at Shane, shovel raised high.

Shane looked for another rock. He found one, but his fingers fumbled with the sling. The chunk of coal fell, bounced, and rolled directly under Xi's charging feet.

Xi's foot slipped out from under him. He reeled forward, stumbling and crashing, swinging the shovel wildly as Shane rolled out of the way, glancing behind him just in time to see Xi tip and tumble headfirst through the large cast-iron opening of the blazing furnace. The fire hissed and spat, engulfing Xi and his agonized screams.

Shane caught sight of the remaining silver grenades still strapped to Xi's belt as flames consumed him. "Oh, shit!" he muttered. He leapt up, running for the rear of the open engine compartment, but his feet only carried him so far. The explosion did the rest.

The blast was deafening. The squeal of the metal from the engine ripping and twisting away in orange-peel strips was ear-piercing. And the wave of intense heat that emanated from the blast was flesh-melting.

But Shane only felt the heat for a fraction of a second before the shock wave picked him up and hurled him straight out of the engine compartment, sending him flying over a corner of the coal car and sailing naked into the snow-covered forest by the side of the tracks.

With a grunt he broke several low-lying branches and hit the ground hard and fast, rolling down a short embankment. He tried to pull himself up, but the train thundered away without him, shooting a lava burst of fire into the night from its erupted stack.

Shane heard hurried steps in the snow and turned to see an elderly couple from a nearby shack, rushing through the blizzard to investigate the commotion. They saw Shane, naked, bruised, and covered in snow and coal dust, and simply stared wide-eyed.

Shane quickly covered himself with both hands.

"Howdy," he offered awkwardly with a coy wave of one

hand. Then with a broad-shouldered shrug he said, "It's a long story."

The blast shredded the sides of the engine compartment completely and shot a vertical jet of fire into the night. At the same time the front wheels of the engine left the tracks, pointing the ruptured nose upward, pouring on the speed. When the wheels slammed back down on the tracks, the train was moving at almost twice the speed it was before.

It was as though the train itself had transformed into the wrath-filled dragon god of the underworld, possessed by the spirit of Fucanglong, tearing down through the serpentine curves of the mountains, ready to destroy the city that now lay in its path.

In the master carriage everything rocked with the sudden burst of speed, including the crate holding the zidium bomb. The crate tipped, and the silver ball rolled out of the wooden box and knocked gently against the back wall of the car, then continued to roll free like a giant pinball over the carpet, tempting fate. Its fail-safe mechanism assessed the risk level of every bump, just waiting to switch into defense mode and reset the counter to a 10-minute countdown.

The explosion of the engine knocked Mya off her feet and sent Bradley rolling across the floor of the exhibition carriage, the red velvet curtain unfurling and spitting him out. Mya hit the floor and dropped the gun. It slid up to Bradley. He grabbed it, but Mya already had one of the sacks of diamonds in her fist and struck him across the face with it before he could aim the pistol at her. The seams of the black velvet bag broke and hundreds of tiny diamonds burst through the air.

Bradley fell backward but didn't let go of the gun. He picked himself up, expecting Mya to fight him for it. But she had more important things on her mind.

The cabinet door was open and Mya's hand was already

inside the display cabinet, snatching the Eye of Fucanglong from its delicate perch.

Bradley fired off a shot.

The glass of the cabinet shattered.

But Mya was gone, unlocking the door of the car, taking the Eye and the black velvet bags full of diamonds with her, running back to the master carriage, back to protect her delicate, deadly bomb. She slammed the door to the car shut behind her, then Bradley heard a click as the door between cars was locked from the outside.

Doctor Cyclops opened the incisors of the rib-cutters as wide as they would open, but as he lowered the sharp teeth toward the base of Luca's throat, the naked Italian suddenly jerked his hand as hard as he could, pulling the rope long and tight and far enough to hook it around the lower incisor of the cutters.

That's when the engine exploded, jolting the car.

The already unsteady doctor lurched forward, accidentally snipping the cutters shut and severing the rope clean.

Luca's arm pulled free, then swung straight into a punch that hit Doctor Cyclops in the face so hard it knocked the eye patch off his head. He fell to the floor and stared up at Luca screeching, his one eye full of anger. "I'll kill you! I'll kill you!" he shrieked. But Luca managed to untie his other hand and was already working on the ropes binding his ankles.

Doctor Cyclops rose unsteadily, pulling himself up the wall, coming face-to-face with the rusted saw that hung there.

Luca threw the ropes loose and leapt off the bed, only to feel the jagged teeth of the saw come down on his shoulder and sink themselves into his flesh. Doctor Cyclops yanked the saw back, ripping a deep gash in Luca's shoulder. Luca caved to his knees, where he caught sight of the rib-cutters.

Before Doctor Cyclops could make another hack in his flesh, Luca jumped up, rib-cutters in hand. Doctor Cyclops squealed and ran, making a beeline for the front door of the car, racing onto the landing between the bedroom carriage and the exhibition carriage. He tried to open the door to the next car, but Mya had already locked it from the inside to prevent anyone from disturbing her while she filled her bags with diamonds.

Doctor Cyclops turned in a panic. Through the open, swinging door of the bedroom carriage he caught sight of Luca storming toward him. The doctor had nowhere to go but up. He dropped his saw onto the rushing tracks below, grabbed the rungs of the ladder to the roof, and flew up it as fast as he could.

Chad whipped Will with the length of chain again.

More blood burst from Will's lips. More pain. More reason to get up. He struggled to his knees, his arms quivering.

Chad smiled and whirled the chain in circles above his head, enjoying the heavy, whooping sound it made, when suddenly there was a deafening blast. Up ahead, the dark sky lit up in a bright orange burst as the engine exploded, followed by a tower of flame and a jolt as the entire train rocketed down the tracks, knocking Chad off his feet.

Already down, Will clung to the flatbed car, watching as Chad lost his chain and tumbled dangerously close to the edge of the platform before grabbing hold of a landing skid on the chopper and pulling himself up.

As Will pulled himself painfully to his feet, Chad unstrapped the last remaining chain tying the chopper down, hauled open the cabin door, and climbed inside, locking the door behind him.

In the pilot's seat he glanced at the helicopter's instrument panel, trying to think back, back to the hundreds of times he'd seen Richard or Xi fly this damn thing. His eyes danced frantically. Fuel, Airspeed, Np, Rotor Nr, Tail Rotor, KIAS … *"Fuck!"*

Then he saw it, a switch labeled simply *Engage*. Chad flicked the switch and the bird fired up.

Outside, Will heard the slow-building whir of the engine, then the sound of ice sliding off the rotor blades as they began to spin faster and faster.

Then he heard a more disconcerting sound: A grind and crunch. A quavering whir, the sound of something wrong.

Chad looked through the rear panel of the fuselage to the tail's boom and saw the cable trailing from it. Worse still, he saw it tangle itself in the tail rotor blade. As the blade continued to spin faster and faster it began to chew up the long, flickering cable, winding it in. Sparks burst from the churning rotor blades. Smoke began to pour from the tail as well as the engine mount just behind the fuselage.

Will looked through the windshield at Chad and shouted, "Shut it down!"

But it was too late. Quickly Will pulled back, trying to get as far away from the chopper as possible, the terrible grinding sound of the churning cable getting louder and louder.

Doctor Cyclops crabbed his way along the rooftop on sliding hands and feet until he heard the sound of the chopper fire up.

"Don't leave! Don't leave without me!"

It was enough to launch him to his feet and stumble his way toward the rear of the car's rooftop.

Behind him Luca hurried up the ladder and sprang onto the roof.

Cyclops looked back and whimpered, then continued his precarious race toward the rear of the car, seeing the blades of the chopper spinning madly—seeing Chad alone inside the cabin, his face lit up by the glow of the instrument panel, his hands desperately trying to shut the chopper down. Now the smoke was beginning to fill the cabin.

Behind the train, the cable snapped tight between the rear of the car and the tail of the chopper as the hook snagged on the rear coupling of the flatbed, but the tail rotor continued to spin, trying to reel in the hooked cable.

When the end of the cable wouldn't come to the tail rotor—

—the tail of the chopper pulled itself down to the end of the cable. With a bang the tail's boom dropped down hard, lifting the front of the helicopter clear off the flatbed.

Inside the smoke-filled cabin, Chad tried to find the door handle through the choking smoke, but all he could do was scream.

The tail pulled itself all the way down to the rear of the flatbed, flipping the front of the chopper all the way up in the air, where it somersaulted, clearing the back of the flatbed completely and smashing upside down onto the tracks behind the train in a fiery explosion. Burning, splintered shards of chopper sliced the air, flipping and shooting in all directions.

Will hit the deck of the flatbed once more, covering his head from the blast.

Doctor Cyclops stood with his mouth agape atop the roof of the car as a rotor blade cut through the air, heading straight for him. He had no time to scream or duck as the blade spliced straight through his scrawny throat, sending his head flying through the air and his diamond eye popping out of its socket. His decapitated body quivered and spasmed momentarily, then fell from the roof onto the tracks before being churned up by the wheels of the flatbed.

As the burning helicopter jumped on the tracks and spat charred shrapnel into the night, Luca dropped flat onto the rooftop of the carriage but slipped on the icy surface. Desperately he tried to cling to the roof railings, but another buck from the chopper sent a quake through the flatbed and the carriage, lifting both into the air momentarily before slamming the train back down hard onto the tracks.

Luca's fingers slipped. He had nothing else to grab on to and tumbled off the roof completely, arms grabbing in vain. In a blur he was thrown from the train and saw the snow coming at him.

He balled himself up as tight as he could and hit the ground in a fountain of ice, turning into a human snowball, rolling out of control through the forest, his wounds leaving pink trails in the snow. He hit a tree and unraveled with a grunt, twirling and twisting through the snow, sliding to a halt. Bleeding. Racked with pain. But alive.

He sat up as best he could and hurriedly limped back to the tracks.

He saw the train, ablaze at both ends now, disappear down the line.

And far beyond that, softly glowing in the distance— Beijing.

Will clung to the flatbed for dear life. The train jumped and crashed back down onto the tracks, flipped into the air by the thrashing, burning chopper. Out of the corner of his eye he saw Luca thrown clear, sailing off into the forest.

Will glanced behind him. He knew if he didn't get rid of the blazing helicopter it would soon derail the entire locomotive. If that happened he knew at least Beijing would be saved. But not the mountain villagers. Will would have to find another way out of this, and fast, before the chopper ripped the train clean off the tracks.

Something was about to rip the train clean off the tracks.

Mya fell to the floor of the master carriage with another violent jolt, seconds before she was able to place the zidium device carefully back into its padded crate. It slipped from her hands as she hit the floor. With a rumble it rolled across the floor, headed for the base of the life-sized statue of Sen.

Mya dived and grabbed it, inches before it hit.

If the fail-safe countdown triggered now, it would dash all hopes of destroying Beijing. As her plans continued to fall apart, minute by minute, Mya Chan made herself two promises. No matter what happened, the Eye of Fucanglong would be hers—

—and tonight, Beijing would become history.

She picked up the silver ball once more and carefully eased it into the crate, then hurried to a window, rattled it open, and looked outside. Ahead, the night was glowing orange with the tower of flame still shooting from the ruptured engine. She glanced back and saw more flames, this time spitting and leaping from the blazing chopper, which slammed up and down on the tracks and clung to the back of the flatbed, bucking the entire train.

At the same time that Will realized he had to get rid of the chopper, Mya made the same decision. But there was no need to get to the flatbed to do it. Mya could simply uncouple the back half of the train. After all, she had the diamond and she had the bomb—all the power she ever wanted.

Bradley steadied himself as the train tilted, rocked, and threatened to jump the tracks. He shook the door handle once more, trying to get out of the exhibition carriage and into the master carriage in pursuit of Mya, but the door was locked tight.

He took Mya's pistol and fired two shots at the lock. The second almost broke the handle free, but Bradley was denied a third shot. The petite pistol clicked—empty.

Bradley shook the handle of the door as hard as he could, then put his boot into it, kicking the handle until it finally gave and fell to the ground. He pulled the door to the car open, and suddenly across the gangplank joining the two cars he saw Mya, leaning down with both hands, pulling the pin lever that uncoupled the two cars.

Mya looked up, her hands covered in grease, and smiled at Bradley as the gangplank slowly slid apart and the exhibition carriage slid away from the master carriage.

"Goodbye, Bradley." Mya waved at him with her grimy, oily fingers.

The gangplank parted completely, the distance between the two cars growing foot by foot.

"Not so fast, bitch!"

To Mya's great surprise, Bradley dropped the gun, backed up, then launched himself through the doorway of the exhibition car, over the rushing tracks, and into the doorway of the master carriage.

Will leaned as low as he could, holding on tight as the flaming chopper continued to kick and fight. It wasn't the chopper itself he was trying to release; it was the entire flatbed car he intended to detach from the bedroom carriage.

He pulled the lever. The pair of couplings opened like yin and yang parting. Released from the chopper, the bedroom carriage suddenly leveled out on the tracks and the bucking stopped. The flatbed continued to be tossed about on the tracks more violently than ever now that it no longer had the rest of the train to weigh it down.

With a thump and a bang the chopper bounced high, lifting the detached flatbed car clear off the tracks and bringing it down on an angle that cracked three wheels. Sparks flying, it twisted and capsized completely, sending both the chopper and the car into a fiery spin and eventually crashing to a roaring halt across the tracks.

Will watched as the train left the charred remains of Chad Chambers far behind, then he jumped to his feet and raced through the bedroom carriage. He shouldered open the locked door of the exhibition carriage, raced to the front of the car, and then—

—pulled himself to a stop just in time before falling onto the tracks.

He quickly realized he'd been severed from the front half of the train. He looked ahead to see the blown-apart engine, the coal car, and the master carriage pulling away. And inside the master carriage, wrestling on the floor, were Bradley and Mya.

"Bradley!" Will glanced at the tracks being devoured beneath him. The distance between the exhibition carriage and the master carriage was too far to jump now.

As Bradley turned at the sound of Will's voice over the rumble of the train and the howl of the storm, Mya took the chance to slug him, her fist connecting with his jaw so hard it dropped Bradley to the floor unconscious.

Mya pulled herself off the floor, shot Will a triumphant look across the gap that grew between them, then from between her breasts produced the shimmering Eye of Fucanglong. She winked and blew Will a farewell kiss before slamming the door shut.

"Fuck!" Will swore through gritted teeth. Mya had the bomb. She had the diamond. And she had Bradley.

Will sized up the gap again, but attempting the jump would be suicide. The distance between the two cars was at least 15 feet and increasing by the second. There was no way Will could stop the front half of the train now. He watched the train pull further and further away, a tear of rage welling in his eye. Suddenly he felt more alone than he had ever felt in his life. More helpless and worthless than ever before.

Until—

—the front half of the train ahead suddenly jerked right.

Jerked right? It took a precious second for Will to figure out what just happened, and then—

A track switch. He looked ahead and saw the fork in the tracks. The front half of the train veered along the right-hand track. And on the left, running parallel, was a second track. A track that cut a tighter turn around a curve up ahead. A track that Will would miss if he didn't somehow hit the switch that was fast approaching off to the side.

He looked around desperately. Saw Mya's pistol lying on the ground. He snatched it up, took aim at the switch, pulled the trigger.

Click!

Nothing. "Damn it!"

The split in the tracks sped toward him. If he didn't switch the tracks now he'd follow behind the first half of the train until he petered to a halt, unable to do a thing. He needed to get on the tighter track to gain ground. He needed to hit that switch *now!*

With the gun his only hope, Will took aim and hurled the diamond-studded pistol as hard as he could at the oncoming switch. It slammed into the switch panel with all the force he could muster. The switch turned and the tracks locked onto the new path, inches before Will's half of the train hit the turn. The exhibition carriage jerked left, running onto the alternate tracks.

"*Yes!*"

Mya stood over the unconscious body of Bradley, and for a second she considered taking the lamp off the desk and bludgeoning the irritating, self-righteous fool to death with it, right here and now. But why mess up her dress and break her nails when she had so many reasons to smile. Several trillion reasons, it seemed. For it suddenly became apparent to Mya Chan that everyone else in the consortium was dead.

Which left the entire investment portfolio and all its riches in her hands. As well as the Eye of Fucanglong. Her plan. Her prize.

She returned the large diamond to the snug nest of her

cleavage, deciding she had more important things to do right now, like secure the bomb and get off this runaway train. With her slippery greased hands she picked up the crate and placed it on the marble desktop, beside her black velvet bags of diamonds.

Then she began to pace, thinking of her next step. The bomb, of course, would stay on the train. The diamonds, including the Eye, would accompany her in her escape. She'd have to secure them to herself somehow. She'd have to leap from the train and manage not to lose a single diamond in the jump. Or alternatively throw them from the train now, right now, and go back for them. Mya opened the curtains on the left-hand side of the car, convinced that this was the best plan. Her only option.

But as she hauled the red velvet curtain aside and dropped the window open beside the desk, instead of seeing forest and villages rush by, what she saw made her gasp—

The second half of the train rattled alongside her.

It had run the tighter course around the bend and had caught up on the parallel track, speeding alongside the master carriage now. And on its roof was Will Hunter.

He shot one glance at Mya. This time he was the one who winked. Then, without a moment's hesitation, he threw himself off the roof of the moving train and crashed shoulder-first through the open window of the master carriage, taking out the frame, smashing the glass, sliding across the desktop, and sending Mya, the diamonds, and the zidium device hurtling across the floor.

Will shook his head and looked up, blood trickling down his messed blond hair.

Mya glanced across at the crate, which had spilled on the floor and once more sent the bomb ricocheting through the car. It hit a tipped-over footstool, bounced off a wall, then slammed against Bradley's unconscious body, causing him to stir. Groggily, he opened his eyes to see Mya make a dive for the rolling silver bomb at the same time Will made a dive for her.

Outside, the second half of the train began to roll to a stop as the parallel tracks straightened out and switched back to a single line. Only three cars long now, the Zhang Diamond Express thundered toward the Lake of a Thousand Stars.

Inside the master carriage, the bomb barreled across the Persian carpet.

Will tackled Mya to the ground, pinning her down till she cracked his forehead with a head butt that knocked him away.

She crawled on her hands and knees and saw the dagger-like letter opener lying at the foot of the desk. She grabbed it in one hand and grabbed a still dazed Bradley by the throat in the other.

At the same time, Will—head spinning and forehead bleeding—tried to blink away his star-filled vision, pulling himself up by the red velvet curtains.

Mya pulled Bradley to his feet, the letter opener drawing blood from a prick to his throat.

Will felt the bomb roll across the floor and nudge the back of his legs. He had to do something. He had to save everyone. But how?

Then his eyes focused. He saw the frozen lake. He felt the bomb resting against his heels. And he heard her voice.

"Give me the bomb! Give it to me now or I'll kill him!"

Will looked from the bomb at his feet to Mya, her greasy hands already slipping on the letter opener. He glanced sideways to the frozen lake as the train started around it. And at that moment he knew what he had to do.

He knew he had to trigger the fail-safe mechanism on the bomb, he had to activate the 10-minute countdown, and he had to hit that bomb with something hard to do it. And he couldn't think of anything harder in this room than Mya Chan.

287

"Oh, I'll give it to you, all right."

Suddenly Will took three steps back, then ran at the bomb as if he was about to kick the goal of his college career.

His boot slammed into the silver ball. Mya tried to jab the letter opener into Bradley's throat as he did so, but the letter opener slipped harmlessly down her greasy palm. Bradley dropped to the floor.

The silver bomb soared through the air until—

CLUNK!

It hit Mya Chan directly in the forehead, instantly triggering the 10-minute countdown and knocking her clean off her feet. She was out cold before she even hit the Persian carpet.

At the same time, the bomb bounced across the car, its red digits now racing toward certain doom.

Bradley pulled himself off the floor. "What just happened?"

"We just saved Beijing," Will answered. "Now help me save everyone else's asses, including ours!"

"How?"

Will grabbed Bradley and pointed out the window, through the ice-covered trees, to the frozen lake. "We need to derail this train. Now!"

The remaining three smashed and burning cars of the Zhang Diamond Express raced through the snow and curved around the lake. Inside, with the unconscious body of Mya Chan lying on the floor, Bradley opened the front door of the master carriage while Will tipped over one of the Louis chairs and pushed it out the door. The chair fell between the master carriage and the coal car and splintered apart under the hot spinning wheels.

Will looked at Bradley. "We're gonna need something bigger."

He pushed one of the Parisian lounges out through the door. The wheels of the train devoured it with little more effort than the parlor chair.

They would soon pass the lake. Will looked around the car desperately, then his eyes came to rest on the lifeless bronze eyes of the statue of Zhang Sen. He got behind the statue and pushed it to the floor. As he started to put his back into it and push it across the carpet, Bradley joined in and helped. As the blazing train veered around the frozen lake, Will and Bradley pushed the heavy bronze statue closer to the door, inching it out over the edge toward the speeding tracks, until finally—

—the statue tipped.

The head of Zhang Sen hit the tracks first and cracked off. The body hit the wheels. The car bounced upward, lifting the coal car with it, then the flaming engine. The three cars jackknifed in the air.

Will grabbed Bradley and the two of them hit the floor of the master carriage, holding on to one another as tight as they could.

The cars flew up into the air and came down with a crash, but not on the tracks. They landed in an explosion of snow on the steep embankment heading down toward the frozen lake, the cars twisting around each other, spitting out chunks of steel and buckled wheels, taking out trees as they smashed their way through the forest before hitting the frozen lake. All three cars tipped on their side as momentum sent them sliding clear across the lake's icy surface.

The engine continued to shoot its jet of orange flames, now blasting horizontally, turning the top layer of frosty ice to glistening glass as the train skimmed across the lake.

The tipped master carriage left a trail of shattered glass and scattered diamonds all the way from the shore to the middle of the frozen lake, where the three cars eventually skidded to a stop, fire erupting from the burst engine and quickly melting the frozen surface.

The first crack appeared within seconds.

Will was the first to pull himself together, pushing the remaining Louis parlor chair off of him. The ceiling was now a row of broken windows, their red velvet curtains hanging down through the car. He saw snow falling in through the shattered windows above and realized the car was on its side now. Quickly he looked down. Underneath him was another row of smashed windows. And beneath that—cracking ice. Starting with a series of small streaks, sprinkling across the white surface of the lake.

"Bradley!" Will uttered urgently, reaching across to shake Bradley's shoulder, unable to take his eyes off the ice.

The streaks spread. There was a loud *crunch!* And suddenly, like a thunderbolt, a giant crack shot across the frozen surface directly beneath the shattered windows. And the freezing waters of the lake started to gush upward.

"Bradley!"

Crack!

"Bradley, get up!"

Crack-crack!

The split turned into a delta, cutting across the surface of the lake in a dozen different directions.

As the freezing water rushed inward, Bradley began to stir, then he was suddenly hauled to his feet by Will, who had jumped over the unconscious body of Mya and was now dragging Bradley to the door of the car, now dangling open at the far end, its hinges busted.

"We gotta get outta here!" Will cried. He pulled Bradley past the zidium device as its counter ticked down past the three-minute mark.

Then, suddenly, Bradley saw something else on the floor: The Eye. The Eye of Fucanglong. It had fallen from Mya's bosom in the crash and was now resting beside the ticking bomb. Shining. Shimmering. Calling. Bradley pulled back on Will's hand.

"What are you doing?" Will asked, feeling Bradley's hand leave his.

But Bradley was no longer looking at Will. He was looking into the Eye of Fucanglong. "The diamond," he breathed.

Suddenly there was another deafening *CRACK!*

A huge sheet of ice directly beneath the car gave way. One end of the car dropped into the lake and the other end sank into the rushing water, dragged down by the weight of the engine and coal car. The icy currents rushed upon Mya, whose confused eyes shot open as she spluttered and coughed and slid under the rushing water.

From outside came several explosions of steam as the lake snapped and broke apart, ice erupting in violent cloud-bursts as the blazing fire battled the freezing water.

The hypothermic currents swirled around the bomb—its timer now down to *2:16*—and carried the silver orb down into the depths, rolling toward one end of the sinking car.

The Eye of Fucanglong bounced and rolled down the length of the shattered, fast-flooding car, teetering in slow motion as it was dragged under.

Will tried to grab Bradley, but before he could reach him Bradley dived into the freezing water after the diamond. There was another ear-splitting *crack*, and another ice shelf outside split and dropped them further toward a frozen grave.

"Bradley!"

Will pushed his way through the water and found an arm. But it wasn't Bradley he pulled to the surface—

It was Mya.

"Where's the diamond?!" she hissed.

"Where's Bradley?!"

In the same instant they both turned and dived into the sinking car. Beneath the water Bradley was running out of air, bubbles billowing from his mouth as he tried to dig beneath the sliding desk and broken Parisian lounges to the far corner of the car where the Eye of Fucanglong concealed itself.

Suddenly Mya appeared next to him. She elbowed him in the chest and forced the last bubbles of air from his lungs, then pulled at his arms, fighting him for the diamond. She didn't have to fight for long; behind both of them Will grabbed the seat of Bradley's trousers and hauled him back to the surface.

Will and Bradley both came up gasping.

"What the fuck are you doing?" Will spat water, shouting over the splintering sound of ice cracking.

"You don't understand!" Bradley snapped back.

The car groaned perilously. "Understand what?"

Bradley panted, still trying to fill his lungs with oxygen. "Don't you get it? That diamond! It's the only thing that's left of my family."

Will grabbed Bradley fiercely by the back of his head and held his face close. "No! *You're* the only thing that's left of your family. Don't die for a stupid rock!"

There was another monstrous *SNAP* of ice outside. The car dropped further into the water. Bradley slid backward, teetering back toward the deep. But Will reached for him.

"Take my hand and don't let go."

As he began to fall backward into the water, Bradley slapped his palm against Will's. Their hands locked. With all his strength, Will began to drag Bradley from the sinking, burning train wreck.

Under the water, Mya's air began to run out. She pushed past the desk and the lounge and dug her arm deep beneath the pile of splintered, sunken furniture, until finally she reached the diamond. She couldn't see it, but she could feel it. Small. Cold. Sharp. Just like Mya herself. She gripped it in her fist. Then suddenly another section of ice cracked and the car dropped even deeper into its watery grave, tipping on even more of an angle.

The desk slid down further, trapping Mya's hand. Then came the silver ball. Rolling through the water, bouncing to a stop directly in front of Mya's face. Its red digits were ticking down faster than ever.

0:56

0:55

0:54

She tried desperately to pull her arm free, but it was stuck. Her lungs pushed out plumes of bubbles.

At the other end of the car, the water rushed up through the open door, pushing Will and Bradley up through the hole. Will looked around quickly. They were in the middle of the lake, 600 feet or more from shore. The jet of fire from the overturned engine was quickly melting the ice, forming a black hole of freezing water in the center of the lake. All around them the ice plates were cracking and exploding.

Will jumped from the edge of the sinking car onto a dipping, tilting sheet of ice. Bradley quickly followed. Behind them, air, steam, and bubbling water gushed from the three connected cars.

Will and Bradley leapt from one floating ice sheet to the next until they were no longer standing on broken, floating ice. But they were still too far from shore.

"We'll never make it," Will said, glancing back at the sinking train.

That's when he heard Bradley say, "Take my hand and don't let go!"

Will looked at him.

Bradley simply held out his hand. "Never give up. Right?"

Will nodded, smiled, then put his hand in Bradley's and watched, confused, as Bradley began stomping his boots into the ice.

Suddenly Will realized—it wasn't the ice Bradley was stomping on. It was the trail of diamonds left behind from the crash, the diamonds that had been thrown from Mya's black velvet bags, now scattered from the shore to the sinking train. Will followed suit and he and Bradley pounded their shoes down on every last diamond they could see.

As the frozen surface of the lake collapsed behind them, Bradley tightened his grip on Will's hand. Then, with dozens of razor-sharp diamonds embedded in their soles and Will in tow, Bradley began skating.

He skated faster than he had ever skated in his life, his family's diamonds cutting across the ice, his legs pumping toward the shore, thighs burning, left shoe sliding far and strong, then the right, one hand behind him clinging tightly to a precariously sliding Will.

Behind them the center of the lake split apart completely. Fractured chunks of ice sent water and steam ballooning into the air as the train and its fiery engine finally plunged into the freezing water. The train spiraled into the deep dark of the lake.

In the master carriage, her arm stuck and clinging to the diamond, the red digits of the bomb counting down in her face, Mya Chan released the last bubble of air from her lungs and smiled.

If the diamond couldn't belong to her, it would belong to no one.

As she sucked in her first lungful of frozen water, her body spasmed and the red digits on the bomb finished their countdown.

0:00:02

0:00:01

0:00:00

Bradley and Will were halfway to shore when the icy lake erupted like a volcano behind them, shattered ice blasting upward, forcing the snow that fell from the heavens back into the sky.

Will glanced behind him and saw giant sheets of ice flip

into the air before the cracks of destruction ripped across the lake toward them.

Bradley heard it; he didn't have to look back. With more power and strength than any Olympian could muster, he shot across the frozen surface, pulling Will behind him. Cutting long strides in the ice. Moving as fast as he could.

Faster. Faster still! The entire lake was rupturing from its epicenter. Bradley felt the surface beneath his diamond-studded shoes pitch and tilt. He kept skating.

The fracturing white around him broke up completely. The shore came closer and closer until—

—the last blast of the zidium sent the entire surface of the frozen lake shooting up into the air.

And the Lake of a Thousand Stars turned into the lake of a trillion tiny crystals of ice and diamonds, bursting skyward, up into the falling snow, turning that terrible, fateful night into something more beautiful than anyone could have possibly imagined.

As the blast wave shot toward shore, it picked both Will and Bradley up off the ice and sent them flying into the forest, tumbling through the snow, rolling and crashing, before they landed at the foot of a large tree—

—still holding hands.

Slowly the shining debris from the lake sailed down from the sky.

Bradley watched, heaving for air, the glistening ice and raining diamonds lighting up his eyes. "I've never seen anything like it," he whispered.

But lying in the snow beside him, Will didn't answer. Bradley looked over and saw that Will had passed out, utterly drained and exhausted. Bradley kissed him on the cheek. Then he continued to watch the stars fall.

In the shed atop the crumpled and deformed mountain of the Zhang diamond mines, Jake heard the distant *poomfh!*

He left the Professor for a moment and made his way outside, across the displaced earth and cracked ice, to see the distant burst of light far down the mountains. It rose into the snowy night sky like a glowing dome of light more beautiful than anything he'd ever seen—a thousand stars launching into the night.

"Jake?"

He heard the shivering voice of the Professor behind him and raced back into the shed. He wrapped his arms around the old man.

"I want everyone to be all right," the Professor whispered.

Jake thought about the blast he'd just seen, and wished for the same thing. "I'm sure they are," he whispered back into the Professor's ear.

"Eden too."

Jake nodded, his heavy heart searching for hope. "Eden too," he said. "Especially Eden."

The Professor took a long sharp breath then, feeling the pain and discomfort inside. "Take me home, Jake. Please, take us home now!"

Jake kissed the Professor on his freezing cold forehead.

"I will. I'll find the others. We'll go home together. Just as I promised him. Just as I promised Eden we would."

XX

San Francisco General Hospital, California

THE ELEVATOR AT THE END OF THE CORRIDOR PINGED.

Even before the doors could fully open, Jake wrestled his way free and was first to charge down the hall toward Dr. Dante, Sam, and the puffy-eyed Elsa, followed by Will sliding recklessly along the waxed linoleum floor, and behind him, Shane and Luca helping the wounded, anxious Professor along.

They all looked badly beaten and bruised. The doctors in Beijing had patched them up as well as they could, but no amount of pain could stop the five of them from returning to San Francisco as fast as possible.

Dr. Dante looked at the frazzled, injured men, a little startled and concerned.

Jake seized Sam so tightly by the shoulders that he almost dislocated them, then leapt from Sam to Dr. Dante. "Doc, please, tell us. Is he okay? Is he alive? Is he..."

Dr. Dante looked from Jake to the scathed, scared faces of

all the rest. "As I told your friends, we tried everything." He sighed, himself visibly exhausted. Then he managed a weary smile. "And we believe we've been able to stabilize him."

Jake drew breath. Hope. Without another word he bolted to the window into the intensive care unit just as a nurse inside drew open the curtain. And there on the bed, being carefully monitored by no fewer than four hospital staff, was Eden.

Unconscious. Tangled in tubes. But alive.

Jake turned quickly to Dr. Dante, trying to catch his terrified breath. "Thank you!" he whispered.

"You can thank me once he's made a full recovery, which we hope won't be too long. He's strong. In no time he'll be a completely new person. Trust me."

Jake stepped up to the glass and placed his sweaty, trembling palm against it. And as he did, Eden's eyelids fluttered open, his eyes dancing in and out of consciousness. His lips quivered and turned up at the sides, forming something like a smile.

Something like love.

XXI

Hong Kong, China

WILL ARRIVED AT DAWN AND MADE HIS WAY THROUGH Hong Kong's already bustling morning traffic, heading for the Zhang Diamond Tower.

"You've been busy," he said, dropping his overnight bag in the doorway of the newly built boardroom. Bradley turned from the window overlooking the skyscraping city and mountains beyond, and smiled at the sight of his American friend.

He rushed toward him and the two embraced.

"What do you think?" Bradley asked, gesturing to the restored room.

Will pushed his messy blond hair out of his eyes. "You've gotten rid of that charred-to-a-cinder look—"

"—and gone for a more relaxed and friendly feel," Bradley added.

Indeed, the boardroom had a much less corporate feel to it. There were flowers and plates of fruit on the new boardroom table, and cozy lounge chairs scattered around the place. "Welcome to the brand-new Zhang Diamond Corporation. A place where everyone's treated equally. A place where anyone can feel at home. I'm steering the company in a whole new direction. I'm going to make good on all of my uncle's false promises. I'm going to rebuild the Shandong mines and start up the Montana Project, but not for wealth or power. I want to repudiate the corruption of this business and turn it into an industry based on fair trade and equal rights for all. I can do it, Will. I know that now."

"What about skating?"

Bradley smiled. "I've lived that dream now. And won."

"Then perhaps you and I can get down to some unfinished business."

Will stepped up to Bradley, took his head in his hands, and kissed him on the lips, gently nudging him back against the edge of the boardroom table. He grabbed his T-shirt at the hem and quickly pulled it off over his head, then wriggled Bradley's tie loose and began unbuttoning his shirt. He stripped it open, then slowly knelt, kissing Bradley's brown, hairless flesh all the way down his chest and stomach before unbuckling his belt and unzipping his trousers.

At that moment, the cell phone in the pocket of Will's jeans began to chime. Reluctantly he pulled it out, only to check if the Professor was calling with another emergency. But the caller ID read *Home*.

Will decided Felix could wait a few minutes. He put the phone down on the floor and went to press OFF, but his finger slipped and he inadvertently answered the call. Felix went straight to speaker.

"Master William? Are you there?"

"Oh, shit." Will panicked, then stammered, "Ah, Felix, h-hi. Listen, this is kind of a bad time."

"Dear Master William, I think when it comes to you, time defies any sort of description."

Will couldn't help but smile. Old Felix—as unruffled as ever. "You're calling to ask if I'll be home for dinner, right?"

"Correction, home for your favorite dinner. And also to let you know your college lecturer, Professor James, called to inform you that your latest assignment is overdue."

"Oh, shit," Will whispered, but suddenly Bradley took his cares away by reaching inside his own unzipped trousers and pulling out his hard, upward-tilting cock. It instantly rose to meet Will's lips.

The young American melted. He reached inside Bradley's trousers and took Bradley's full, writhing balls in both hands, then took a mouthful of that warm, sweet dick.

On speaker, the unflummoxed Felix, completely unaware of what was occurring on the other end of the phone, said, *"Don't worry, Master William, you've been granted an extension. I told Professor James you had your hands full at the moment, and would sink your teeth into the task as a matter of urgency."*

Will spluttered and slid Bradley's cock from his lips. "Ah. Uh, Felix, can I call you back?"

A heavy sigh came down the line. *"Very well. As you say, I'll catch you later."* The words sounded so wrong in Felix's plum accent that Will couldn't help but smile.

"Catch ya, dude!" This time Will managed to hang up the phone successfully, before looking up at Bradley. "Now, where were we?"

Bradley responded by taking Will by the shoulders, lifting him back up to his feet, and unbuckling the young man's jeans.

Will's cock sprang into Bradley's hand. Bradley smiled and eased himself up onto the boardroom table, taking Will by the hips and pulling him up with him. The two kicked off their shoes and pants as Bradley slid on his back to the center of the table.

Will crawled over the top of him. The two kissed each other on the lips, the chin, the nose, as Will lowered his body on top of Bradley's. Their heaving chests met. Their stomachs rose and fell and rose again, touching softly as they breathed. Their cocks rubbed gently, tenderly against each other.

Will whispered in Bradley's ear. "Whatever you do, don't light any candles."

The two laughed, then kissed again.

XXII

San Diego, California

FELIX HUNG UP THE PHONE AND SIGHED AGAIN. HE WASN'T annoyed with Will; he knew his extracurricular activities kept him busy. He simply, genuinely, missed young Master Hunter's company—despite the infernal roar of that motorcycle he insisted on riding and the loud music he played while he studied, on the few occasions he actually did study, and the strange hours and secretive company he kept.

Yes, despite it all, Will Hunter was the only family Felix had. And he worried about him constantly. He loved him. And he missed him.

Just as Will was about to miss the cheeseburger and homemade fries that Felix had fixed for him. He was about to garnish the meal with a sprig of parsley on top of the bun when the doorbell rang.

Strange, thought Felix. He wasn't expecting any deliveries or messages, or least of all, company. He untied his apron and hung it on the oven rack, rather untidily and very much out of character, but he had every intention of returning to it as soon as he attended to the caller at the door.

On his way down the hall he straightened his shirt and vest and made certain his tie was knotted high and tight. Then he opened the door.

There before him stood a silver-haired gentleman in his sixties. By his side was a woman, tall and attractive. Felix guessed by her beautiful yet stern high-cheekboned features that she was Eastern European, possibly Russian.

"Felix Fraser, I presume," the silver-haired visitor stated rather confidently.

The butler glanced at them both for a moment, then replied, "May I be of any assistance?"

The older gentleman smiled assuredly. "Oh, I most certainly believe you may. My name is Caro Sholtez. And this is Natalya."

Natalya smiled also. Then by way of introduction she pulled a pistol and aimed it directly at Felix.

The shocked butler gasped, eyes now fixed on nothing but the gun.

The reaction sent a ripple of sheer amusement through Caro that almost made him laugh. Almost. "Tell me, Mr. Fraser, are you a good traveling companion? Because if you're not, Natalya will happily put a bullet in your brain right now."

With a quivering nod, Felix whispered, "Yes. I love traveling."

The power-hungry smile spread even further across Caro's thin, bloodless lips. "I have a feeling you're just saying that. But I do like cooperative captives. So come along then—among many other things, I have no tolerance for dawdling. We still have several more 'traveling companions' to collect along the way, and trust me when I say—"

Caro leaned in close, close enough to hear the tremor of

Felix's heart, close enough to feel the butler's shallow, terrified breaths against his sunken cheek.

"—Time is of the essence."

XXIII

Vatican City, Italy

THE DRAGON WAS FROZEN IN ITS MOMENT OF DEFEAT, pinned down by the hooves of the horse and the point of Saint George's lance about to pierce its heart. Ordinarily the pontiff's personal visitors would pause and admire the giant canvas hanging in one of his many private halls. But this particular visitor didn't so much as glance sideways.

The sound of his brisk, sweeping steps echoed through the halls and chambers. Portraits of popes past, the grim faces of archbishops, the mournful gaze of martyrs and saints watched from the confines of their elaborate, solid-gold frames as the man hurried through room after room, delving deeper and deeper into the Vatican until he came to a tall, ornate door manned by two of the finest Swiss Guards in the pope's personal army. One of the guards recognized the man immediately and opened the door for him.

"He's expecting you."

"Thank you," the man said. He was panting.

He entered the room, immediately intimidated by its size, his soul seemingly swallowed up by its high-vaulted ceiling and cold sparseness. There was very little furniture in the room and even less light. A single sliver of sun broke through the drawn curtains, illuminating little more than a large desk with a marble top and ornate gold legs at one end of the room. In the dim light, the man could make out a figure sitting in a high-backed chair behind the desk. He made out a second figure, short and hunched, looming in the shadows by the curtains.

The man slowed his stride and tried to control his nervous, exhausted breathing, walking respectfully toward the desk now.

"You have done well, my son," the figure in the high-backed chair said, his voice old and slow, yet weighted with knowledge and power.

"Thank you, your Holiness," the man said, stopping in front of the desk and genuflecting. "The subject is alive and seems to be responding well to the treatment, although his condition needs to be monitored."

In the dim light, the figure in the chair—the most powerful man in the Catholic world—smiled. "Excellent. The correction has begun. Wrong shall be made right. Let God's will be done."

"Your Holiness, we still need to find the tigers. There's not enough of the elixir to—"

The old man held up his hand and silenced the visitor with a comprehending nod. "And we shall," he said. "We have information on the whereabouts of the shipwreck. We will find the map. God is on our side."

He leaned across the desk and placed his hand on something folded neatly on its marble surface. He slid it across the desk, and in the dim light the man could see that the object was crimson in color.

The old man said, "Dr. Dante, this is for you."

The man who stood before him, Dr. Angelo Dante, asked, "What is it?"

From behind him came a slurred and zealous voice, a thick Cockney accent present despite the time he had spent convalescing in the Vatican. "It's da robe. Da robe of da Crimson Crown. You are now one of us."

Dr. Dante turned. The figure hunched by the curtains stepped into the sliver of light. He had only one arm and his face was horribly scarred, the flesh disfigured by fire. Nonetheless he smiled as best he could, sucking in the drool that pooled in his mottled mouth, before laughing maniacally as he spattered—

"Vengeance is mine. So say da Lord!"

About the Author

GEOFFREY KNIGHT's Fathom's Five adventure series is the result of watching too many matinee movies in small-town cinemas as a child, before embarking on his own adventures as an adult, traveling the world from the palaces of the Rajasthan Desert to the plains of Africa to the temples of Kathmandu. The Fathom's Five series, which includes *The Riddle of the Sands* and *The Curse of the Dragon God*, will continue soon with the fourth adventure, *The Temple of Time*. Geoffrey lives in Sydney, Australia.

Rousing, Arousing
Adventures with Hot Hunks

Buy 4 books,
Get 1 *FREE**

The Riddle of the Sands
By Geoffrey Knight

Will Professor Fathom's team of gay adventure-
hunters uncover the legendary Riddle of the
Sands in time to save one of their own? Is the
Riddle a myth, a mirage, or the greatest engi-
neering feat in the history of ancient Egypt?
"A thrill-a-page romp, a rousing, arousing
adventure for queer boys-at-heart men."
—Richard Labonté, Book Marks
ISBN 978-1-57344-366-1 $14.95

Divas Las Vegas
By Rob Rosen

Filled with action and suspense,
hunky blackjack dealers, divine drag
queens, strange sex, and sex in strange
places, plus a Federal agent or two,
Divas Las Vegas puts the sin in Sin
City.
ISBN 978-1-57344-369-2 $14.95

The Back Passage
By James Lear

Blackmail, police corruption, a diz-
zying network of spy holes and secret
passages, and a nonstop queer orgy
backstairs and everyplace else mark
this hilariously hard-core mystery by
a major new talent.
ISBN 978-1-57344-423-5 $13.95

The Secret Tunnel
By James Lear

"Lear's prose is vibrant and colour-
ful...This isn't porn accompanied by
a wah-wah guitar, this is porn to the
strains of Beethoven's *Ode to Joy*, each
vividly realised ejaculation accompanied by a fanfare and the crashing of
cymbals."—*Time Out London*
ISBN 978-1-57344-329-6 $13.95

A Sticky End
A Mitch Mitchell Mystery
By James Lear

To absolve his best friend and sometimes lover from murder charges,
Mitch races around London finding
clues while bedding the many men
eager to lend a hand—or more.
ISBN 978-1-57344-395-1 $14.95

* **Free book of equal or lesser value. Shipping and applicable sales tax extra.**
Cleis Press • (800) 780-2279 • orders@cleispress.com
www.cleispress.com

Ordering is easy! Call us toll free or fax us to place your MC/VISA order.
You can also mail the order form below with payment to:
Cleis Press, 2246 Sixth St., Berkeley, CA 94710.

ORDER FORM

QTY	TITLE	PRICE
_____	_____	_____
_____	_____	_____
_____	_____	_____
_____	_____	_____
_____	_____	_____

	SUBTOTAL	_____
	SHIPPING	_____
	SALES TAX	_____
	TOTAL	_____

Add $3.95 postage/handling for the first book ordered and $1.00 for each additional book. Outside North America, please contact us for shipping rates. California residents add 9.75% sales tax. Payment in U.S. dollars only.

* Free book of equal or lesser value. Shipping and applicable sales tax extra.

**Cleis Press • Phone: (800) 780-2279 • Fax: (510) 845–8001
orders@cleispress.com • www.cleispress.com
You'll find more great books on our website**

Follow us on Twitter @cleispress • Friend/fan us on Facebook